PRAISE FOR DHARMA KELLEHER

"Kelleher's characterizations and voice are fresh and new, the action comes fast and furious."

— GREG HERREN, AUTHOR OF *BATON ROUGE BINGO*

"Dharma Kelleher has created one of the most unique characters in crime fiction. She takes readers on a thrilling ride that will have you turning pages into the wee hours of the morning!"

— RENEE JAMES, AUTHOR OF *SEVEN SUSPECTS*

The action-packed scenarios don't quit, right up to the story's unexpected, satisfying resolution."

— MIDWEST BOOK REVIEW

TERF WARS

TERF WARS

A JINX BALLOU THRILLER

DHARMA KELLEHER

TERF WARS: A JINX BALLOU NOVEL

Published by Dark Pariah Press, Phoenix, Arizona.

Cover design: JoAnna Kelleher

This is a work of fiction. Names, characters, places, and incidents are products of the author's imagination and are not to be construed as real. Any resemblance to actual events, locales, organizations, or persons, living or dead, is entirely coincidental.

Ebook ISBN: 978-1-952128-06-6

Paperback ISBN: 978-1-952128-07-3

Hardcover ISBN: 978-1-952128-09-7

To my wonderful wife, Eileen.
Even after more than twenty years,
my heart skips a beat every time I see your lovely face.

1

———

The eyes of the diners at the Skyway Café zeroed in on me and my associate, Nathaniel "Rodeo" Kwan. Our body armor, weapons, and other gear tended to attract attention.

The small family-style restaurant overlooking the Payson Airport runway was crowded, thrumming with dozens of conversations and the clinking of plates. The aromas of breakfast and coffee got my stomach rumbling.

Unfortunately, Rodeo and I weren't here for the huevos rancheros or the biscuits and gravy. We were on the job, hunting a bail jumper wanted for multiple sex crimes.

I scanned the tables for the face that matched the mug shot provided to us by the bail bond agent.

"There," I whispered to Rodeo, pointing as subtly as I could. "Third table from the right, two rows back."

He nodded and proceeded around the other side so we could cut off any attempted escape.

I put a firm hand on the woman's shoulder. The other held my Taser, ready to use as a stun gun. "Nancy Turner, you failed to appear at your court hearing. You need to come with us."

Turner's body tensed beneath my grip. She stood slowly. For a moment, I thought this arrest would go easy.

Without warning, she threw a cup of coffee at my face. I dodged the scalding liquid but lost my grip on Turner. She bolted, racing between the tables, knocking over empty chairs in her wake.

I took off after her with Rodeo on my heels. I was tempted to tase her but didn't want to risk hitting an innocent bystander by mistake. Would look very bad on my report.

In an attempt to cut off my quarry, I leapt onto one of the tables but discovered it wasn't as stable as it looked. It toppled, sending me and the dishes crashing to the floor. I landed on my feet and took off after Turner, ignoring the obscenities being yelled at my back. Not that I cared. All that mattered was apprehending Turner.

She reached the side door of the restaurant five seconds before I did and fumbled with the doorknob but stopped cold when she looked out the window. My other associate, Zahara Washington, waited on the other side of the door with her Taser raised.

"Gotcha!" I grabbed Turner's jacket collar, but she twisted out of it and ducked back toward the kitchen.

I signaled through the window for Zahara to cut Turner off at the service entrance, then I continued after her. Rodeo circled around to keep her from reaching the front door.

Turner snatched a large tray of dishes from a server's hands and sent a cascade of eggs, bacon, and other food at me. I dodged it and pursued her through the double doors into the kitchen. The cooks leaped out of the way as we charged through like a tiny stampede of buffalo.

"Give it up, Nancy. My associate's outside that door."

She fervently glanced around for the exit. Realizing she was cornered, she grabbed a chef's knife from a cutting board and pointed it at me. I was sure she'd use it if I got close enough.

"My lawyer wants me to take a plea deal, but I didn't do anything wrong."

"Tell it to the jury. I'm not in the guilt or innocence business. You missed your court date. You go back to jail. That's the deal."

"I'm not going back. I didn't hurt anyone." Her eyes blazed with fury as she waved the knife back and forth.

I raised my Taser. "Look, lady, we can do this easy, or we can do this hard. Your choice. Now what'll it be?"

"No! I didn't do anything bad."

"Hard it is, then." I pulled the trigger.

Her body seized while fifty thousand volts of electricity coursed through her. She grunted in agony through gritted teeth and collapsed to the floor. I snatched the knife from her hand and snapped the cuffs on her wrists.

"Nancy Turner. My name is Jinx Ballou. I am a bail enforcement agent hired by Assurity Bail Bonds after you failed to appear."

She struggled to escape the cuffs, trying to kick me off her. "No, no, no! I didn't do anything wrong."

"Settle down or I will tase you again. Do you understand?"

She stopped struggling and began to sob. "Yes."

Rodeo appeared at my side and helped me get our fugitive to her feet. "You caught her. Well done, boss."

As we frog-marched Turner toward the front entrance, a woman in a staff uniform shouted, "Excuse me!"

I guessed she was a manager here at the Skyway Café. She said something else, but her voice was drowned out by the sound of a small plane landing on the airstrip next to the restaurant.

"What?" I asked when the noise subsided.

"You disrupted our breakfast service. Who's going to pay for the damage?"

"What damage?" I feigned ignorance.

"Shattered dishes and a broken table for starters. Not to mention comping the meals for our customers whose breakfast was so rudely interrupted."

I pulled out one of my business cards and tossed it at her. I didn't have time for her bullshit. "Bill me."

"Hold up, my hat fell off inside." A slim man with an athletic build, Rodeo never went anywhere without his signature Stetson. His fondness for cowboy hats had earned him his nickname when he served in the army.

"My jacket's in there," Turner complained.

"Grab her jacket while you're at it, Rodeo."

"Copy that, boss."

I walked Turner out into the beautiful, if chilly, March morning. The weather was idyllic down in Phoenix. But up here in Payson's high desert, the winter chill lingered. That was one of the things I loved about Arizona. You could have triple digits in Phoenix and still have snow on the ground in the White Mountains, a few hours' drive away.

Zahara met me by the Gray Ghost, my scratched and battered Nissan Pathfinder. She had a wiry physique and reminded me a lot of Grace Jones from that old Conan movie. Before I'd hired her, she had been an MMA fighter until an injury forced her to retire from the sport.

She took one look at Turner, who was now ugly crying, and said, "It'll be okay, ma'am. We'll take you back to Phoenix, get you processed in, and see about getting your bail reset."

Some bounty hunters get all chummy once a fugitive is

caught. I wasn't one of them. Maybe it was because I'd been hardened from years of chasing scumbags who tried to run from the law. Or maybe I was broken in a way that Zahara wasn't.

"Bail reset? Yeah, we'll see about that," I harrumphed. My vest was still wet from where she'd thrown her coffee.

"It's not fair," Turner muttered sullenly as we secured her in the back seat of the SUV. "I didn't hurt anyone."

"Don't worry. Everything will work out." Zahara slid in next to her, draping the woman's jacket over her shoulders and buckling her in. I hopped in the driver's seat while Rodeo climbed in next to me, once again wearing his Stetson.

"Chalk up another win for Ballou Fugitive Recovery," I said. "Let's drop her off at the jail and get paid."

"Amen to that," Rodeo replied.

Zahara started to say something but yawned wide, having been up all night on a fruitless stakeout where we'd thought Turner had been hiding. "Just want to catch some shut-eye."

I drove past the plethora of small businesses that composed downtown Payson. The Northern Arizona town was emerging from its winter slumber. A banner overhead welcomed visitors to the upcoming Spring Festival. I planned to be in Vegas with my friends celebrating my last weekend of being a single woman.

"Everyone acts like what I did was so wrong," Turner whined when the shops gave way to the rolling tree-covered hills along Highway 87.

"Lady, you fucked a bunch of dead bodies." My stomach roiled at the thought.

"I can't help it. It's a compulsion. I've tried to stop, but whenever I see a cadaver laying out on the table, I lose control."

Rodeo made a disgusted face. "Ugh."

"Shut the hell up, Turner!" I snapped.

"No one was hurt."

I glanced back at the woman through the rearview mirror. Tears once again streamed down her face.

"Ease up, you all. Can't you see she's sorry?" Zahara asked.

"Yeah, sorry she got caught," I said with a snort.

"How is it even possible?" Rodeo asked. "I mean, if they're dead, how can they even get it up?"

"Dude, don't ask questions like that," I said. "I don't want to know."

"If we get them early enough and rigor hasn't fully dissipated," Turner explained as if she were talking about anything other than molesting a corpse.

"Shut up, shut up, shut up!" I cranked up my "Bad Girls" playlist on Spotify. The Pink Trinkets' punk rock anthem "Punching Nazis" blared through the speakers.

A few songs later, even I started to get a headache and turned the stereo down to a normal level. Despite the blaring music, a glance into my rearview mirror revealed that Zahara had fallen asleep.

Turner never showed at the house Zahara was staking out. Fortunately, a tip led us to the Payson Airport restaurant where our fugitive was planning to meet a pilot who'd agreed to fly her to Nogales, Mexico.

"You excited about this weekend?" Rodeo asked.

I caught his eyes in the mirror and grinned. "I am. You're still welcome to join us for my bachelorette party."

"Kind of weird for a guy to attend a bachelorette party."

"Well, you are dating my brother. Besides, I'm not exactly a traditional kinda gal."

"Really? I'm shocked!" he joked. "You seem so normal."

"Right. A transgender comic book geek who works as a bounty hunter. Doesn't get much more normal than that."

We both laughed.

"Besides, Easton's coming. They're nonbinary," I continued. "If it makes you feel any better, think of it as a gathering of über-diverse friends. Or if you'd rather go to Conor's bachelor party..."

"No, thanks. I have a feeling Conor's bachelor party will be a bit too heteronormative for my tastes."

"You're getting married?" Turner asked. "How nice."

"Shut up, perv." I'd almost forgotten she was back there.

"Jinx, be nice," Zahara replied sleepily.

"Nice is not in my vocabulary with necrophiliacs." I sighed. "Anyway, I'm glad we could still get rooms, what with StoryCon being this weekend."

"Oh, that's right." Zahara perked up, stretching her arms. "Who are you cosplaying as this time? Wonder Woman or Xena?"

"Asaya Thrax. She's a space marine from *Into the Black*."

"That series on Netflix?" Rodeo asked. "I've watched a few episodes of it but had trouble following it. Gwyneth and Jake like it though." Jake was my brother. Gwyneth was Rodeo's daughter from a previous relationship.

"It takes a few episodes to get into it. I fell in love with the graphic novels a few years back. And the outfit is awesome. Black and royal-blue formfitting space armor."

"You make it yourself?" Zahara asked.

"Absolutely. Not cheap or easy to get right but worth it."

Rodeo laughed. "For a badass chick, Jinx, you sure are a big ol' nerd."

"A girl's gotta have her hobbies," I said. "At least I'm not fucking dead guys."

2

———————

We dropped off Turner at the Estrella Jail and picked up the body receipt, which I would turn over to Assurity Bail Bonds for a fat check.

It was nearly one o'clock when Zahara, Rodeo, and I arrived back at the Hub, a coworking space I worked out of in downtown Phoenix. I parked in the nearby lot between Rodeo's Mazda Miata and Zahara's Ford Explorer.

"Any more jobs?" Zahara yawned audibly and stretched.

I checked the email account on my phone. "Looks like Assurity Bail Bonds has another one for us. Let me see if it can wait until Monday."

I called Sadie Levinson, the owner of Assurity. "Yo, Sadie. We bagged Turner."

"Finally. I have another defendant for you to return to custody," she said with perfect professional diction. "Judge Campos revoked her bail this morning after she threatened a witness."

"Who's the defendant?"

"Blair Marshall, white female. No priors. Originally

charged with aggravated assault. Upgraded to murder one when the victim died a few days ago."

The name sounded vaguely familiar. "My team's exhausted from chasing Turner halfway across the state, and we're headed to Vegas for the weekend for my bachelorette party. Can it wait until Monday?"

She made a noise indicating her displeasure. "It's only Wednesday. The judge wants her apprehended tout de suite. Otherwise, it'll be my tuchus in a sling."

"Yeah, well, I'm flying out tomorrow morning."

"I need this defendant picked up now, Ms. Ballou. She murdered a woman. A transgender woman, I might add."

"Shit. She's the one who killed LaTonya Garrett?" A lump formed in my throat. The Phoenix Gender Alliance, a trans support group I was a member of, had staged a protest at the courthouse when Marshall was released on bail, fearing she would hurt another member of our community. "And you posted her bond?"

"I issue bail bonds for defendants on a wide range of charges, including murder. You know this. But now that her bail's been revoked, I need your help returning her to custody. Neither she nor her attorney have returned my calls."

"Fine. I'll take the case."

"Thought you would. The original bail was set at two hundred grand. Considering the urgency, I'll pay double the standard rate if you apprehend her by Friday."

Double the standard ten percent meant a bounty of forty grand. A nice chunk of change if we could apprehend her quickly.

"Email me the documents, and we'll see if we can't track her down today. If not, I'll have Rodeo and Zahara nab her before the weekend."

"See that you do. This one's a priority."

I hung up and turned to Rodeo and Zahara. "We got another one for Assurity. Big payday but not much time to grab her."

"Darn, I was hoping to catch some sleep," Zahara said. "Last night's stakeout is kicking my rear."

"Go grab some winks, Z," I replied. "Rodeo, how you holding up?"

He had been running leads with me since the wee hours of the morning. "Could use some coffee, but I can manage for a while yet."

"Excellent. Careful driving home, girl," I called after Zahara.

"Will do." She climbed into her Ford Explorer and drove out of the lot.

"Come on," I told Rodeo. "Let's see if we can't track down one more before the weekend."

The Hub was housed in what was once a car dealership. The shape of the tall glass-fronted building reminded me of an inverted boat hull. The interior featured a cavernous open space with the only walls in the back where the restrooms and a few meeting rooms were located.

Dozens of computer workstations occupied ten-foot-long folding tables. Neon artwork installations mounted on the exposed steel infrastructure gave the space a cyber-industrial look, sort of a "disco meets the Terminator" vibe. EDM played over the sound system.

Rodeo and I navigated through the tables to the one I shared with Becca Alvarez, my best friend since sixth grade and now my maid of honor. She had been my first friend after coming out as transgender.

These days, she freelanced as an IT security consultant and also skip traced fugitives for me, often providing information that most of the online skip-tracing databases didn't offer, some of it not entirely acquired legally. She sat nestled among three flat-screens, typing away madly. Empty drink cans and food wrappers lay cluttered among stacks of file folders, loose papers, pens, and computer parts.

"Hey, Becks! How's it going?" I asked.

Like me, Becca had long dark hair and tan skin. When we were growing up, people often mistook us for sisters. Despite our lack of a blood relation, we were family.

"Morning, you two. Been busy checking a suspected vulnerability on a client's server. You catch that creepy woman with the corpse fetish?" Her lip curled in disgust.

"We got her." Rodeo pulled up a chair next to my workstation. "The dead can rest in peace once again."

I opened my laptop and printed the documents that Sadie Levinson had sent on Blair Marshall, including the arrest report, her bail application, a credit report, and the recent order from the judge revoking bail. "She was a serious whack job. Absolutely convinced she'd done nothing wrong. Had to tase her when she came at me with a knife."

"Oh my gourd! Glad that locasita's locked up. You packed for our flight tomorrow?"

Prior to the bachelorette party, Becca and I were getting our geek on at StoryCon, a sci-fi/fantasy convention being held in Vegas over the extended weekend. My other wedding attendants would arrive on Saturday for the party.

"Just about. I was ready to call it a day, but Assurity has one more fugitive for me. Blair Marshall."

"No shit. That psycho puta who murdered the trans woman in the Save Mart restroom?"

"That's her. Judge revoked her bail for threatening a witness. Hoping Rodeo and I can pick her up by the end of the day."

I labeled a manilla folder and studied the documents I had printed.

Blair Marshall was twenty-seven, five-five, drove a 2016 Chevy Malibu, and lived with her significant other, a thirty-eight-year-old woman named Naomi Hoffman in the north valley off Happy Valley Road. She had good credit, a couple thousand dollars in the bank, and ran a nonprofit organization named Womyn Born Womyn whose mission was spreading harmful lies about transgender people.

In her mug shot, her feminine features and long blond hair belied a stony expression.

In the past year, Marshall's little nonprofit hate group had tried to push a bill through the state legislature that would have forced trans people to use public restrooms based on their assigned sex at birth. The measure died in committee only after someone pointed out that doing so would force trans guys—many of whom were bearded and muscular—to use the ladies' rooms.

Not that trans guys were a threat to cisgender women either. But the bigots realized their proposed legislation would have had the opposite effect of "keeping men out of women-only spaces."

And now Blair Marshall, self-appointed gender defender of the valley's restrooms, had brutally murdered a Black transgender woman. Well, if she was going to continue her crusade against my community, she'd have to do it from behind bars. I intended to put her there.

"You need me to skip trace Marshall?" Becca asked.

"Let me go knock on her door, see if we can do this the easy way. I'll call you if I need any skip tracing."

She nodded. "Okay, chica. If I don't hear from you, I'll see you tomorrow morning at Sky Harbor."

I gave her a hug. "See ya then, bestie."

"Take care, Becca," Rodeo said. "Have fun in Vegas. And keep our girl outta trouble."

I elbowed him and led him out of the building. We climbed back into the Gray Ghost and drove north.

3

I pulled off the Black Canyon Highway at Happy Valley Road and turned south into a residential area after a few miles. Rodeo helped me navigate through a labyrinthine neighborhood filled with McMansions.

Naomi Hoffman, who owned the house, worked as the creative director of a media marketing company. Must've made some serious bank, because no way Marshall could've afforded a place like this running a nonprofit. Not unless she was earning serious money under the table somehow.

I blocked off the driveway with the Gray Ghost to prevent an escape. It wouldn't stop anyone who was determined. The crushed-rock landscaping that was ubiquitous throughout the valley didn't have any large cactuses or palm trees to keep Marshall from cutting across it, but it might discourage her.

When we stepped out of the SUV, I adjusted the straps on my vest, unsnapped the retention strap on my ankle holster, and double-checked my Taser. I'd once forgotten to put on a fresh cartridge and nearly got my clock cleaned by an ill-tempered fugitive.

"SOP," I said to Rodeo. "Go around back. Keep an eye out for dogs. I'll take the front."

"Copy that." He tilted his Stetson to block the sun from hitting him in the eyes and grabbed the beanbag shotgun along with a two-foot pry bar from the back of the SUV.

I pulled out a thirty-pound battering ram, closed the truck, and turned on my two-way radio. "Channel four as usual."

"Roger." He turned his on and crept around the house to the gate that led to the walled-off backyard.

When I reached the front door, I called on the radio. "Front door ready."

"Back door ready. There's a doggy door in the back but no sign of a pooch."

"Let's hope it stays that way. Watch yourself."

I pounded on the front door, punched the doorbell a few times, and shouted, "Bail enforcement. Open up now!"

I waited, but there was no response. It was nearly three on a Wednesday afternoon. Most people working a nine-to-five weren't at home. Which didn't necessarily mean Blair Marshall wasn't in there hiding.

"No answer," I said into the radio.

"You think she's inside?"

"Only one way to find out."

I tried knocking and rang the doorbell a few more times. When I was convinced no one was coming, I hefted the ram and pounded the door. It cracked on the first hit. The second blow splintered the frame and knocked it open.

"Front door breached."

A series of clunks came from the back of the house. Rodeo prying open a sliding glass door, no doubt. His voice crackled over the radio. "Back door breached."

According to a U.S. Supreme Court case from way back, bounty hunters were allowed to enter a fugitive's home without a warrant because, even while on bail, they were still considered in custody.

I lay the ram by the doorway, drew my Taser, stepped inside, and saw a kitchen to my left, a living room to my right. On the wall, a security system touch pad indicated an open front and rear door, but no alarm was triggered. Either someone was home or Marshall and Hoffman had forgotten to set the alarm.

I turned to the kitchen and began my search. Fugitives were remarkably creative in choosing places to hide. I've found people in kitchen cabinets and tucked into closet shelves, laundry baskets, and attics.

Based on the physical description and mug shots in her file, Marshall could probably squeeze into some tight spots, so I checked in cabinets high and low, as well as in the walk-in pantry. No joy.

"Arizona room clear," Rodeo said over the radio.

I replied a moment later, "Kitchen clear."

We proceeded through the house systematically. I explored the living room, checking under couches and chairs, under tablecloths, and behind the entertainment center.

When the living room was cleared, I joined Rodeo in the bedrooms. He'd already cleared the master bedroom and bath. I took the guest bath, checking behind the shower curtain and the cabinets under the sink.

"One side of the master bedroom closet is empty," Rodeo said as we met in the hallway. "Looks like someone packed up some clothes and moved out."

"Or wants us to think she did. Check the third bedroom." I pointed to the trapdoor in the ceiling that led to the attic. "I'll take a peek up top."

"Copy that."

I pulled down the trapdoor and unfolded the ladder. My pulse accelerated. Checking attics was dangerous with violent suspects. Sticking your head up into the dark made one a prime target for someone with a weapon.

There had been no indication that either Marshall or Hoffman was a registered gun owner, but they could have bought one from a private dealer. Or Marshall could be lying in wait with a baseball bat or other weapon.

I grabbed a flashlight from my utility belt, climbed a few steps, and made a quick assessment of the dark expanse. Wooden struts, stacks of boxes, and other personal belongings provided a playground of hiding places that stretched the length of the three-thousand-square-foot house.

I mounted the remaining steps, scanning the attic for movement and keeping an eye out for anything that seemed out of sorts. I drew my revolver, since my Taser was limited to a thirty-foot range.

The air was stuffy and warm. Dust motes floated in and out of my flashlight's beam. The plywood floor creaked as I stepped onto it. It wasn't secured to the crossbeams. One wrong step and I'd go plunging through the main floor's ceiling.

I approached a cluster of camping gear next to boxes marked with the words "Naomi's china" in permanent marker. Didn't find anything of interest except a pissed-off family of roof rats that went scurrying away into the dark.

Despite the high intensity of the situation, the hunt was my favorite part of the job. And I was good at it.

When I'd checked out every shadowy corner, my instincts were telling me no one was home.

"Attic clear," I called into the radio.

Rodeo replied, "Third bedroom clear except for a very frightened little Chihuahua."

"Remember, Rodeo, they're only Chihuahuas if they're from Chihuahua, Mexico. Otherwise, they're just yappy ankle-biters."

"Good one, boss."

I climbed back down to the main floor and found Rodeo rechecking one of the bedrooms.

"Looks like no one's home," I said.

"Copy that. What's our next move?"

I wanted to call it a day, but I also wanted to find Marshall before I left in the morning.

"The nonprofit hate group that Blair Marshall runs is down on Camelback and Third Street. Let's go say hello."

Something outside the window caught Rodeo's attention. "Uh-oh. Looks like we got company."

"Whoever's here, I'm calling the cops!" called a female voice from the entryway.

"Go right ahead," I replied when we found a stocky woman in her forties with shoulder-length hair standing by the shattered door. I flashed my bail enforcement badge and ID. "We're here to enforce a judge's order."

She held up her phone in such a way that it was clear she was video recording our presence and the damage to the door. "What the hell's going on? Why are you in my house?"

"You're Naomi Hoffman, right?" I asked.

She turned the phone toward me. "Who's asking?"

"Ballou Fugitive Recovery. We're looking for Blair Marshall."

"She's. Not. Here." Hoffman enunciated each syllable.

"Where is she?"

"Why should I tell you? You people broke down my door. And I'm recording this to show the police."

"Be my guest. The judge revoked Marshall's bail. Assurity Bail Bonds hired us to return her to custody. So, where is she?"

She shrugged unconvincingly. "How should I know? I just got back from a dentist appointment."

"You live with her. I'm guessing you're in a relationship, judging by the portraits in the hallway. If anyone knows where she is, it's you."

She put her hands on her hips. "I recognize you. You're that tranny bounty hunter who was featured in *Phoenix Living* a few years back."

Ugh. One of the worst mistakes in my career as a bounty hunter was being interviewed for the weekly alternative newspaper's cover story. I had no idea at the time that the journalist writing the story would out me. We never discussed my being trans. But he'd dug it up, nevertheless.

"You put your home up for collateral. If she fails to surrender herself, you lose your home," I replied, refusing to take her bait. "And for harboring a fugitive wanted for murder, you could face a hefty prison sentence yourself. So, go ahead and call the police. We'll wait."

"She's not here. Just leave."

"Tell us where she is."

"I'm not telling you anything, *sir*!" She glared at me. "Now get out of my house."

Rodeo put a hand on my shoulder. "Let's go, boss. She's not here."

"Suit yourself. Maybe after Assurity Bail Bond takes your house, I'll buy it." I walked out the broken front door. "Though I'd want to get rid of the roof rats first."

"You're going to pay for my door!"

"Tell us where Blair Marshall is, and I'll consider it." I waited as she glared at me. "No? Okay. Later."

"Bitch!" she shouted as we strolled to the Gray Ghost.

4

"She was not a happy camper," Rodeo joked while I drove out of the neighborhood.

"Ya think?" I pulled onto the southbound Black Canyon Highway. "Not that I care, considering her girlfriend murdered LaTonya Garrett. Let's see what we can find out at the so-called nonprofit of hate she runs."

Shortly after the Peoria exit, traffic came to a halt, although we were heading into town during the afternoon rush hour. I turned on the radio and learned that there had been a multi-car pileup near Bethany Home Road, a few miles south.

"This doesn't look good," I said.

"Maybe pull off the highway at Dunlap," Rodeo suggested.

It took forty minutes to reach the exit and another ten before we got through the light on Dunlap Road. Even then, the surface streets were gridlocked from all the other drivers escaping the blocked highway.

By the time we reached the Womyn Born Womyn office,

situated in a small strip mall, it was a quarter after five. The office was closed and dark.

"Shit." I pounded on the glass door. "Fucking traffic."

Rodeo put a hand on my shoulder. "Don't worry. Zahara and I will track her down. If we don't have her by the time Z leaves for Vegas on Saturday, I'll keep looking. Maybe have Byrd or one of Conor's other guys as backup. Go enjoy your weekend."

I sighed. "If it was anyone but one of these fucking TERFs."

TERF was short for transgender-exclusionary radical feminist, a term the radfem community came up with to describe those who didn't consider trans women to be women and who treated trans men as traitors to the butch lesbian community.

"Don't let her live rent free in your head," Rodeo replied.

"You sound like my dad."

"Well, he *is* a psychologist."

"Yeah, yeah. Let's go back to the Hub."

It didn't take us long to return downtown, which had emptied for the day.

"See you Monday," Rodeo said, giving me a hug. "Have a pleasant flight and have fun this weekend."

"I intend to."

"But not too much fun." He winked.

"Yeah, yeah."

I headed home to get ready for my crazy extended weekend in Vegas. With a little luck, Rodeo and Zahara would track down Marshall in a day or so, making Sadie a happy woman—or at least less grumpy than usual—and the rest of us a little richer.

Home was a cozy house in the overpriced Willo District

in central Phoenix that backed up to McDowell Road. I had nicknamed it the Bunker because my fiancé Conor Doyle had installed inch-thick polycarbonate windows, bulletproof walls, steel-reinforced doors, and an underground tunnel that led from a tattoo parlor on McDowell to a trapdoor in our coat closet. He'd made the extreme modifications after a drug gang had tried to level the place in a drive-by shooting.

My two-year-old golden retriever Diana greeted me with sloppy, wet doggy kisses at the door when I arrived.

"Hey, baby girl. You need to go for a run?"

"Just got back from one," Conor called from the kitchen.

I found him relaxing and drinking a bottle of Jarritos Mandarin soda at our antique kitchen table rumored to have once belonged to the pirate Jean Lafitte, one of my ancestors.

Like me, Conor was a bounty hunter. In fact, he was the one who introduced me to the business before I started my own company. He greeted me with a hug and a kiss when I walked in.

"What's the craic, love?"

Despite all the years I'd known him, his curly red hair, emerald eyes, and Irish brogue never failed to turn me on. The man had a sexy ruggedness that a lot of cisgender women dreamed their men had. The fact that he loved me, a transgender woman, still blew my mind.

I sat opposite him and took a sip of his soda. "We got Nussbaum finally."

"The barmy lass who shags corpses?" His upper lip curled in disgust. Even that was sexy. "Good for you, love."

"Over one hundred counts of abuse of a human corpse. But her perversion is my profit. Two-hundred-thirty-thou-sand-dollar bounty."

"Brilliant! Try not to blow your entire cut gambling in Las Vegas." He winked when he said it.

"Not a chance. Though I may have to bring an additional suitcase for all the comics, books, and other merch I plan to buy."

My stomach rumbled. I hadn't eaten since we caught Nussbaum, and I was starving. I pulled a banana from the bunch on the counter only to realize it was an empty peel.

"Dammit! Got me again with the empty banana trick."

He nearly choked on his soda laughing. Recently he'd discovered that he could open a banana from the middle and the peel wouldn't wilt. Now it had turned into an ongoing prank.

I smirked. "Laugh while you can, smarty-pants. You'll get yours."

"Sorry, love. I ate the banana early this morning. Been waiting all day for you to grab it." He continued to chuckle.

"Anyway," I said, trying to recover my dignity. "How was your day? You were on a stakeout, right?"

"Aye. The bloke was a no-show at his girl's place. I think we'll check with some of his co-workers at the construction site." His eyelids drooped. "Until then, I gotta get some shut-eye. I'm knackered."

My phone rang. The caller ID showed the name Marie Lafitte. I took the call.

"Grand-Mère Marie! How are you?"

"Oo ye yi, cher. I fear I may not make it down for the wedding."

"Why? Are you sick?"

"No, no, it's Guimauve. She's not her usual perky self, and she hasn't been eating. I fear she may be ill."

"Oh, Grand-Mère, I'm so sorry. Any idea what's going on?"

"She's at the veterinarian now. They're running tests."

My heart felt heavy. I so wanted her to come out for the wedding. But she loved that dog, and it was a long trip from New Orleans for a woman in her late seventies.

Conor eyed me with a concerned look.

"Do what you feel is best. If you can't make it, I will understand. I know how much she means to you. And maybe I'll fly back to New Orleans sometime soon."

"I would hate to miss your wedding, cher. You're my only granddaughter."

"I would miss you too. Let me know when you hear from the vet."

"I will. Bye-bye, cher."

I hung up and sighed.

"How's Grand-Mère Marie?" Conor got up and hugged me from behind.

"Not good. Her dog, Guimauve, is sick."

"Gwee-what?"

"Guimauve. It's French for marshmallow." I shrugged. "She's not sure whether she'll make it to the wedding or not."

"Poor woman must be wrecked. What kind of dog is it?"

"Shitza-poo."

Conor spewed orange soda across the kitchen table, barely missing me. "A what?"

"A shitza-poo. It's a cross between a shih-tzu and a poodle. What else would you call it?"

"I dunno. Maybe a shih-poo?" He grabbed a kitchen towel and mopped up the mess.

"A sheep-poo? Oh yeah. That sounds tons better."

"Well, I hope the poor pup gets to feeling better. I know how close you are with your grandmother."

I trailed a finger along the grain of the antique wooden table. She had given it to me years earlier. Supposedly,

Captain Jean Lafitte had eaten off it in his ship's cabin. "Yeah, we're close."

"Well, love, I'm gonna hit the sack."

I felt a twinge of sadness about leaving him for the weekend. Since he'd come back into my life a year earlier, I'd become clingier for fear of losing him once again. "Care for some company?"

His eyes twinkled with anticipation. "Aye! Can never say no to you."

As we undressed, both our bodies reflected the violent and potentially lethal nature of our chosen profession. The coppery curls of hair on his chest couldn't hide the multiple scars from bullet wounds, knife attacks, and an IED he survived while working for Dark Horse Security in Iraq.

My body wasn't much better. I'd been shot, stabbed, beaten, and battered from my countless encounters with suspects, both as a bounty hunter and in my one-year stint as a patrol officer with Phoenix PD.

The scars were a hazard of the trade. But one scar on his leg still pulled at a deeply held trauma in my soul. A year and a half ago, Conor and I were trying to stop a white nationalist paramilitary group from bringing down Phoenix City Hall with a truck full of explosives. Conor had forced the truck over on the Piestewa Freeway. Still, the driver set off the explosive during morning rush hour, killing dozens of people and injuring hundreds more.

For a week, I believed Conor had been killed in the explosion. But on Christmas morning, he called me from Mexico on a burner phone. Seconds before the detonation, he'd leapt off the bridge into the Arizona Canal. He avoided the blast but suffered a compound fracture from the fall into the canal.

With help from a document forger named Picardo,

Conor escaped to Mexico to evade the Northern Irish police who had tracked him to Phoenix as part of their investigation into the Omagh bombing that Conor's father had been involved with when Conor was seventeen.

I visited him down in Mexico but declined his offer to start a new life under assumed identities. Without me by his side, he surrendered to the Northern Irish authorities and was eventually cleared of the terrorism charges after two decades of living on the run.

Months later, Conor's U.S. citizenship was restored. He never explained how, but I gathered that his former employer, Dark Horse Security, had greased the path with Homeland Security.

The four-inch scar where the Mexican surgeon repaired his shattered leg still reminded me of the sense of loss I'd experienced, both when I thought him dead and when I walked away.

Our lovemaking now was even more passionate. Gratitude was a helluva drug. Soon I would marry this amazing man. The impossible dream was finally coming true.

Despite all the shit we'd been through, both together and separately, I had no reservations about spending the rest of my life with this kind, funny, sexy man. The refrain from Carole King's "Natural Woman" played through my mind.

After a post-coital cuddle, he fell into a much-needed sleep while I packed for my weekend of cosplay, fangirling, and bachelorette festivities.

Becca, her significant other Easton St. Claire, and I would spend Thursday, Friday, and part of Saturday doing the StoryCon thing. Going to panels, buying comics, talking to creators, and probably getting my photo taken with other fans of the *Into the Black* franchise who loved the character I was cosplaying.

Zahara, my friend and lawyer Kirsten Pasternak, and my mentor Juanita Valdez would join us on Saturday afternoon. Juanita, a trans woman who owned Phoenix's largest drag bar, was in charge of the bachelorette party. I had no idea what outrageous things she had planned, but knowing her, it would be memorable. Assuming I didn't get too drunk.

5

———

I sat doom-scrolling the latest news on my phone in Phoenix Sky Harbor's Terminal 4 when a high-pitched squeal pierced the din of conversations and occasional boarding announcements. Becca strode toward me with arms outstretched, wearing a white Hawaiian-style shirt decorated with flamingos and hibiscus flowers. I jumped up and ran into her embrace.

"Oh my gourd! I can't believe this is happening, hermana." Becca's voice was choked with emotion. "Our last weekend with you as a single woman."

"Don't worry, nothing's changing but my legal marital status," I reminded her. "I promise to continue to hire you as my skip-tracing guru."

"Oh, is that all I am to you?" she asked with a smirk.

"You mean there's something more?" I replied with a grin.

Her nonbinary significant other, Easton St. Claire, approached, pulling both their suitcase and Becca's. Easton wore a green-striped button-down shirt and dark denim jeans.

"How's it going, Easton?" I gave them a hug.

"Good. This is going to be one wild weekend. Especially once Juanita shows up."

Becca chuckled. "The woman is a force of nature."

"But in a good way," I replied. "Most of the time."

She gripped my shoulders and looked me straight in the face. "You nervous?"

I scoffed. "About flying? Course not. I've flown hundreds of times."

She slapped my shoulder. "¡Idiota! Nervous about getting married."

"I probably should be, but I'm not. More nervous about what Juanita has planned. As for my feelings about the wedding, I'm grateful it's finally happening. He's sexy. He's sweet. And he makes me laugh. What more could a woman want?"

"Good for you," Easton replied.

We sat down near the gate where our flight would board. Becca pointed to a television mounted on a nearby column. "There she is."

The TV screen showed Blair Marshall's scowling face from her mug shot. The volume was turned down, so we couldn't hear what the news anchor was saying.

"Who is that?" Easton asked.

"Blair Marshall," Becca explained. "She murdered a trans woman in a Save Mart restroom."

"She's a TERF." I glared at the screen, which now showed the woman speaking at a rally. "She runs Womyn Born Womyn. Judge revoked her bail after she threatened a witness. Her bail bond agent hired me to drag her scrawny, transphobic ass back to jail. I'm hoping Z and Rodeo can pick her up before the weekend."

"Now I remember." Easton nodded with a frown. "What a horrible person."

A static voice came over the comm system. "Pacific Airlines Flight 5461 to Las Vegas will begin boarding in ten minutes."

"That's us," I said.

~

The flight to Vegas only took an hour and was uneventful. By noon, we'd checked into our rooms at the Pandora Hotel and Casino. For the time being, I had a room to myself. Juanita would take the other bed when she arrived on Saturday. Becca and Easton bunked together across the hall.

I changed into my Asaya Thrax body armor, and the three of us went downstairs to join the throng of StoryCon attendees. I felt like a kid in a candy store, marveling at the wide array of creative costumes from all fandoms, many of them more elaborate than mine.

We attended a few early panels then wandered the vendor marketplace, where one could purchase nearly anything related to comic books, sci-fi, and fantasy. I shelled out more money than I should, and at one point wondered how I was going to get some of my booty back home. I bought Conor a *Firefly* T-shirt so he wouldn't feel I'd completely forgotten about him. Periodically, a fellow Thrax fan would stop me to pose with them for a selfie.

After an exhausting day of panels, shopping, and fighting crowds, the three of us returned to our rooms.

Before taking off my costume, I collapsed into a chair and called Conor.

"Hello, love. How's the con?"

"Good. Having loads of fun. Went to an interesting panel on the science of *The Expanse*. Saw Jodie Whittaker talk about her experiences being on *Doctor Who*. On Saturday, we're going to see Hannah Jakes."

"Who's she?"

"She wrote the *Spellbound* YA fantasy comic book series. Very popular. Amazon Prime's working on a TV series based on the books. Rumor is they're previewing the trailer. I had to reserve tickets ahead of time."

"That's brilliant. I'm wrecked with not seeing you till Sunday."

"I miss you too. But I'll be back Sunday night."

"Seems like ages away. But I'm glad you're having fun with your mates."

"How are things with you?"

"Bloody good. A lad at the construction site gave us a solid tip on our fugitive's whereabouts. Apparently, the two of them had a serious falling-out over a woman. He was happy to give up his former mate. Deez, Byrd, Tommy Boy, and I are on our way to pick the guy up now."

"That's great. I'm hoping Rodeo and Zahara can arrest Blair Marshall tomorrow."

"If they need a hand, have them ring my mobile. Byrd or Deez could provide any extra backup."

"Thanks, babe. I better let you go. Easton got us tickets to see one of the cabaret shows at the hotel, and I'm still in my space marine costume. I'll talk to you tomorrow. Good hunting and watch your six."

"Aye. Always do. Love ya, babe."

"Love you too." I felt a knot in my chest when I hung up. I was smitten like a schoolgirl and had no regrets.

While I was slipping into a sunset-orange silk dress to wear to the show, my phone rang. It was Rodeo.

"Hey, boss, how's Vegas?" he asked.

"Fun but tiring." I hurriedly touched up my makeup

while holding the phone. "How goes the search for Marshall?"

"We checked the nonprofit and tried pressing the staff for info. No joy so far."

"Run her girlfriend through the SkipTrakkr database. Check their bank statements and phone logs for leads."

"Will do."

"If you need any additional manpower, call Conor. He's agreed to lend a hand if necessary."

"Thanks. I'll keep it in mind. Hopefully, we'll grab her tomorrow."

"Sounds good. See you Saturday."

I finished getting dressed and met Becca and Easton for the show. It wasn't bad, but I was glad Juanita wasn't with us. As a trans woman who came up through the drag scene, she would've read those showgirls to trash. Probably a hazard of the trade when you're a former performer like her.

The next day, the three of us were back at the con. My pile of books and merch was growing large. I wondered if it would be cheaper to ship some of it home or buy an additional suitcase. I made a couple of trips to the room so that I wasn't hauling it around from panel to panel.

Around noon, I found myself in a section of the marketplace known as Author's Cove, while Becca and Easton went off in search of sustenance. I stopped at a booth where Malorie Cooper, the openly trans author of the Aeon 14 sci-fi series, was selling her books.

"I love your costume," Malorie said when I picked up one of her latest titles. She wore a long rainbow-colored wig and a sapphire-blue catsuit. My pulse quickened seeing her in person.

"Thanks. I love your books. I read the Intrepid Saga a

couple of years ago and have been working my way through the multiple series."

"Aw, thanks. What drew you to my books?"

"A cis friend recommended them. I love the diversity of your characters. I'm trans, like you. Not enough books by openly trans authors out there."

"Very true. You write?"

I blushed. "Me? No. Just a reader."

"Can't have too many of those. You attending the *Into the Black* panel?"

"Definitely. I've been a fan of the books for years. And the Netflix series is off the hook."

"I hear Gerard Boyce is up for an Emmy. I like his character. No over-the-top macho attitude like so many male sci-fi characters. What's his name? Commander..."

"Corwin," I finished for her. "Yes! He's fantastic, but as you can tell, Asaya Thrax is my fave."

"She's awesome. Badass women are always a draw for me. What do you do for a living?"

I grew nervous, preferring to keep a low profile about my profession. "Bail enforcement."

"A bounty hunter, really? How exciting!"

"It has its moments." I bought some of her paperbacks.

"Who should I autograph these to?" she asked.

"Jinx."

"Jinx the bounty hunter. Wow! I should put you in one of my books."

Now I full-on blushed. "That'd be too cool."

She handed me my signed paperbacks. "You better get going. The *Into the Black* panel's about to start."

"Shit. Nice talking to you." I pushed my way through the crowd as quickly as I could, my plastic body armor clanking and squeaking as I ran.

6

I slipped inside the large ballroom as the volunteers were closing the door. Becca's raised hand caught my eye, and I hurried down the third row to where she'd saved me a seat, trying not to step on anyone's toes with my simulated gravity boots.

Moments later, the house lights went down, the stage lights went up, and the *Into the Black* cast stepped onto the stage to thunderous applause from the hundreds of people packed into the room. The collective body heat made me sweat inside my costume armor.

The moderator spent much of the hour asking questions of the cast and the creator of the show. They were all every bit as entertaining as the characters they played. I was enthralled. I loved learning how the actors brought the characters to life, hearing about funny situations on set, and getting to know these amazingly talented people.

When they opened it up to questions from the audience, Becca nudged me. "Go up and ask a question."

"What?" I was nervous enough talking to Malorie Cooper in person. But to get up in front of the cast and a crowd of hundreds and ask some corny, gushing fangirl question while dressed in my homemade armor? Absolutely terrifying. I'd sooner walk naked into a seedy bar full of murderous thugs. "I'll just listen to what other people ask."

"Come on, Jinx," Easton insisted. "You're an überfan. And you're always wondering about the behind-the-scenes of the show. Go up and ask one of those questions."

I shook my head, trying to play it cool. But Becca kept shoving my shoulder. She could be such a brat. Eventually, I took a deep breath and whispered, "Fine."

I squeezed my way out of the cramped row, nearly falling over onto a guy with long legs. When I reached the end of the long line, I tried to come up with a question to ask. My armor grew uncomfortably warm. Sweat puddled underneath my breasts. I should've figured out a way to install a cooling system.

I could ask Nora Herbert who influenced how she played the character Thrax. Or maybe what was the craziest fan mail she'd received. Or whether she read the books before playing the character. Or...

My brain was a locomotive racing full speed toward a hairpin turn. Ideas for questions kept popping up in my head, each one wiping out the one before, all while the line toward the microphone in the aisle grew shorter.

When I reached it, I was about to ask a question when Gerard Boyce spoke up. "I absolutely adore your costume," he said in a posh British accent, very different from the Texas drawl his character Commander Corwin used. "Did you make it yourself?"

"I... uh... yeah." My brain completely short-circuited.

"It's brilliant. What's your name?"

"Jinx Ballou."

"Is it really? Smashing name."

"Thanks."

"And what's your question, Jinx?" the moderator asked, no doubt trying to speed things along.

"I... um... my question's for... Commander Gerard... I mean, Gerard Boyce." My face felt like it was on fire. Why did I say that? I didn't have a question for him. "Your character, he's a really nice guy." Jeez, what a stupid thing to say.

"Thanks, love." He smiled, and that only made things worse.

Was I fangirl crushing on him? Shit.

"What... what drew you to wanting to play the character?"

"That's a great question." He leaned forward, elbows on knees, meeting my gaze. "Even before casting began for the series, I was a fan of the character from the books. Corwin's compassion, his level-headedness, and his commitment to protecting vulnerable people defined his psyche for me. We need more of that in the real world. So when given the opportunity to read for the part, I jumped at it. Does that answer your question?"

"Uh. Yeah, it does. Thanks."

"I'd love to get a photo with you in your costume after the panel." He shot me a million-dollar smile, and I nearly melted into the floor.

What the fuck was happening to me? I was getting married in a week to the man of my dreams. But here I was gushing over a man who plays dress-up for a living? I was a bounty hunter, for goodness' sake, a tough, smart woman who fought bad guys and put them in jail. I was the real deal. And this guy was turning me into a puddle of goo?

"Yeah, I'd like that," I answered before I realized what I was saying.

I shuffled back to my seat, trying to shake the cotton out of my brain.

"Oh my gourd!" Becca squealed. "You're getting a photo taken with the *Into the Black* cast. I'm totally jealous."

I was torn between the excitement of taking selfies with the cast and the abject terror of making a further fool of myself.

When the panel was over, I turned toward the exit. No need to further embarrass myself.

Easton stopped me. "Wait! Aren't you getting photos made with Boyce and the rest of the cast?"

"He was just saying that."

"No," Becca corrected. "He was serious. The next panel's not for an hour, anyway. We'll wait for you. This is your weekend. Cut loose. Check off some items from your bucket list. You've always wanted to get up close and personal with the cast."

"Okay." I took a deep breath and regained my cool. An actor wanted to get a photo with me. It was all good. No need to lose my head. I didn't have a real crush on him. We were two adults who enjoyed a well-written television series.

I reached the curtain and met a volunteer who invited me to follow her backstage where Boyce, Herbert, and the other cast members were relaxing with drinks and snacks.

"There she is!" Nora Herbert studied my costume. "Wow. This is great craftsmanship. You made this?"

I nodded.

"Amazing. Better than the one I wear for the show. The costume department should totally hire you. Do you work in fashion?"

I chuckled nervously. "No, I'm in bail enforcement."

"Wow! How badass is that? I should get *your* autograph."

"Just a job like any other."

"Let's get some photos," Boyce said.

The cast gathered around. We took some shots with me posing with Herbert, flexing our biceps, then with Boyce, his arm around me. He smelled great. Finally, some group shots. I gave their publicist my email address so she could send me copies of the photos.

As Herbert and the others walked off with a volunteer, Boyce added, "The cast and a few crew members are getting together for drinks later tonight in my hotel room. Care to join us? We always like to kick back with our more ardent fans."

A red flag triggered in the back of my brain, but I ignored it. Boyce wasn't like some celebrities. He respected women. Besides, it would be a group situation. No big deal.

"Sure, what time?"

"Around nine o'clock. Room 3466."

"Should I come in costume?"

"No, wear something elegant but comfortable. We're real people, after all."

"Sounds fun. I'll see y'all at nine."

I returned to Becca and Easton, who were waiting in the empty ballroom.

"So?" Easton asked.

My phone pinged. Email received from the show's publicist. I opened it and showed them the attached pics.

"Look at you!" Becca gasped as she flipped through the photos. "Mingling with the fancy Hollywood types."

"Gerard Boyce invited me to join them for drinks later tonight. Only I forgot to ask if it'd be okay if you come too. Maybe I should forget about it. Hobnobbing with actors isn't really my scene."

"Are you kidding?" Easton asked, straightening their suspenders. "You totally have to do it. We'll be fine. I was thinking of playing the blackjack tables in the casino tonight. Go have fun."

"You sure?"

"Absolutely," Becca reassured me. "All this running around has me low on spoons, anyway. This is your weekend. Why shouldn't you hang out with some of your favorite celebs?"

"But I want photos," Easton insisted. "Lots of photos."

I still felt a little guilty, but what the hell. In a week, I'd be marrying the love of my life. Might as well have some innocent fun. "I promise."

7

We attended a few more panels then hung out in Becca and Easton's room and ordered delivery from an Italian restaurant at the Venetian. Rodeo called in the middle of dinner to say he and Zahara hadn't apprehended Marshall but had a good lead and were feeling lucky.

After dinner, I bought a black cocktail dress at a shop in Pandora's lobby and a six-pack of Death Adder beer from a nearby liquor store. I'd never tried that microbrew. But Easton had recommended it, and I didn't want to show up to a party empty-handed.

I had just enough time to get back to my room, change into the dress, and take an elevator up to Boyce's suite. My pulse raced when I knocked on the door. Out of habit, my knock was more of a pounding designed to intimidate occupants inside. That only fueled my embarrassment.

Boyce opened the door. "Huh-ho! For a moment there, I thought you were the bloody cops," he said with a whimsical wobble in his speech. His gaze dropped to my chest then down to the six-pack in my hand. "What have we here? Death Adder, eh? Sounds darkly delightful. Come join the party."

I followed him into the enormous suite. The place looked like a luxury apartment with an amazing view of the Strip below and the city lights extending out to the horizon. Unlike my little box of a room twenty floors below with an excellent view of the parking lot.

The lighting was subdued. Ravel's "Bolero" played on the stereo, the repetitive, marchlike refrain of percussion and woodwinds slowly building in intensity.

Instinctively, I assessed the room as I always did when I entered a place. The practice had been drummed into me since my days at the police academy. A tingle of wariness ran down my spine that had nothing to do with my previous fangirl shyness.

My situational awareness should have been at condition yellow—alert but relaxed, no immediate threat present. Instead, I found myself at condition orange. Something was wrong here. It took me a moment to realize Boyce and I were alone. I didn't have to check the adjoining rooms. I simply knew it.

"Shall I pour you one of your beers?" He strode over to a wet bar.

"Sure. Where's everyone else?" I wandered around the suite and studied a framed black-and-white print on the wall. Looked like one of Ansel Adams's photos of mountains in Yellowstone or Yosemite National Park. Never could keep them straight.

"They'll be along. A few of them wanted to try their luck at the tables before joining the party."

"I see." I returned to the wet bar.

He handed me the mug of beer, downed what remained in his tumbler, and poured himself another three fingers of bourbon. "In the meantime, love, it's just you and me. Cheers."

"Cheers." I clinked my mug with his glass.

The beer was cold with a rich, hoppy flavor and notes of coffee and cherry but had a bitter aftertaste. I failed to see why Easton liked it. I sipped it to appear social.

"Tell me, Miss Jinx, what does one do as a bail enforcement ossifer?" he slurred, locking eyes on me.

"Bail enforcement *agent*," I corrected, if a bit rudely. "When defendants fail to appear in court or the judge revokes their bail, their bail bond agent hires someone like me to return them to custody."

"How exciting!" He leaned closer. "And if they don't come along nicely, is it all guns blazing, bring 'em back dead or alive?"

"Not usually. It's no longer the Wild West. We bring them back alive, or we don't get paid."

I hated talking about my work to anyone not in the business. Most civilians had wild romantic visions of what a bounty hunter did and were disappointed to learn it wasn't nearly as exciting as movies liked to portray it.

"I ask because I've been cast as a bounty hunter in an upcoming movie," he explained, straightening up, perhaps to appear more sober than he was. "Brett Ratner directing, no less. And between you and me, one Mr. Weinstein is the executive producer, but that's kind of hush-hush because of all the... you know." He made an exaggerated gesture with his hand, apparently hinting at the consequences regarding Weinstein's abusive history.

"As a professional, I take my craft very, *very* seriously, you understand. I'm not some tosser who jumps willy-nilly into a role. No sirree. I do my research. And when I learned you are a professional bail enforcement agent—see, I was listening—I said to myself, Gerard old boy, you must talk to this girl and pick her brains. Indeed, I want to know all about your work."

He leaned in again, and I caught a full whiff of whiskey breath with a hint of B.O. Not nearly as nice as he'd smelled earlier that afternoon. "Now then, Miss Jinx the bounty hunter, how do you do that voodoo that you do? How do you catch these rapscallions who jump their bonds?"

"Bail," I corrected.

"Jump their bails." He placed a hand on my thigh.

In an instant, I went from condition orange to red. I pushed his hand away and stepped off the stool. "Maybe we should wait for the others."

I strolled toward the picture windows looking down on the city and felt a little woozy. It wasn't the dizzying view of Vegas below that bothered me but something else. Was I coming down with the flu?

"The others? The others can sod right off! This is you and me, love. Two single adults in a city of decadence. What's the saying? 'What happens in Vegas, stays in Vegas?'"

The music changed from Ravel to Wagner's "Ride of the Valkyries." A wave of nausea plowed through me. Something was very wrong. I pulled out my phone and texted Becca. *In trribl Helo Rm 3466.*

The phone fell out of my hand and landed silently in the white deep pile carpeting. I leaned against a couch and gazed out at the city lights, trying to keep the room from wobbling.

"Oh, Jinxie," he crooned from across the room.

"Gimme a moment, Mr. Boyce."

"Aw, Little Gerry wants to come out to play."

I felt a hand on my ass. With lightning speed, my training and instincts kicked in. I wheeled around, grabbed his wrist, and twisted with all my strength. Bones snapped, and Boyce yowled in pain.

"Fucking cunt! You broke my bloody wrist!" He stood there cradling his wrist with his dick hanging out of his zipper.

I stumbled into an end table and knocked over a lamp. The room was really spinning now, and my abrupt pivot to defend myself from my indecent host didn't help.

8

————

I woke with a fifty-megaton nuclear warhead exploding in my head. "Oh fuuuck."

"Hey look! Snow White's waking up," said a harsh female voice somewhere nearby.

Another voice cackled. "What you think she in for? I say DUI. She looks like a drunk."

"Naw! I say she got her white ass busted for assault. Prolly put a beatdown on some ho gettin' cozy with her man."

More laughter.

"Fuck." I gritted my teeth, sat up, and opened my eyes.

Bars. Why are there... shit. I'm in jail. Why am I in jail?

Two scantily clad women sat on the other side of the holding cell.

I tried to remember how I got here, but my memories were jumbled in bits and pieces. A hotel room. Not mine. Bigger. A man yelling. Bitter-tasting beer. City lights. Sin City. I was in Vegas. For StoryCon and my bachelorette party. But I wasn't in my Thrax costume. I was in a dress that seemed only vaguely familiar.

"What you do, Snow White?" asked the woman with the harsh voice. Sounded like a four-pack-a-day smoker. She was the taller of the two.

"What'd I do?"

"Yeah, to get yo'self locked up," the shorter one asked.

"I... I don't remember."

They laughed like I'd told the best joke they'd heard all year.

"Musta been having a real good time," Smoker replied.

"Maybe she got herself roofied."

"Don't explain why she here."

Shorty pointed at me. "Looka them muscley arms she got. Them some serious guns. Bet she kicked somebody's ass. You kick somebody's ass, Snow White?"

"Kicked somebody's..." *Did I?* It was like stumbling through a fog. "I dunno."

I checked myself. My left shoulder was sore, but there were no bruised knuckles or other obvious injuries.

I spent an hour trying to piece together the evening's events, while the two women sharing the holding cell chatted quietly to each other and cast the occasional glance in my direction and chuckling.

An electronic alarm blared for a moment, then the main door to the holding area clanked open. A female Las Vegas Metropolitan Police Department officer stepped into the room followed by my friend Kirsten Pasternak, who, besides being one of my bridal attendants, was also my attorney.

She stood an inch shy of six feet, which never stopped her from wearing heels. She wore a lilac suit and carried a leather briefcase.

"Kirsten? What the hell's going on?"

"Not here." She nodded to the officer, who opened the cell door and beckoned me.

"What about my lawyer?" Smoker asked.

"He'll get here when he gets here, sugar," the officer replied.

Smoker flipped her off then crossed her arms.

The officer led Kirsten and me to a cramped interview room and left us there with the door closed.

"What happened?" Kirsten asked me now that we were alone.

I told her what little I recalled. Going to Boyce's hotel suite expecting a party but finding him there alone. Me having a lousy-tasting beer. Classical music. He started screaming. Then nothing. A gaping hole where my memories should have been.

"Boyce claims you showed up at his hotel room drunk as a skunk, forced your way inside, and then broke his wrist when he tried escorting you back out the door."

"Broke his wrist? Why would I do that? I'm a fan. Of him and the show. And I didn't push my way in. He invited me to join him and the rest of the cast for a party at nine o'clock. I even brought beer."

"What kind of beer?"

"Death Adder. It's a microbrew that Easton recommended."

"When did he issue this invite?"

"After meeting them backstage earlier today following the *Into the Black* panel. Is it still today? What time is it anyway?"

"One o'clock, Saturday morning."

"So, yesterday."

"Did anyone else hear him invite you to this party?"

"Sure." But then I thought more about it. "No. The other cast members had left when Boyce invited me."

"And no one else was at this party?"

"I only remember seeing him."

"How many beers did you have in his suite?"

"I only remember taking a few swigs of one because it tasted like shit. I started feeling woozy soon after. I walked toward the window and looked out on the city lights below, hoping to clear my head."

"Did you have anything to drink before you showed up?"

"No. Becca, Easton, and I had dinner in their room. But all I drank was iced tea."

"And you don't remember arguing with Boyce or getting physical?"

"No." I stared at the table and tried to replay it in my mind, but there was too much mental static. "Wait. I think I called Becca. No, I texted her. I was in trouble. The room was spinning. Like I was coming down with something."

"Becca mentioned getting your text. She called the police only to learn you'd been arrested. That's when she called me. I grabbed an earlier flight. Tell me, Jinx, could Boyce have drugged you?"

"Drugged me?" I tried to relax and let the memories come. "He poured a beer into a glass mug from the wet bar and handed it to me."

"Did he put anything into the mug either before or after pouring the beer?"

"I don't know. I was staring at a framed Ansel Adams photo. One of them from Yellowstone or Yosemite."

"What happened after you started feeling woozy?"

A body memory hit me like a gut punch. "I was staring out at the city with my back to him. Then he grabbed me."

"Grabbed you how? By your arm?"

"No, he grabbed my ass. Hard. And I..." I closed my eyes and rotated in my chair, recreating the scene in my mind. "I spun around and reached for his wrist. He was standing there with his dick sticking out of his pants. I was woozy and scared." I looked up at her. The memories were falling into place. "Shit. He drugged me and..."

A chill ran through me. Had he raped me? I felt the outside of my dress. I still had panties on. And I wasn't sore down there.

"Did he rape you?"

"I don't think so."

"I could request a rape kit."

"I don't think that's necessary. I stopped him. I grabbed his wrist. Twisted. Hard. Something snapped. Shit. That's how I broke his wrist. If I was defending myself, then they can't charge me with assault, can they?"

"They can charge you, but if you were in fear of being raped, that's a valid legal defense. The catch is we have to prove it."

"How?"

"I'll request a blood sample be taken for a tox screen, though it's been about five hours. There may or may not be anything left in your system, depending on what he gave you. Rohypnol is hard to detect and has a short half-life. That's why it's so often used as a date-rape drug. Do you have any injuries? Did he hit you?"

"Not that I know of. My shoulder's a little sore. I think I landed on it when I collapsed." A tidal wave of emotion hit me, and I started bawling. I'm not normally a crier. "This is supposed to be my bachelorette party."

She put a hand on my shoulder. "We'll get this worked out, okay?"

I wiped my face and nodded.

Kirsten knocked on the door. A moment later, a man in a dark suit walked in carrying a legal pad and an electronic tablet. The red light on the ceiling-mounted camera blinked to life.

9

"I'm Detective Mark Danville from the Las Vegas Metropolitan Police's Assault Division interviewing Jenna Christine Ballou, represented by Kirsten Pasternak, counsel. Do you know why you're here this morning?"

"You tell us, detective," Kirsten answered before I could. "You put an unconscious woman in a holding cell?"

"Ms. Ballou was fully conscious when we brought her in and talking up a storm, saying things like, 'He had it coming,' repeatedly. She was intoxicated, but we figured she'd sleep it off once we put her in the cell."

"What's the deal, detective. Why are we here?" I asked.

"Jenna Ballou, you are being charged with assaulting Gerard Boyce. You broke multiple bones in his wrist."

"Before we go any further, my client requests her blood be screened for narcotics that Mr. Boyce gave her without her knowledge or consent."

"You think he drugged you?" Danville asked me.

"He put something in my drink. I brought a six-pack of

Death Adder beer. He opened one while I was looking around his suite. After he brought it to me, I started feeling woozy after drinking only a little."

"That's a serious allegation, Ms. Ballou."

"So are Mr. Boyce's unfounded claims that my client assaulted him when he knows she was acting in self-defense."

"I have video of your client admitting to the assault. Care to see?"

"That's impossible," I insisted. I had no memory of the arrest.

Danville pulled up a video on his tablet, hit play, and set it on the table. I recognized an echoey recording of my voice. The video was jumpy, but I was flailing around drunkenly in Boyce's suite while two uniformed officers tried to cuff me. I guessed it came from an officer's body cam.

"You can't do this. The fucker had it coming. He got what he deserved," my recorded self shouted.

Danville leaned back after it played, arms crossed. "Pretty damning, if you ask me."

"I don't hear my client admit to any criminal act, detective. She appears intoxicated, most likely against her will. And again, I insist my client be given a drug screening."

"We can look into a tox screen. But first I'd like to get a better understanding of what took place last night in Mr. Boyce's suite."

"Detective, with all due respect, due to how quickly certain drugs can clear a person's system, I ask that we make the tox screen a priority. Until that happens, you will get nothing from my client."

"Very well. I'll send someone in to take a blood sample and submit it to our crime lab."

He stood up and walked out.

"What happens if the drug Boyce used is already out of my system?"

"We'll deal with that when and if it happens."

We waited another thirty minutes before a technician came and took three vials of blood. I wanted to make a snide remark about them taking their fucking time, but Kirsten gave me a look that kept my mouth shut.

When Danville returned, I explained about Boyce's invitation, my surprise at him being alone in the suite, and Boyce assaulting me when I was feeling woozy. "I acted in self-defense out of fear of being raped. Same as any woman would do."

"It is your assertion that you broke Mr. Boyce's wrist after he grabbed you first. Is that correct?"

"Yes."

"Do you have any proof to support this allegation?"

"Proof that he grabbed me? No. Wait, I remember. I sent a text message."

"A text message? To whom?" Danville asked.

"Becca Alvarez. She's my best friend. She's here in town with me."

"She's in the lobby, in fact," Kirsten added. "She can corroborate that Mr. Boyce invited my client to meet the cast of *Into the Black*. I'm sure the other cast members can also confirm that. Ms. Alvarez can also confirm my client told her Boyce had invited her to a party with the cast. The claim that she forced her way in is nothing but a blatant attempt to cover up his intention to rape my client. He should be in jail, not Ms. Ballou."

"Okay, I'm going to look into your story. Wait right here."

"Be sure to check the suite for the beer if it's still there."

A few hours later, Danville returned. "I've spoken with Mr. Boyce's attorney. He has agreed to drop the charges provided you apologize to him and agree to pay for all medical expenses and lost income related to his broken wrist."

"No," I said firmly before Kirsten could speak.

"No?" Danville looked incredulous. "It seems like a fair offer."

"Not just no, but fuck no!"

"Jinx..." Kirsten cautioned. "Language."

"I will not apologize to him. He may play a nice guy on the show, but the man is a predator. If I hadn't defended myself, who knows what might have happened? I won't apologize for protecting myself against that scumbag. He's lucky I didn't do more than break his wrist. I'm a former police officer myself. I will not be railroaded by some celebrity predator."

Kirsten put a calming hand on my shoulder. "Did you get a result on the tox screen?"

"We did. It came back positive for ketamine and Valium."

"He put that shit in my drink!"

"Did you find the beers in Mr. Boyce's suite?" Kirsten pressed.

"We found five bottles of Death Adder beer in the suite's mini-fridge. Boyce claims they are his."

"What about the sixth bottle? Or the glass mug my client was drinking from?"

"We found no sixth bottle. All the mugs in the suite appeared to be clean and unused."

"He washed it out. No doubt because he didn't want anyone to find the ketamine he put in it," I said. "Piece of shit."

"And what about Boyce's false allegation of my client

forcing herself into the suite? Did you speak with Ms. Alvarez?"

"We did. The text you sent her was nonsense." He looked at his notepad. "It reads 'In tribble. Hello. Rm 3466.' In tribble? Is that a *Star Trek* reference? Something to do with the convention you've been attending?"

"No, you twit!"

"Jinx..."

"I was trying to text 'In trouble. Help. Room 3466.' The shit that asshole slipped into my beer was affecting my ability to text."

"Detective, it's clear that Mr. Boyce is covering up his intention to sexually assault my client. Only she turned out to be more than he bargained for. I doubt this is the first time he's tried this with female fans. Therefore, out of courtesy to a former police officer, drop the charges before you embarrass your department."

He studied the two of us for a moment. "I'll tell you what. I will release you for now and let the district attorney decide how she wants to handle it. In the meantime, stay local."

"I'll be here until Sunday afternoon. Then I'm returning to Phoenix. I have a fugitive murderer to apprehend. If the DA's office wants to charge me, they know where to find me."

"I thought you said you're no longer in law enforcement."

"I'm a licensed bail enforcement agent."

"A bounty hunter?" He sniggered derisively.

"That's right. Or maybe you think murderers who threaten witnesses should run free, never facing the consequences of their actions."

"Jinx, settle down."

"I'm sure you are a credit to your profession," he replied when he stood up and opened the door.

I couldn't tell if he was being sarcastic or not.

"You're free to go. You can reclaim your personal possessions on your way out."

"Thanks for a great time," I said with dripping sarcasm.

It was nearly five o'clock in the morning when we reached the lobby of the precinct. Becca and Easton, both as bleary-eyed as I felt, rushed and hugged me.

"Oh my gourd, Jinxie! Are you okay?" Becca asked.

"Yeah, for now."

"As soon as I got your text, I called 911. The dispatcher told me the police were already on their way. Did you really break Gerard Boyce's wrist?"

I told her and Easton the story as best I remembered it when we got into Kirsten's rental car and drove back to the hotel.

She was in tears by the time I finished. "I'm so sorry that happened to you. And on the weekend of your bachelorette party."

I took a deep breath, gazing out at the early-morning traffic. The sun was turning the eastern sky from black to apricot. "I've been through worse. And at least I have you and Kirsten and Easton and everyone else coming later today. Plus, there's the Hannah Jakes panel this morning. I've been really looking forward to her talk."

Easton cleared their throat and leaned back from the front passenger seat. "About that. I saw on Twitter that Hannah Jakes has gone full TERF."

I turned to them, feeling like yet another shoe had dropped. "Are you serious?"

"Afraid so. She posted a link to a right-wing blog claiming how kids are getting brainwashed into thinking they're trans, and that allowing them to transition is child abuse. The usual transphobic straw man arguments and gaslighting bullshit."

"Why would she do that? Her Spellbound series has such diverse characters."

Becca put a hand on my shoulder. "Yeah, but even a lot of her so-called diverse characters were problematic. A lot of harmful stereotypes. Butch Meyers, the token lesbian character, was always hitting on straight girls. And Pedro Garcia, the only Latinx character in the entire series, is the son of the school's groundskeeper. Because apparently landscaping is the only thing my people know how to do. At least in her mind."

I sighed. "You're not wrong. I'm still disappointed. Why do people have to be such shits?"

"We're still going to have a helluva time tonight," Kirsten said. "Forget about those assholes. They write about heroes or play them on TV. But you, my dear, are the real thing. You've caught serial killers, stopped a terrorist plot, brought down human trafficking organizations, and saved countless lives. It's one reason I'm always proud to represent you. You're one of the good ones."

"Does this mean you'll represent me for free?" I half joked.

"Not a chance, my dear. If you were destitute, I'd consider it. But you make good money at what you do. But I promise not to charge you for the extra plane fare I paid to move my flight up by twelve hours."

"Thanks."

Becca handed me her phone, which had the StoryCon schedule for the day. "Hey, weren't you talking about having met Malorie Cooper in the Author's Cove?"

"Yeah, why?"

"She is speaking on a panel about the science behind science fiction. We could go to that at least."

I met her eyes and couldn't help but smile. Despite all the bullshit and truly despicable people in the world, I was lucky to be surrounded by such amazing people who had my back. People who had proved yet again that I could count on them when the shit went down.

"Sounds like fun," I said.

10

————

I spent the next four hours trying to sleep in my hotel room. There was a message to call the front desk, but I opted to deal with it after I'd had some rest and was in a better emotional state.

What little sleep I managed was fitful with panic-inducing flashes from the night before. Goddamn that motherfucker Boyce! Robbing me of an enjoyable weekend. I hoped his broken wrist hurt like a mofo and would trouble him for the rest of his life.

At ten o'clock, I lay awake in bed, staring at the curtains and trying to get my mind to focus on things that made me happy. Playing with Diana the Wonder Dog. Making love to Conor. Slapping the cuffs on a fugitive.

A knock on the door tore me out of my bizarro version of *The Sound of Music*.

"Ms. Ballou, it's hotel security."

I sighed. *What now?*

I shuffled to the door and opened it. "What?"

A stocky man in a black bespoke suit glared at me as if he'd caught me spray-painting graffiti in the hallway. Next to him stood what looked like a white gorilla in a Pandora Hotel security uniform.

"Ms. Ballou, I'm Mr. Katsura, the Pandora Hotel's chief of security. I'm afraid we must ask you to leave the premises immediately. Hans here will escort you from the building."

A fireball of anger erupted inside me. "Why?"

"You assaulted one of our VIP guests last night."

"News flash, dude. I was the one who was assaulted. Gerard Boyce roofied me and tried to rape me. I merely defended myself. Call Detective Danville at Las Vegas Metro PD if you don't believe me."

"Nevertheless, we must ask you to leave. Please don't embarrass yourself by creating another disturbance."

"Hold that thought." I bounded across the hall and knocked on Kirsten's door then stepped next door to Becca and Easton's room.

A minute later, Kirsten and Easton joined me and the security guys in the hallway.

"Becca's sleeping," Easton said. "What's up?"

"Hans and Franz here are forcing me to leave after Gerard Boyce tried to rape me last night."

"I think you better reconsider," Kirsten told Katsura.

"This matter doesn't concern you, ma'am. This is between Ms. Ballou and the hotel."

"I'm Ms. Ballou's attorney. She was assaulted on your property, making you liable for injuries she sustained. And now you're trying to kick her out for being a sexual assault victim?"

"We are removing her from the premises for breaking a VIP guest's wrist. We have a zero-tolerance policy regarding violence."

"And what exactly is your policy regarding sexual assault?" Kirsten asked. "That asshole drugged Jinx and tried to date-rape her. He isn't the victim. He's the perpetrator."

"If you force her to leave, I'll contact KVGS Channel 5," Easton added. "Their consumer watchdog, Noah Cameron, is a college buddy of mine. I'm sure he'd love to do a story about how the Pandora Hotel protects sexual predators and treats their victims like criminals."

Hans grunted.

Katsura turned purple. "That is a lie."

"Is it?" Kirsten pressed. "Are you forcing Mr. Gerard to leave?"

"That is not your concern."

"In other words, no!" I said.

No one said anything for several minutes. Eventually, Katsura said, "Fine. You can stay. Your reservation states that you were planning on leaving tomorrow morning, anyway. See that you do, or we will remove you."

Katsura and Hans the blond gorilla trudged back down the hallway.

"Thanks, you two." I let go of a breath I'd been holding. "That's another one I owe you."

Easton gave me a side-hug. "You got it. We should also report it to the con organizers. They claimed that they'd be cracking down more on sexual harassment and assault. Let's find out if they're true to their word."

"No, I'd rather not."

"Jinx," they insisted. "If you don't report him, he could do the same to another fan, only she may not be able to defend herself like you can."

"Easton's right, Jinx," Kirsten added. "Don't let anyone else become a victim by staying silent."

My insides twisted at the idea of telling a bunch of strangers how I'd been victimized. But they were right.

Boyce had probably done this countless times before. And would continue to do so once his wrist healed.

"Okay, let me get some food in me. Then I'll go down-stairs and report the incident."

"You want me to come with?" Kirsten asked.

"I wouldn't complain if you did. Off the clock?"

"Absolutely. I may be your lawyer, but I'm also your friend."

"How's Becca?" I asked Easton.

"Last night was rough on her. She's trying to get some sleep so she has enough spoons for tonight's festivities."

For years, Becca had lived with myalgic encephalomyelitis, better known as chronic fatigue syndrome. Under normal conditions, she functioned fairly well. But stressful situations could put her in bed for days. Even though the night before wasn't my fault, I still felt guilty that she was suffering after I fangirled my way into a dangerous situation.

"Let me know how she's doing."

A few hours later, Kirsten and I met with two StoryCon organizers. To their credit, they took the situation seriously and would not only ban Boyce from this and future cons but would inform the hotel and the organizers of other conventions without mentioning my name.

Kirsten had originally planned on doing the touristy thing in the city, but with Easton taking care of Becca, she insisted on hanging with me at the con during the day. Two trans women taking in the panels and the sights. The lines between our personal and professional relationship felt blurred at times, but I was grateful for her friendship.

Shortly after two o'clock, Juanita called, saying that she and Zahara had arrived at the hotel. I hoped Z had good news for me on the Marshall case.

11

Kirsten and I met them down in the lobby.

"Please tell me you caught Marshall," I said to Zahara. "I could use some good news."

She frowned. "Sorry, girl. No luck so far. We called the numbers on her phone logs. No one admitted knowing where she was hiding out. Next, we contacted a few former employees. One of them, Amie Summers, gave us an alternative phone number Marshall used to use. I called it and left a message. Some guy called back, saying he recently got a phone with the number. Doesn't know Marshall or anyone connected to WBW."

"Damn."

"Rodeo's still looking, so don't give up."

"I know, but Sadie's offer of a twenty percent bounty has expired. Oh well. The usual ten percent is still twenty grand."

"Okay, okay, people," Juanita said, waving her arms dismissively. "Enough shoptalk. We are in Sin City to party. Not play cops and robbers."

She was a statuesque dark-skinned woman who,

despite being in her sixties, could still turn heads. Originally from Puerto Rico, she had a regal bearing on par with the likes of Tina Turner and Rita Moreno.

Having originally come up through the drag scene under the moniker tía Juana, she eventually came out as transgender. Soon after I met her at the Phoenix Gender Alliance, she adopted me as my fairy drag mother. She was smart, snarky, and the owner of the biggest queer club in Phoenix, The Main Drag.

"Fine, no more shoptalk," I agreed.

"Good, now how is my sweet little bachelorette?"

"Tired but hanging in there. Last night was a long night." I opted not to bring down the scene by going on again about the situation with Boyce. Best to put it in my rearview and not look back.

"Then you best start chugging some energy drinks, mi'ja. First, we're taking a limo to dinner at Wing Lei's, the best Chinese restaurant in the city. Then on to be entertained at Cirque du Soleil's *Mystère*."

"Wow! I've always wanted to see a Cirque du Soleil show."

"And finally—" She paused for dramatic effect. "No bachelorette party would be complete without male strippers, so we're going to see the Thunder from Down Under."

Zahara smirked. "Just what every lesbian dreams of seeing. A bunch of greased-up men in Speedos prancing around."

"I'm sorry that my plans do not meet with the approval of the bull dyke contingent," Juanita snapped back with a glare. "But this is Jinx's weekend. Not yours!"

Zahara held up her hands in surrender. "You're right. Sorry."

I was stunned by Juanita's plans. "Tía, I don't know what to say."

"I'd settle for gracias. And naming your first child after me."

I laughed and kissed her cheek. "Muchas gracias, tía. But I wouldn't hold your breath on me having any children."

"Miracles happen every day, Miss Thang. Everybody thought I was a goner after those pinche terrorists shot me in the head. Then the doctors said I'd never walk again. But look at me now, putas." She twirled and struck a pose worthy of New York's ballroom scene.

I laughed. "Juanita, you are a force of nature. Nothing can kill you."

"Damn straight, chica."

"Well, I'm going to grab a few winks before this shindig gets started," Kirsten said. "I'd hate to miss out on some hot Aussie men by falling asleep in the middle of their show."

"I second that," I said.

We went up to our rooms. Juanita put away her clothes then went downstairs to lay by the pool awhile. I fell asleep on the bed. Somehow having all of my friends there helped keep the nightmares at bay.

I woke around five o'clock when the phone rang.

"Jinxie, it's Becca."

"What's up?"

"I don't have the spoons for tonight. I'm sorry."

My heart sank. "If you'd rather, we can cancel and hang out in your room and watch movies and drink. Maybe Juanita can hire a few male strippers to show up."

"No, you all go out. I'll be fine. I need some downtime. Sorry to bail on this special night."

"You were there for me last night when it really mattered. You've always been there for me when it mattered. When Barclay Dietz nearly killed me. When I thought Conor was dead. This is just a night with friends. Is Easton staying with you?"

"No, I told them to go with you all. I'll be fine on my own. Going to order some room service."

"Love you, Becks."

"Love you too, compa. Have a good time tonight."

I hung up with a lump in my throat. I hated her missing out on the fun because a celebrity I once respected turned out to be a perv. But I knew she'd be okay and was glad she was taking care of herself. I would've felt worse if she had pushed herself to come out with us only to be miserable.

I called Conor, since I'd forgotten to earlier. I opted not to tell him about the Gerard Boyce fiasco, not wanting to worry him. He told me that Diana was whining a lot, no doubt missing me.

I missed the two of them as well. I'd never been away from my dog for this long before and couldn't wait to see her. And I sure couldn't wait to feel Conor's muscular arms wrapped around me. Among other things.

We met up in the lobby and stepped outside to a waiting limo. Dinner was both beautiful and delicious. The costumes, music, and performances in Cirque du Soleil's *Mystère* were bizarre, beautiful, and mesmerizing. I felt like I'd been transported to another world entirely.

By the time we made it to the Thunder from Down Under show, I was having trouble keeping my eyes open despite my nap earlier and enough coffee to give an elephant kidney failure.

But partway into the performance, one of the dancers announced, "Before our next number, I'm told that we have a lovely bride-to-be in the house." I had to admit his Aussie accent was sexy as hell.

I caught a mischievous grin on Juanita's face. The room grew uncomfortably warm as this buff man in tight jeans stepped off the stage and into the audience right up to where I was sitting. The spotlight was blinding. My heart was doing a little thunder of its own, nearly drowning out the cheering crowd.

"G'day, ma'am. What's your name?" he asked, reaching out his hand.

For a second, I couldn't remember my name. "Uh, Jinx."

"Jinx, huh? That's a very sexy name. Pleasure to meet ya, Miss Jinx. I'm Trevor."

"Hi, Trevor." I was plotting a thousand ways I would murder Juanita for embarrassing me like this.

"Now, a little birdie told me you're getting married next weekend. Is that right?"

"Yeah."

"Your fiancé here tonight?"

"No, he's back in Phoenix."

"Phoenix, eh? All the women in Phoenix as hot as you?"

Wow, that spotlight was like a convection oven. "I... I guess."

"Would you care to join me and my mates on stage for a little dance?"

"I don't know." I was a decent dancer, but joining a group of professionals onstage was way out of my comfort zone.

"Come on, mi'ja!" Juanita called. "Go on up there! They won't hurt ya."

I took his hand and let him lead me onto the stage. The music started, and I went with it, following his lead, mesmerized by his gleaming smile. Before I knew it, the song was over.

"Everybody, give it up for our blushing bride-to-be, Miss Jinx, for being such a lovely sport, and wish her all the best for her big day next Saturday."

Juanita, Kirsten, and Zahara patted me on the back when I got back to my seat.

By the end, I was thoroughly exhausted. Zahara helped me back up to my room. Even Juanita's snoring didn't keep me awake. Much.

12

"Breakfast!" I called when room service arrived with an enormous platter of culinary wonders including a pile of bacon, a tall stack of pancakes, oatmeal, scrambled eggs, fruit, and a few bagels. And of course, a large carafe of coffee.

It was Sunday morning. I'd managed about six hours of sleep, but they were good solid hours of deep, dreamless zonkage. Besides, there were a few panels I wanted to attend before StoryCon wrapped up.

"Juanita, breakfast!" I repeated.

"Mmphnrph," she replied into her pillow. As the owner at The Main Drag, she rarely woke before noon.

I poured a cup of coffee, black, and brought it over to her. She wore a black silk sleeping mask. But her nose twitched at the scent of the coffee.

"Que hora est, mi'ja?"

"Ocho de la mañana, tía. Time to get up, sleepyhead."

"Ay-ay-ay. Is that any way to treat your fairy drag mother? Waking her up before the crack of noon?"

"Checkout's in two hours. Come on. There's coffee and lots of delicious food."

She pulled herself up into a sitting position and slid the sleeping mask off her face. "Dios mio! What's with all the food? You could feed an entire family with all of this."

"I wasn't sure what you'd like, so I went a little crazy. Besides, I wanted to show my thanks for an amazing time last night. You're the best fairy drag mother a girl could have." I offered her the cup of coffee.

She sipped it and sighed. "Damn straight, mi'ja."

"I'll see if the others want to share in this bounty."

She shuffled off to the bathroom, and I stepped out and knocked on Becca's door. She opened it, looking much better than I'd seen her the previous day.

"How you feeling?"

"Better. Functional." A devious smile crossed her face.

"What?"

She handed me a thumb drive. "I got bored and did a little skip tracing on Ms. Blair Marshall. Tried to ping her phone but couldn't get a location. Ran call logs on her, her girlfriend, and a few other numbers that she frequently called before she went dark. Compiled a list of names and other relevant data on the people she's been talking to."

I hugged her. "Thanks, Becks. You're the best."

"How was last night?" She still sounded fatigued but more like her healthy self.

"A lot of fun. You able to fly home today?"

She nodded. "We're getting packed. Or rather Easton's packing for us."

"Come to my room when you're done. I ordered a ton of food."

"Will do." She gave me a peck on the cheek. "Can't believe you'll be an old, married lady this time next week."

"Yeah, yeah. A crotchety thirty-two years old. Amazing I can still walk without a cane."

"See ya in a few." She shut the door.

I hustled over to Kirsten and Zahara's room and invited them over.

I held on to the thumb drive like it was a precious gift I couldn't wait to open. If I'd brought my laptop with me, I would have scanned over the information that Becca had compiled. I was eager to get back on the hunt and put that murderous TERF behind bars.

While the six of us chowed down on the smorgasbord, sharing with each other the less traumatic events of the weekend, someone knocked on the door to the room.

I opened the door to once again find Katsura standing there. Alone this time.

"Come to harass me some more? Checkout's not for another hour."

Becca appeared beside me, recording our interaction with her cell phone.

"I wanted to make sure you and your little group were leaving, as agreed," Katsura said with a sneer.

"What's your problem, dude?" Becca asked. "We did nothing wrong. Gerard Boyce roofied Jinx and tried to rape her. But somehow that's her fault?"

"She broke his wrist."

"In self-defense," I replied. "What was I supposed to do? Let him rape me? I used to be a cop. I know the law."

"You kicking that pendejo Boyce out of his suite?" Becca pressed.

"How we deal with our other guests is none of your concern, little lady. Be sure you're all out of your rooms by eleven. Otherwise, we will forcibly remove you from the premises and have the police arrest you for trespassing." He turned on his heel and disappeared down the corridor.

"Asshole," I said loud enough for him to hear.

"Cabrón," Becca added.

The flight back to Phoenix was only an hour but seemed to drag on. There was a delay after we landed, and we sat on the tarmac for half an hour. Even the company of my best friends couldn't cut through my overwhelming desire to see Conor and Diana again. And then get back to work.

13

———

Relief washed over me when I walked into the Bunker. Diana bounced around and ran through the house, barking and showering me with slobbery doggy kisses. Good to know I was missed.

Conor jumped up from his recliner and wrapped his arms around me. A soccer game played on the TV with the crowd roaring as I kicked the door closed behind me.

"Glad you're back, love." He smelled so delicious it was all I could do to keep from weeping with joy.

"You don't know how good it feels to be home." I kissed him deeply for what had to have been at least an hour. Would have continued if Diana hadn't been jumping on the both of us, desperate for attention.

"Can I get ya some lunch? I know it's nearly three but wasn't sure if you'd had something on the way over."

"I had a big breakfast, but I could eat."

Over a sandwich and beer, I shared all that had happened in Vegas, the good and the bad. He listened intently to all of it without interruption.

"Glad ya taught that wanker a lesson," he said, anger evident in his voice. "Is the DA prosecuting him?"

"Kirsten phoned Detective Danville earlier today. Doesn't look like Boyce will be charged. On the upside, they're not charging me either."

"Oi! I'd love to have a go at that wanker. Do more than break his bloody wrist, I'll tell ya that."

"It's done, Con. Nothing more we can do. The StoryCon organizers have banned him from future events and reported the incident to the producers of *Into the Black*. Maybe they'll shit-can him."

"He bloody well deserves it. And worse."

I remembered the thumb drive Becca had given me. "Just a minute." I hopped up from the table and ran into the guest room that we used as our home office.

"Oi! Where ya going, love?" Conor called from the living room.

"I gotta check something."

"Ya just got back."

"Come on, come on, come on," I told my laptop, wanting it to hurry and boot up.

With the thumb drive inserted, I sorted through the contents and opened the reports Becca had compiled. Marshall had shut off her phone, which was why Becks couldn't get a location. I guessed she was either using a burner or staying with someone who either was passing along messages or letting Marshall use their phone.

On the list of recent contacts was a woman named Elise Holbrook. According to the report, she was second-in-command of Womyn Born Womyn. With Marshall on the lam, she was currently acting chair. The two had been communicating by phone until this past weekend. Nothing recently. But my gut told me the two were still in touch.

The question was how to get Holbrook to give up her boss. I didn't think the intimidation approach was going to work. Sure, technically if she knew where Marshall was, she was harboring a known fugitive. But getting her arrested for that was unlikely, no matter how many times I threatened it.

A bit of deception was called for. There were a number of techniques that I often employed, like calling the fugitive and claiming they had won a prize like a cell phone or a car then arranging to meet them somewhere. It worked more often than it should with my less-savvy fugitives. From what I had gathered of Marshall's bio, she was smart. Graduated with a bachelor's in women's studies from Smith College and an MBA from Stanford. Holbrook had comparable bona fides. The "You're a Winner" gambit probably wouldn't work now that she knew we were after her.

That's not to say they couldn't be conned. The key was to offer the right bait. A cell phone or a car might be enticing, but it also could come across as too good to be true. And then there was the issue of having a place to meet where I could set up the ambush. It would have to be in an office environment. Not even something like the Hub would be likely to draw Marshall or Holbrook.

I needed to offer something they really wanted, something that wouldn't seem too good to be true, something where it would make sense to meet with them either on their territory or neutral ground like a coffee shop. I thought about it a while but wasn't coming up with any viable ideas. My brain was still exhausted from the past few days. But I stuck the question in the back of my mind. Sometimes that was what I had to do to allow my subconscious to come up with a workable solution.

"Hey, ya all right?" Conor stepped in the room. "Ya ghosted on me."

"Sorry, we're still trying to locate Blair Marshall."

"Aye, ya mentioned that Rodeo and Zahara hadn't found her."

"No, but Becca did a little of her magic to point me in the right direction."

"She uses some dodgy methods to track your skips. Pinging phones and the like without a warrant."

Conor tended to steer clear of the legally gray areas of our business. I preferred to push the limits. It worked most of the time.

"Becca knows what she's doing. I'll admit it's not entirely legal, but if it gets people like Marshall off the streets, I'm not complaining."

"Any good leads?" He started to rub my shoulders, and my mind turned instantly to mush. His strong hands felt so good on my knotted muscles.

"Eh, what?" I imagined other places they'd feel good as well. "Just... just need to... god, that feels good. I need to formulate a game plan."

He leaned down and kissed the back of my neck. Light, gentle kisses that made the hair on my arms stand up and send chills down my spine.

"A game plan, eh?" he teased. "What's your next move, love?"

I took him into our bedroom and showed him. Twice.

14

———

The next morning, I sat at my computer at the Hub. Becca was home, still recovering from our trip to Vegas. A chronic fatigue flare-up could sideline her for a few days. I felt bad that she skip traced for me Saturday night but was still grateful she had.

Pima Bail Bonds had sent me a job for a new skip who was charged with vehicular homicide, DUI, and driving the wrong way on the Loop 101. Rodeo and Zahara were out tracking him down.

I was going back through the documentation I had on Blair Marshall and formulating a strategy. By the time my eyes were crossing from staring at the screen, I had a plan. Not a great plan. Hell, it probably wouldn't work. But sometimes, I had no choice but to try shit and see what worked.

I called Elise Holbrook, Womyn Born Womyn's assistant director.

"Womyn Born Womyn. This is Elise."

"Hi, Elise. My name's Liz Windsor," I replied, using one of my favorite aliases. "I'm a journalist working on a story for *Phoenix Living* about how your organization is trying to protect the women of Arizona from the intrusion of men in women-only spaces and women's sports. I was wondering if you'd have time to talk."

The words sickened me to say, but echoing their propaganda was a good way to ingratiate myself.

"Liz Windsor, you say? Not familiar with the name."

"I work mostly freelance. But with Blair being railroaded for protecting women and the mainstream press turning her into a pariah, I felt obligated to write a story to set the record straight. I'd really love to sit down with you and get your perspective."

I wanted to suggest a meeting with Marshall, too, but didn't want to overplay my hand. I'd play that card once she thought she could trust me.

"Sure. Do you know where our office is located?"

"Camelback and Third Street, right?"

"Right. I've got some time at ten. Will that work?"

"Absolutely. See you then."

That gave me an hour. It would only take me about twenty minutes to get there. With the extra time, I rushed home to the Bunker to change up my look enough that she wouldn't recognize me from that dreaded cover story *Phoenix Living* did about me years earlier.

Juanita had taught me some makeup, hairstyle, and wardrobe techniques that created enough of a change that most people wouldn't recognize me from the old photos.

After giving my closet a thorough look-see, I slipped a sport coat with a rainbow lapel pin over a purple-and-white striped shirt, tucked my hair under a stylish felt hat, and tried a few new things with my makeup to change the shape of my face and look more professional than my usual minimalist style.

"Here goes nothing," I told my reflection.

I grabbed a notebook and some pens, hopped in the Gray Ghost, and drove north to Camelback. I feared I would be late when I had to wait for the light rail to pass and caught another red light after that. The main lot for the tiny strip mall that WBW called home was already full, forcing me to park a couple doors down.

I walked in the door a few minutes after ten. A woman with straw-straight hair, no makeup, and a business casual outfit sat at the receptionist's desk. "Can I help you?"

"I'm Liz Windsor," I replied. "Elise Holbrook's expecting me."

"One moment." She fielded an incoming call then called Holbrook to let her know I'd arrived.

A woman in her thirties with a teal-blue side-shave haircut and a pleasant face came down the hallway. She immediately set off my gaydar. "Ms. Windsor?"

"Yes, an absolute pleasure to meet you."

"Elise Holbrook. Likewise. I like your pin."

That was always a coded response between members of the queer community. Rather than asking, "Hey, are you gay?" we compliment one another's subtle queer cues. A butch haircut, a rainbow bracelet, a queer pride T-shirt. Although if this woman found out which letter in the LGBTQIA acronym I represented, she'd be less enthusiastic about talking with me.

I forced a blush. "Thanks. Bought it at Pride last year. Gotta represent, right?"

"Absolutely. Follow me back to my office."

Her office was small but tidy. Framed photos of Holbrook, Marshall, and others attending various events decorated the wall. I recognized her standing underneath the Michigan Women's Music Festival banner in one.

"What would you like to know?"

"How did you become a part of Womyn Born Womyn?"

"Blair got me into it. She and I are cousins."

I studied her for a second and saw the resemblance in the eyes and nose. I hadn't noticed it earlier because of the vastly different hairstyles.

"I told her about encountering a tranny in a women's restroom at a Pink Trinkets concert. It really shook me up to see him there. I felt so unsafe."

"Why, what happened? Did the trans person attack you?"

"No, he didn't. But he was this big guy, must've been six-four. Prominent brow. No amount of makeup could hide that. It felt so invasive. I'm not transphobic. But he didn't belong there. What was to keep him from raping me?"

I forced myself to ignore the deliberate misgendering and the insinuation that trans people were inherently violent or a threat to cis women. I had a role to play, so I swallowed my anger, hoping to get close to Marshall.

"And you told this to Blair?" I tried to sound empathetic.

"I did. She and I have always been close. She told me she was starting a local chapter of WBW to help protect the women in the valley. And to protect the kids."

"The kids?"

"When some parent starts listening to the TRA propaganda—"

"TRA?"

"Sorry, the trans rights activists. They're indoctrinating parents, who then convince their impressionable kids that they are trans. It's nothing short of child abuse, forcing them to take hormones and undergo irreversible surgery. They're kids, for Goddess's sake."

"Have you met with any of these children?"

"A few noncustodial parents have talked with us, explaining how their kids have been brainwashed."

I went through a list of questions I'd come up with earlier that had enough of a trans-exclusionary, pseudo-rad-fem bent to elicit her sense of trust.

I learned that the paid staff of the organization was small. Only a half dozen people. The rest of the membership were volunteers who showed up to rallies, protests, and other events to spread their transphobic propaganda.

It was all I could do to play along while she went through the usual litany of bogus anti-trans conspiracies, absurd leaps of logic, straw man arguments, and disproven medical and psychological claims. I was impressed in an odd way. To the ignorant, they sounded totally legit until you started poking holes in them with facts based in science and reality.

No one had brainwashed me to be trans. I had known I was a girl since I was five. I was the one who had to convince my family, as is nearly always the case. And kids not allowed to transition too often committed suicide, especially when unsupportive parents resorted to conversion therapy to "fix" their queer kids. I was one of the lucky ones, having survived a suicide attempt and having supportive parents.

I moved on to talking about LaTonya Garrett's murder in the Save Mart's women's restroom and Blair Marshall's subsequent arrest. Holbrook trotted out a tale that completely contradicted the police report. But still I smiled and nodded as if every word was gospel.

"This is great stuff, Elise."

"Thanks." She was smiling. A good sign.

"You know what would really sell this story? If I could speak with Blair herself. How can we make that happen?"

The smile faded into a pained grin. "With the judge illegally revoking her bail, it's hard for her to meet publicly."

"Of course, I understand. The last thing I want to do is compromise her situation. At the same time, it's hard to present her side of the story without hearing from her directly. After all, she was the one in that restroom at Save Mart, not you or me."

I let her digest that for a moment. She looked genuinely torn.

At last, she said, "Let me talk with her. Hold on a sec."

She stepped out of the office and made a call on her cell, though I could still see her. She appeared earnest when the person on the other end answered the call. Holbrook soon became more animated, clearly pleading my case for an interview. When she hung up, her shoulders slumped.

"I'm sorry, Liz. She's not interested in doing an interview right now. Simply too risky. There's a bounty hunter looking to lock her up again."

Damn. So much for that idea. "Well, I have to say I'm disappointed. Without Marshall on the record, I'm not sure if *Phoenix Living* will even publish the story."

"They have to. Children are being forced to take untested hormones and are being mutilated by quack surgeons. Women's safety is being threatened by men invading our spaces. These mentally ill invaders must be stopped."

It was all I could do not to slug her for spewing such blatant lies. I stood up, feigning disappointment. "I'm sorry, but I can't sell the story with just this. Have a good day, Ms. Holbrook."

I walked out, expecting at any moment she would stop me and convince Marshall to meet with me. But she didn't.

Time for Plan B. Or more like Plan D if I included our previous week's failures. At this rate, I'd run out of letters.

Then I got an idea.

When I reached the Gray Ghost, I punched Holbrook's cell number into my mobile SkipTrakkr app. Her call log appeared. The number that Holbrook had called to speak with Marshall wasn't familiar. Most likely a burner.

"Gotcha!"

15

———

I replaced the hat, the sport coat, and the slacks with my body armor, tactical gear, and cargo pants. The tinted windows provided enough privacy that no one could see in. At least I hoped not.

Once changed, I called Becca and asked if she was up to pinging Marshall's new number.

"Hold on a minute. Lemme get logged into the system." Becca sounded positively exhausted. I felt bad about calling. "Mierda. The user I've been mirroring changed their password. Un momento."

"Don't worry about it, girl. Get some rest."

"¡Espere! I can get in there." A moment later, she said, "Okay, I'm in. Entering Marshall's number. Must be a burner. No user information coming up."

"Can you get a location?"

"Yes, the phone is at Gila Valley Office Park in Buckeye."

"Wow, way out there. At least it's not all the way up in Payson or Show Low. Send me the coordinates. Thanks, Becks."

"Any time."

"And get some rest. I won't bother you again today. I promise."

"Watch your back, compa."

"Always."

When Becca texted the geo location of Marshall's burner, I punched the coordinates into my map app, then called Rodeo. "Hey, man! How's it going with our wayward wrong-way driver?"

"Target acquired. Found him at home completely hammered. Guy nearly puked in the back of Zahara's Explorer. We're at the Chandler Jail now waiting for the body receipt. You at the Hub?"

"No, I'm down by Womyn Born Womyn. I've got a location for Marshall."

"Excellent. Where is she?"

I gave him the address of the office park in Buckeye.

"Wow, that's the other side of the valley. Be an hour before we get there."

"Do what you can. I'll head out now and make sure she doesn't vanish before we can apprehend her."

"Copy that, boss. See you there."

I took Seventh Avenue to the I-10 then out past the White Tank Mountains to Buckeye, roughly thirty miles from downtown Phoenix. It boggled my mind how much the metro Phoenix area had expanded in the past decade, especially with the addition of the Loop 303 and the extension of the Loop 202. In fact, Buckeye was one of the fastest growing cities in the country. I was sure it was a nice place to live, but too remote for my tastes.

The Gila Valley Office Park comprised six beige stucco buildings, each housing a dozen businesses. The location of the phone ping was specific enough for me to narrow my search to Building D, probably one of three businesses—Sunburst Telecomm, Baseline Accounting Professionals, and Ramdeen Food Enterprises. My money was on the accounting office since one contact on Marshall's bail bond application worked as a CPA.

I sat across the lot in the Gray Ghost, watching the building through binoculars. The accounting office was getting a lot of foot traffic. Hardly surprising considering it was mid-March. People were rushing to get their taxes done, unless they were like me and waited until the last possible minute.

But no one coming or going from any of the businesses looked familiar.

With every minute, I grew more restless, worried Marshall had left before I arrived. I didn't want to have to track her down all over again. After a half hour, I called Becca again.

"Sorry to bother you again. Would you ping that phone again? I want to make sure she's still there."

"Sure, gimme a sec." A moment later, she said, "Phone's still there."

"Okay. Thanks." The news should have provided some relief against the growing tension but didn't. What if she had dumped the burner there?

I hated sitting on my ass when I was this close to bagging my quarry. I chambered a round in my Ruger in the cross draw, snapped a cartridge onto the Taser, and gave the watch another glance. "Come on, guys! Get here already."

A cluster of people strolled out of the accounting office. Through the binoculars, I spotted Blair Marshall among them. She wasn't a tall woman, but she moved like she knew how to handle herself in a fight. The horrific photos of LaTonya Garrett from the arrest report bore this out. Normally I had a lot of respect for women who could kick ass but not when they hurt innocent people.

The three women with Marshall had bulky corrections-officer physiques. Did they meet in a weightlifting gym and bond over a mutual hatred of trans people? Why in the world would these brawny butches feel threatened by trans women?

As the fearsome foursome marched across the lot, I realized I couldn't wait any longer for Rodeo and Zahara. I stepped out of the Gray Ghost and intercepted the group with Taser drawn.

"Blair Marshall. You need to come with me."

The women turned and glared at me. Marshall's friends formed a wall between me and her.

One tossed her a set of keys. "Go, Blair! We'll hold her off."

Marshall dashed into the driver's seat of a Volvo. I was tempted to fire the Taser at one of the women blocking my path, but if I did, the others would be on me. With my martial arts training, I might fend them off. Or I might not. Meanwhile, Marshall would get away.

I rushed back to the Gray Ghost, determined not to lose her. I fumbled with my keys but soon got the engine going. When I attempted to drive through the parking lot after Marshall, the Butch Patrol blocked my path.

"Get the fuck outta the way!" I shouted.

They smiled and crossed their arms. One flipped me off.

Fuck!

I slammed the Gray Ghost in reverse, did a three-point turn at the end of the lane, and drove out the other exit.

Blair was already a half mile down the road. I pushed the accelerator to the floor, whipping around slower cars on the rural two-lane road and nearly scraped paint with a panel van coming the other way. As the distance between us narrowed, the drone of a train's horn filled the air, followed by the clanging of a railroad crossing ahead.

Marshall cleared the crossing seconds before the arms of the railroad crossing gate blocked the road. I had no choice but to stop. I pounded the steering wheel until my hand ached. "Fuckity fuck fuck fuck!"

When the train was halfway through the crossing, it slowed. Slower and slower until it stopped completely, still blocking the crossing. I craned my neck forward and pulled out my binoculars to figure out what the hell was going on.

A few empty auto carriers sat on a spur next to an enormous lot full of shiny new automobiles. The train was picking up railroad cars. It could be another fifteen minutes before I got across. I had no chance of tracking her now. She was long gone.

My phone rang. "Hello?" I answered, making no effort to disguise my annoyance.

"Hey, boss, we're at the office park. Where are you?"

"Down the road a bit. She got away."

"Shit."

"Yeah. I'll be there momentarily." I made a U-turn and returned to the office park.

The three butch women were gone when I arrived. Maybe they'd gone back inside the accounting office. Or maybe they'd driven off in another vehicle. Didn't matter. They weren't my target, and they wouldn't give her up even if I pressed them. Of that, I was sure.

Zahara's Explorer was parked near the exit by Building A. I pulled alongside.

Rodeo, sitting in the passenger seat, lowered his window. "No joy, huh?"

"No joy. A few of her buddies helped her get away. Would have caught her, but a goddamn train cut me off and then started doing that whole back-and-forth, do-si-do bullshit to pick up new railroad cars."

"Darn, that stinks." Zahara shook her head.

"What now, boss?"

I really hated to call Becca back, but the sooner we got her location, the sooner we could bag her. "Let me call Becks to ping her phone."

I called, and she answered right away. "You get her?"

"No. You mind pinging her phone one more time?"

"All right. Let me save my work." She paused a moment. "Okay, we have a new location. About three miles northwest of the office park on Fourth Street, north of Baseline."

"Is she moving?"

"Um, no. Doesn't appear to be. Looks like she's parked on the side of the road."

"Maybe she figures she lost us. Okay, thanks."

I punched the longitude and latitude into my GPS then leaned out my window. "Follow me!"

Once on Fourth Street, I kept an eye out for the Volvo. Right before I crossed Baseline Road, my GPS device announced I had reached my destination. There was nothing around but a vacant lot.

I pulled to the side of the road. Zahara stopped behind me.

It took some searching, but I soon found the burner phone amongst the scraggly weeds and sun-parched earth. The screen was cracked but was still on, sending its signal to the cell towers.

"God fucking dammit!"

16

Zahara put a hand on my shoulder. "Don't worry about it, Jinxie. We'll find her."

"Yeah, she won't escape us for long," Rodeo added. "She might be smart and have help, but we're professionals. How many fugitives have you caught over the years? Hundreds, right?"

"I know. But this one's personal. She murdered a member of my community. All while acting like we're the danger to society. We're the ones getting murdered so often we have a candlelight every year to honor those who've been killed."

"I hear ya, girl. Don't let the resentments cloud your judgment," Zahara added. "We'll get her."

"You're right. We've got the tools, the experience, and the savvy to track her down and send her back to the Graybar Hotel."

My phone rang, and I answered it without checking the ID.

"You get her?" Becca asked.

"Nope. She tossed the burner."

"Shit. I'm sorry, Jinxie."

"Me too."

"I'll keep digging and see what I can come up with. But there's something you should know." Her tone sounded ominous.

"What's that?"

"You're on TDG."

"What the hell's TDG?"

"*The Daily Gossip.* It's the television show from the tabloid of the same name. Basically, two guys standing in a newsroom sharing the latest gossip about celebrities."

"Why the hell am I on it?"

"They were doing a story on Gerard Boyce. How he got booted from StoryCon for trying to sexually assault you. They didn't mention you by name. Only referred to you as the mystery woman. But they aired the grainy security video of you screaming 'He got what he deserved' when the cops arrested you."

"How the hell did they get the security footage?" But I knew. "I'm surprised that fucking security manager didn't give them my name as well."

"We hope. But the two so-called news anchors were questioning why he was the one who got banned from the con when you broke his wrist. I got the impression they're still digging for the dirt. I'll set up an alert for anything else popping up related to it."

"Thanks, Becks."

"Any time."

I hung up and looked at my crew. "News of the Boyce situation popped up on the daytime TV gossip shows."

Rodeo gave me a dismissive wave. "Don't let it bother you. It's all bullshit anyway. The case is closed. We need to stay focused on arresting Blair Marshall."

"You're right." I considered our next move. "Marshall's

bail was revoked after she threatened a witness. I wonder if this witness might know where Marshall might be hiding."

Zahara asked, "You think the witness knows Marshall?"

"It's a long shot, I know. I can't help wonder how Marshall knew how to contact the witness."

"Possible," Rodeo replied. "But Womyn Born Womyn have a history of doxing people who cross them. Maybe they have a SkipTrakkr account."

He had a point. But at the moment, all I had were long shots.

I grabbed the case file from the center console of the Gray Ghost and flipped through it. According to the arrest report, a friend of Garrett's was waiting outside the restroom when the assault began. I recognized the name.

Ciara Vanderbilt was a friend of mine from the Phoenix Gender Alliance who worked as a freelance bookkeeper. She was also the property manager at a house I owned that served as a home for displaced trans people. Was she the witness that Marshall had threatened? Had she had prior contact with Marshall? Only one way to find out. I pulled out my phone.

"Ciara? It's Jinx."

"Jinx, hey! How was Vegas? Sorry I couldn't come. After what happened to LaTonya..."

"No, I understand. Vegas was... well, let's say it had its high and low points."

"I'm looking forward to your wedding. You and Conor make such a cute couple. So, what's up?"

"I've been hired to return Blair Marshall to custody."

"Really? Well, do me a favor. Don't be gentle with that psycho bitch when you catch her. You should've seen what she did to LaTonya." Her voice broke with emotion. "It was so, so... brutal. I kept hoping LaTonya would pull through. But..."

"I'm so sorry. Were you two close?"

"Close friends. Nothing romantic. But she was such a good person. And that fucking animal beat her to death with an aluminum water bottle."

"The judge revoked her bail because she threatened a witness. Were you the witness?"

"Yeah. She threatened to out me to my bookkeeping clients if I testified against her."

"Did you know each other prior to the incident?"

"Not personally. Before the attack, Blair had been trolling LaTonya online. I don't know why Blair focused on her in particular. Maybe because Tonya was Black as well as trans. You know how those TERFs are. Most are as racist as they are transphobic."

"So, no idea where she might be hiding?"

"Ha! I wish. If I did, you'd be the first person I'd tell. I'm not normally a violent person, but I hope she dies a slow, painful death."

"Okay, well, I'm going to do everything in my power to put Blair Marshall behind bars."

"Thanks, Jinxie. You're a real asset to our community."

"I try. Take care, Ciara." I hung up and punched the Volvo's plate number into the SkipTrakkr app on my phone.

The car belonged to Mandy Hudson, who worked as a CPA at Baseline Accounting and lived there in Buckeye. She was one of the three women who had blocked my way. According to her social media, she was also a member of the Womyn Born Womyn group.

Further skip tracing on the app allowed me to identify the two other women who had stood between me and Marshall—Ashley Carroll and Nicci Fiorello. These were promising leads for a stakeout.

"Zahara, drop Rodeo off at his car, and stake out Ashley

Carroll's place. Rodeo, monitor Nicci Fiorello's house. I'll stake out Mandy Hudson's." I gave them the addresses and the plate number of the Volvo Marshall drove away in. "If you see Marshall or the Volvo, call me. Don't make entry alone."

"You might also want to call Picardo," Rodeo suggested. "Marshall has to know this isn't going away. Might be considering leaving the country."

"Not a bad idea."

Picardo was the best forger of documents in the valley. I didn't know how he did it, but after every attempt by government agencies to combat forgery, Picardo figured out how to foil it and create flawless documents, be they passports, driver's licenses, even birth and death certificates.

For years, Picardo and I had had an agreement. I wouldn't turn him into the authorities. In exchange, he'd give me a heads-up on any of my skips and allow me to grab them.

"Good hunting, you two. I'll be in touch."

They drove off, and I called Picardo. I got a generic outgoing voicemail message, as I always did. One can't be a document forger and not screen incoming calls. I told him to call me back then called Conor.

"Hey, babe."

"Hello, Jinxie, my love. How goes the search for your TERF friend?"

"Friend? That's funny. Frustrating so far, but I've got some new leads. I wanted to let you know I'll probably be out most of the night on a stakeout."

"Glad you've got a lead. Care for some company?"

"Tempting. Stakeouts are always better with another person to keep me awake. But make sure you keep your hands to yourself, buddy," I teased. "Don't wanna miss my fugitive just 'cause you get a little frisky."

"I promise I'll be a perfect gentleman." I could hear the grin in his voice.

"Very well. You can come. I'm near Hudson's place, so I'll pick up the snacks." I gave him the address.

"Copy that. I'll see you there."

17

______

The cool afternoon was so intoxicating, I drove with the windows down and let my mind wander as I stopped to pick up some snacks for the stakeout.

My wedding was only five days away. It still hadn't fully sunk in. Not even with all the trying on of dresses, choosing cakes and hors d'oeuvres, picking out flowers, and all the rigamarole that comes with planning a wedding.

My mother had wanted me to hire a wedding planner. It would have been easier for sure. But there was a certain satisfaction in making the arrangements myself.

Despite our mutual Catholic connections, neither Conor nor I were religious. We had settled on having the wedding at Dragon Tree Gardens, which was a mystical botanical oasis unlike anything else in Phoenix.

Our friend Samantha West, a Unitarian minister, had agreed to officiate the ceremony. My mother had wanted to have Father Martin from her Catholic church as well, but he refused because I was transgender. He told her he couldn't "condone my sinful lifestyle." My mother, who hadn't missed Mass once in my lifetime, told him to stick a crucifix where the holy light of God doesn't shine.

During the flurry of all the planning, combined with my erratic work schedule, I had suggested to Conor that we elope. He told me he was game but encouraged me to talk to my dad, the psychologist, first.

"Cher, a wedding—for all its pageantry—is nothing but a glorified party," he reminded me with his sweet Louisiana Cajun accent. "It is a celebration of your relationship, but do not confuse it for one second for the relationship itself.

"The two of you have been through hell and back. Still, you are here now with a love every bit as strong as the bond between your mother and me. Don't get so caught up in the arrangements that you forget what is truly important."

"You're suggesting we should elope?"

"I would be sad to miss out on that special moment, but you do what you feel is best."

"Thanks, Dad."

That moment from a month ago buoyed me now and helped push away the day's frustrations and failures.

It was approaching five o'clock when I pulled into Mandy Hudson's neighborhood. The houses were small, probably less than a thousand square feet by the look of them. A few were double-wide manufactured homes. A wide swath of gravel extended for about ten feet between the road and the yards, which some apparently used as overflow parking since the covered carports usually only accommodated one car each. Many residences had small decorative brick walls around the front yard.

I parked a couple doors down in front of a house for sale. Convenient, as long as a real estate agent didn't show up asking questions.

I looked through the binoculars at the house. There was no sign of the Volvo anywhere on the street. Nor was Blair Marshall's 2016 Chevy Malibu. I guessed at least three-quarters of the vehicles in the area were pickup trucks, mostly large domestic models.

With its faded paint, collection of scrapes and dents, and peeling stickers in the back window, the Gray Ghost looked like every other soccer mom's SUV. But under the hood, I had a high-performance engine and suspension, which came in handy unless I got cut off by a damn train.

Conor's team, on the other hand, took the opposite strategy. His company vehicles bore a strong resemblance to the Maricopa County sheriff's vehicles with light bars, push-bumper grill guards, and flashy gold decals on the side.

Fortunately, he pulled up in his 1968 restored Dodge Charger. It attracted more attention than I would like, but at least it didn't look like a damned patrol car.

He parked behind me and climbed into my passenger seat.

"Any sign of your fugitive?"

"Not so far."

"How're ya handling what happened in Vegas? With that gobshite Boyce, I mean."

Not what I wanted to spend the evening chatting about, but I figured what the hell. It'd help pass the time. I tore into a bag of tortilla chips.

"I'm okay. I fought him off before he could rape me. Maybe that broken wrist will make him think twice before he tries it on someone else. Still, I keep kicking myself for not seeing the signs sooner."

"Not your fault he's such a fecking prick."

"I know. But I should have had more presence of mind.

As soon as I got in there and realized he was the only one there, I should've bowed out right then. Instead, I was such a stupid fangirl, conflating him with the nice-guy character he plays. Even his public persona is an act."

"He's an actor. They're good at making people think they're someone else."

"There's more though." I told Conor about what Becca had shared about TDG airing the video footage of me drugged out of my skull, getting arrested while shouting that Boyce got what he deserved.

Conor shook his head, his upper lip curling in disgust and anger. "Have ya told Kirsten about it?"

"No. I'd just as soon let the story die. If I get her involved, it could turn into a bigger thing."

After a couple of long, boring hours, the street grew dark, devoid of streetlights except on the corner about a block away. I was thinking this was going to be another bust when a vehicle approached from behind us. We scooched down in the seat to avoid being seen.

It was hard to determine the make of the car. All models looked so much alike these days. But the license plate was a match to the Volvo. It pulled into Mandy Hudson's driveway.

"Looks like we got company," I whispered.

We both peered through our respective binoculars and watched two women get out of the car under the dimly lit carport.

"That your perp?" Conor asked.

"Hard to tell from this distance. She and her buddies all had that classic soft butch physique." I watched the two kiss before disappearing inside the house. "Unless Marshall is polyamorous or cheating on her girlfriend, it's probably not her."

"Ya want to go check it out, anyway?"

I considered it. I wasn't sure if either of the two women were Blair or not. But I wanted her in custody pronto!

"Yeah, that's the car she was in earlier. Either one of those two was Marshall or they know where she is. Time we kick a little ass and bring this bitch in."

18

———

We approached the house, both of us in full gear with Tasers drawn and radios on. Conor agreed to watch the back in case Marshall was inside and tried to make another run for it, taking the battering ram with him. I grabbed my pry bar, in case I had to get through the security screen door.

"Front door in position," I called on my radio once I was on the porch.

"Back door, ready when you are, love."

I pounded on the front door. "Open up! Bail enforcement!" I always loved doing that. I punched the doorbell several times.

The main door opened, but the woman with the buzz cut remained behind the safety of a mesh steel security door. I recognized her as Mandy Hudson from her driver's license photo. She was about my age, maybe a few years older. Had the physique of someone who was an athlete in college but whose toned muscles were now turning flabby.

"What?" she asked.

"I'm here for Blair Marshall. The judge revoked her bail."

"Blair who? Don't know nobody with that name. Sorry."

Yeah, two can play at that game. "Funny. You gave her the keys to your car earlier today. You often give your car to perfect strangers?"

"That car? I don't know what you're talking about. Now get off my porch before I call the real cops."

"Let me fill you in on a little thing about the law. Harboring a known fugitive is a felony in these parts. Even out here in Buckeye. So go right ahead and call the cops. I'm sure they'd be happy to help me arrest Blair and you. I get paid either way."

"Ain't no one named Blair here. Now fuck off, bitch." She slammed the front door.

"Hey, Conor. The resident refuses to let us in. Claims our girl Marshall isn't here."

"Your call, love. We can push our way in. Or we can continue to watch the place. Or call it a night."

"She lied about knowing her. I'm guessing she's as likely to be lying about her being here. I'm taking the pry bar to this door and going in."

"Ya sure know how to show a guy a good time, dontcha?"

"What can I say? I like things that are long and hard."

"I know that's the truth."

Now it was my turn to blush.

I pounded on the door once more. "Last chance, ladies. Let me in or I force my way in."

"You can't do that," Hudson replied from inside. "You ain't got no warrant. And she ain't in here."

"Suit yourself." I inserted the pry bar between the doorframe and the flange protecting the security bolt. It took some serious strength, but eventually, the welds gave way. The security popped out of position.

"You're gonna fucking pay for that door, bitch!"

"One down. One to go!" I replied.

"I'm calling the cops."

"Be my guest." I slipped the end of the pry bar between the door and the frame. It shattered easily and creaked open.

I drew my Taser and called over the radio. "Front door breached."

Mandy Hudson stood in the kitchen, shouting into the phone at her ear. "They're breaking in! They're breaking in. Please send someone now!"

"I'm bail enforcement!" I shouted back, hoping the 911 operator could hear me. "I'm here for Blair Marshall. Judge Campos revoked her bail and ordered her returned to custody. Now where is she?"

I heard a large crack from the back of the small house. "Back door breached," Conor said over the radio.

"She ain't here!" Hudson shouted back at me, trying to block my entry.

"Back off or I will tase you."

"She's threatening me!" Hudson yelled into her phone.

"Fine. Be like that." I pulled the trigger. With the fwap-fwap-fwap of the current, Hudson dropped to the floor and collapsed with a sharp cry of agony.

I replaced the cartridge with one from my tactical belt and proceeded to look for Marshall, opening all the cabinets I could see. "Kitchen clear."

"Master bedroom clear," Conor said over the radio.

In the nearby den, I checked behind chairs and under couches and opened the sliding doors of an old entertainment center circa 1970. "Front room clear."

"We got someone in the guest bath."

"Be right there," I said.

"Leave her alone, you bitch."

I turned to see Hudson back on her feet, unsteadily stalking toward me with a baseball bat. Shit. I should've cuffed her.

"Put it down, Mandy, or I'll tase you again. You want that?"

She hesitated, her eyes full of tears and fire. "Just leave her alone."

"Put the bat down. Now!" My finger put a small amount of pressure on the trigger.

She dropped the bat. In a flash, I cuffed her to the arm of the couch. "Stay!"

"You can't do that! I ain't done nothing wrong."

"Sit there until we get this sorted out."

I followed a short hallway to where Conor stood at a closed wooden door.

"She claims she ain't Marshall."

"Yeah, right. Is there a window she can escape through?"

"Glass blocks. Doesn't open."

I pounded on the door. "Listen up, Blair. It will go a lot easier for you if you open the door and surrender. Your friend Mandy's in cuffs. I'll let her go as soon as you surrender."

"I'm not Blair," said the woman on the other side of the door.

"You sure about that? We saw you drive up."

"I'm telling you I'm not her. She isn't here."

"Show us some ID and prove it. Then we'll leave."

"Just leave now."

"Can't do that, Blair," Conor replied. "The judge revoked your bail. We got no choice but to take ya back to custody."

"I am not Blair. I've told y'all a thousand times."

"We already broke down two doors, three if you count the security door," I said. "You want us to make it an even four?"

The lock clicked, and the door opened. My heart sank.

"Shit." I lowered my Taser.

"Not her?" Conor asked.

Elise Holbrook walked out and narrowed her eyes at me. "Liz Windsor? What are you...?"

"The name's Jinx Ballou. I'm a bounty hunter, here for Blair. Now where the hell is she?"

"I'm not telling you. She was only defending herself against that tranny."

"Bullshit." I came dangerously close to tasing her out of spite.

"Go! Go!" Hudson said in a hushed tone from the other room. A door squeaked open and slammed shut.

"She's going out through the carport," Conor said.

"I'll get her."

We rushed out the front door in time to see a figure racing down the street. I took off after her. Unfortunately, the weight of my gear and the bulkiness of my body armor slowed me down.

She jumped into a car parked in a driveway three houses away. The engine roared to life when I reached the car. I recognized it as Marshall's Chevy Malibu. I tried the door, but it had already locked. Our eyes met, and she flipped me the bird.

I smashed the window with the butt of my Taser, but before I could get off a shot, she floored it onto the street and raced it in reverse all the way to the corner then pulled a bootlegger turn and disappeared.

"Fuck!" I had to admit she was one slippery bitch.

Conor caught up to me. "How'd we miss her in the house?"

"I don't know."

Blue and red flashing lights caught my attention from the other end of the street.

"Well, now we got more problems to deal with." Conor put a hand on my shoulder.

"Great. This keeps getting better. We could just leave quietly."

"Except you left Hudson handcuffed to the couch."

"Oops. Okay, we'll deal with these cops. Then I'm going home. That's twice today she's escaped from me."

When Conor and I reached the house, one of the uniformed officers drew his sidearm. "Buckeye PD! Down on the ground."

We complied and then spent the next forty-five minutes explaining that we forced our way in after Marshall entered the house with two other women. They uncuffed us and allowed us to show them our paperwork authorizing us to arrest her.

"They broke into my house and broke down my doors!" Hudson complained. "And handcuffed me to a couch."

"After you approached me with a baseball bat," I replied.

"After you tased me in my own home."

Holbrook chimed in. "And she was impersonating a reporter earlier."

"Not a crime," I said. "Perhaps I should ask these officers to arrest you for harboring a fugitive wanted for attempted murder."

"All right, all right, everyone calm down," answered Officer Medina, a broad guy who had the bearing of a former Marine. He held out his hands in a peacemaking gesture. He turned to his partner, who looked barely old enough to shave. "Officer Vance, why don't you question these two, while I escort our bail enforcement friends outside."

"Suits me," I muttered.

"You're gonna pay for my doors, bitch!" Hudson called after us while we stepped out into the night.

"I'm really not sure what to do with the two of you," Medina said.

I took the lead. "We were here executing a court order to return Marshall to custody. And she would be in custody now, if those two in there hadn't assisted in her escape. We've broken no laws."

"You did tase and handcuff one of them. That could be considered aggravated assault and kidnapping."

"She came at us with that baseball bat," I said. "I assume self-defense still applies out here in Buckeye."

"Don't be smart, ma'am."

"Fine," I replied. "If you want to arrest them for harboring a fugitive, I won't object. But you've got nothing to hold us on."

He glanced at Conor, who had remained silent except when asked direct questions. "Don't I know you?"

Conor shrugged. "It's a small world, mate." There was concern on his face. Perhaps worried Medina recognized him from when he was on trial in the UK for the Omagh bombing.

"Yeah, I do know you. Dark Horse Security, right? Working out of Bagram."

Obvious relief washed over Conor's face. "Aye. I was there."

"Sergeant Medina, 3rd Marines."

"Of course, sergeant. Good to see you again, mate."

"Well, you two get on out of here. Good luck catching your fugitive."

"Thanks," we said together.

He started to walk away then stopped and pulled out a pair of cuffs. "Oh, I suppose these are yours."

I held out my hand, and he tossed them to me.

"Well, at least I'm not spending another night in jail. That would have been twice in as many weeks."

"I think you'd look deadly in prison stripes," he teased, his arm around my shoulder.

I elbowed him in the ribs. "Shut the fuck up."

After we got back to our vehicles, I checked in with Rodeo and Zahara. They agreed to continue staking out their locations for another hour. If Marshall showed up, they would call me. Otherwise, they'd head home.

19

———

The next morning at six o'clock, my phone rang. No caller ID. I hesitated to answer it. It was too fucking early to deal with telemarketers or scammers. But after three rings, Conor started groaning next to me. "Make it stop."

I picked it up. "Hello?"

"Ballou? It's Picardo. You called?"

I breathed a sigh of relief. "I'm looking for Blair Marshall, white female, age twenty-seven, about five-four. Wanted for attempted murder. She contact you for new papers?"

"White female? Not so far. All of my recent clients have been men."

"Okay, well, if she reaches out, let me know."

"Will do. Ciao."

I dragged myself out of bed and sat at the kitchen table with my laptop, researching as much as I could about Marshall and Womyn Born Womyn. Apparently, WBW was a global organization based originally out of London. Marshall was in charge of the Phoenix chapter but appeared to have a lot of contacts overseas. If she did run to London, at least we had an extradition treaty. But unless Sadie at Assurity Bail Bonds wanted to pony up for my travel expenses, I wouldn't be hopping the pond after Marshall.

I spent a couple of days following leads, searching for new burner phones, periodically running call logs on Marshall's known associates, and tracking bank charges for both Marshall and her girlfriend. Rodeo, Zahara, and I took turns surveilling her house, Baseline Accounting, the WBW office, and the homes of some of Marshall's buddies. But we saw no sign of our wayward bigot.

On Wednesday morning, I was back at the Hub running a check through SkipTrakkr when my phone rang. I didn't recognize the number, but it was local and could be a lead.

"Hello?"

"Jinx Ballou?" a female voice asked.

"Yes, who's this?"

"You the bounty hunter looking for Blair Marshall?"

"I am. Do you know where she is?"

"Just fuck off, sir, and leave Blair alone." The caller hung up before I could respond.

I let it go. Sure, I could report the caller for harassment. I had friends in several local police departments and a few with the local FBI headquarters. But I didn't need the distraction. I had to find Marshall soon or Sadie was going to can me and give the case to someone else.

Half an hour later, another call came in from an unfamiliar number. I let it go to voicemail. When a notification popped up, letting me know they left a message, I listened to it.

"Listen up, Mr. Ballou, you freak. Leave Blair alone or you're gonna regret it."

"What the hell?" I deleted the message and pulled up the news as a distraction. Not that it would get me in a better mood. The headlines were always the same. Politicians spewing the party line. People killing each other over stupid shit. Corporations buying each other out. Blah blah blah. It always made me more miserable, but I couldn't break the habit, especially whenever I was frustrated on a job.

Meanwhile, my phone kept ringing. I sent them all to voicemail but didn't bother listening to the messages.

I switched to social media, subconsciously desperate for an endorphin hit. Same reasons. Worse results. I found myself on the WBW page, hoping it might clue me in to Marshall's location. Maybe they'd drop some crumb, not knowing it would give me a lead.

"Oh, fuck me." Bile rose in my throat.

"What's wrong?" Becca asked.

"Womyn Born Womyn doxed me."

"What?" Becca hurried over to my computer.

"They posted my home address. My phone number. My private email address. Shit, they even posted that I work out of here. Fuck." I scrolled some more. It got worse. "What the ever-loving fuck?"

I clicked on a video link. It was the same video of me in Vegas drugged out of my skull and screaming about Boyce. But the bits with me accusing Boyce of drugging me had been conveniently clipped out.

"They're claiming you were charged with assault for attacking Gerard Boyce? What bullshit!"

I read the attached article, which had been posted on the *Las Vegas Times'* website. Holbrook alleged I had been stalking Boyce because I hated his feminist stances, and that any claim that I had been roofied was a lie to smear him.

Becca sat down at her workstation and started doing her own digging. "Hijo de puta! Jinxie, you're gonna want to see this. Or maybe you don't."

"Why, what is it?"

"They posted a video on their blog claiming you tried to seduce a little girl."

"What? You're bullshitting me." I rushed over to her side of the table.

Becca had turned down the volume so that only the two of us could hear it. The video was of me sitting on a park bench I didn't recognize talking to a little girl I'd never met. The words coming out of my mouth made me sick to my stomach. I was dumbfounded.

"I...that's not me. It can't be. I've never said anything remotely like that. I have no idea who that girl is or where this was shot."

"Could be a deepfake."

"A what?"

"A deepfake. A video that uses artificial intelligence to make it look like you were doing something you've never done. Movie magic."

"How can they do this?"

"Didn't you say that Marshall's girlfriend is the creative director at a marketing company?"

"DekaHedron. Yeah, but they make cheesy local commercials. Not something like this."

"Doesn't mean she doesn't have access to the tools. Video AI has come a long way in the past few years."

"So, what do I do?"

My phone started ringing again. I hesitated to answer it. But the caller ID came up as AZ REPUB. Was it someone from the Phoenix newspaper trying to sell me a subscription or to interview me for a story? Or the Arizona Republican party?

"Hello?"

"Is this Jinx Ballou?" The voice was male but unfamiliar.

"Yes, who is this?"

"I'm Jonah Taylor with the *Arizona Republic*. I have some questions about a video that shows you talking with a young girl."

I disconnected the call and blocked the number. It immediately started ringing again with a different number. I sent it to voicemail and changed the settings on my phone to silence all calls not in my contacts list. I wanted to block them, but I didn't want to risk blocking calls from anyone giving me a lead on arresting Marshall. They'd just go to voicemail.

"Jesus Christ on a crutch."

Becca put her arm around me. "Don't let them get to you. They're worried because you're closing in on Marshall."

"Except I'm not. I don't know where she is now."

I tried to focus, but my mind felt like a circus full of crack-addicted squirrels. Monkey mind, my dad called it. I'd never had to deal with this kind of bullshit before. Even on social media, I only lurked, never posted. My handles were generic and my bios nearly nonexistent. Nothing that would identify me.

I called Kirsten and explained the situation. "Okay, don't panic. If this is a deepfake—"

"Of course it's a deepfake. You think I tried to seduce a child?"

"No, of course not. I meant to say that we will get to the bottom of it and prove your innocence, as well as try to bring charges against whoever created it. We'll have to get out in front of the story. Could mean a lot of publicity, which I know you hate."

"Fine. What do we do first?"

"I have an associate who specializes in forensic video analysis."

"What the hell's that?"

"They analyze videos involved in legal matters. They can determine where a video was shot, whether files are authentic or have been altered, help identify subjects, things of that nature."

"Okay, fine. Do that."

"They're not cheap."

"I don't care. I can't have people thinking I'm a child molester. This is an attempt to discredit me while I go after Blair Marshall."

"Assuming we can prove the video has been doctored, we can go after WBW for defamation, invasion of privacy, and harassment. I will also get in touch with a crisis image consultant to determine how best to handle the publicity aspect."

"Okay, thanks."

"One other thing, if you receive any harassing phone calls, emails, or letters, keep them. They will help us build a case on the doxing. We can also turn them over to law enforcement for prosecution."

"Assuming my voice mailbox doesn't fill up."

"Do what you can. You'll get through this."

"Yeah, just what I need a few days before my wedding."

"This will pass. Your relationship with Conor will last a lifetime."

"You sound like my dad."

"Is my voice that low?" Her attempt at self-deprecating humor made me smile. Almost.

"You know what I mean."

"I'll be in touch."

I hung up and saw that I'd received a warning that my

voice mailbox was ninety percent full. I went to my cell carrier's website and upgraded my plan to unlimited voice-mail capacity. It would cost me another hundred a month, but I would not spend the next few days dealing with this bullshit.

Sadie called me around noon. Rodeo and Zahara had spent the morning driving by some of the places we had staked out and were on their way back to the Hub with no success.

"Jinx, where is Blair Marshall? The county attorney is riding my ass. I need her back in custody ASAP. I could lose my shirt on the bail bond."

"I've got my entire team on it, Sadie. She's got a lot of friends helping her out. But we will get her."

"You're getting married in three days and then going on a honeymoon, I assume."

We had planned to spend a week in the Florida Keys scuba diving, seeing the sights, eating fresh seafood, and sipping cocktails while watching the sun set over the water in Key West. I couldn't wait.

"I can't wait another two weeks for you to bring her in," she continued.

"You won't have to. I promise. I will get her before then."

"You better deliver, Ballou. It's not like you're the only game in town. I bet Leroy Drake could find them."

I was tempted to tell her to give it to him. Let ol' Leroy deal with this bullshit. But this had become personal, and I was determined to make them pay for murdering LaTonya Garrett, as well as the harm they'd done to myself and the entire transgender community.

"Leroy Drake couldn't find his asshole in a bucketful of assholes."

"He found Zach Gonzales last December after you spent a month looking for him."

"He got lucky," I replied. "How about all the times I found skips for you after he and a lot of others couldn't? Be real, Sadie. You need me on this one."

"Find her today."

"Trust me. I got it handled."

I hung up and stared across the table at Becca.

"You got it handled?" she asked, a twinkle in her eye.

"No. But what else am I going to say? I have no idea where this Marshall bitch is hiding."

"I may have some good news."

"Hit me. I need it. What'd you find?"

"I got a location on a burner Marshall may be using."

"Seriously? Finally."

20

"Where is she?"

"Deer Valley. Not far from her house. And she's on the move. I can keep pinging her as long as the phone stays on."

"Got it. I'll call you once I'm in the area."

Rodeo and Zahara walked in with bags of food from Mel's. "No time to eat, guys. We got a lead."

They reversed course, and we ran to the parking lot, climbed into our separate vehicles, and headed up the Black Canyon Freeway.

Thirty minutes later, I turned onto Deer Valley Road with Rodeo and Zahara behind me. I called Becca and put it on speaker.

"Where is she?"

"West Apache Lane, just past Fifteenth Avenue heading east. She's not moving fast. Keeps stopping for some reason."

I drove south past Rose Garden Lane and turned east onto Apache Lane, scanning the road ahead.

"I've got you on my screen as well," Becca explained.

"You're closing in on her. She's stopped at Thirteenth Avenue."

"I'm not seeing her," I said. "But there's a garbage truck in front of me. Maybe she's on the other... fuck."

"What's wrong?" Becca asked. "Oh. Right."

"Damn. If I didn't hate her so much, I'd be respecting the hell out of her. I'll be back shortly." I pulled over to the curb and got out.

Rodeo and Zahara parked behind me. I climbed out and met the two of them next to Rodeo's Miata.

"Where is she?" Zahara asked.

I pointed to the garbage truck that was disappearing around the corner. "She must have tossed the phone in the trash right before the truck picked it up."

"Damn. Hate that bitch."

"Maybe you should let this one go, boss," Rodeo said. "I heard about the video and the doxing. We could tell Assurity to give the job to someone else."

"No. I am not letting Sadie give the case to Drake. I swore I would bring Marshall in. I intend to do it."

Zahara put a hand on my arm. "Jinxie, I get it. She and her TERF buddies are doing everything they can to make life miserable for you and everyone in the trans community. Much as I'd like to get paid for bringing this woman in, you don't need this level of aggravation. Not right before your wedding."

"I'm going to have this level of aggravation regardless, so I might as well bring her in. That should solve the problem once and for all."

"I don't see how, boss," Rodeo said. "I get your motivation, but I don't see the upside. No bounty is worth this."

"Maybe you're right. If the situation gets worse, I'll tell Sadie to give the job to Drake. For now, though, let's keep the pressure on Marshall and her associates. Drive past all the places she might go to ground. Knock on some doors, but don't force your way in anywhere. And watch your six." I assigned each of them three locations to check out.

I spent the next few hours staking out Baseline Accounting, Mandy Hudson's house, and the home of another of Marshall's buddies. While I sat, I thumbed back through the case file. Bank records, phone logs, credit reports, text messages, social media. It's amazing the size of the digital paper trail people leave these days. Finding a lead that would turn into something other than another wild goose chase felt like looking for a needle in a haystack the size of a SpaceX rocket.

On the drive home, I tried to assure myself that it would all work out. My team and I would track down Blair Marshall. Kirsten would deal with the legal issues surrounding the deepfake video and the doxing. At least it couldn't get any worse, I told myself.

I was wrong.

My street was clogged with media vans, Phoenix PD blue-and-whites, and a chanting mob of people, some of whom carried signs that said things like Fuck Your Pronouns, Trannyism Is Child Abuse, Sorry about Your Dick, and No Men in Womyn's Spaces. I squeezed the Gray Ghost through the crush of crazed protestors and TV crews into my driveway. As I pulled in, I spotted the words "Tranny Perv" painted on our front door.

No amount of positive thinking could stop the tears from flowing. I was beyond angry. Beyond humiliated. I was crushed.

When I parked in the garage, a few protestors followed me in, preventing me from closing the garage door.

I stepped out with my Taser drawn. "Get the fuck off my property before I light one of you up."

They backed out while shouting their lurid accusations.

A woman in a suit and a detective shield on her belt climbed out of a nearby unmarked Phoenix PD sedan, flanked by two uniformed officers. The officers herded the protestors back into the street.

As she drew closer, I recognized the detective. "Wasserman?"

Rachel Wasserman and I had been in the same squad as patrol officers when I was with Phoenix PD. She was good police. And now apparently a detective.

"Long time no see, Ballou. Can we talk?"

"Yeah, come on in. What about your buddies?" I nodded to where the unis were keeping the mob at bay. How long before the lunatics broke out the pitchforks and torches?

"Officers Reese and Khalid will do their best to keep the media and the protestors off your property."

I closed the garage door and led Wasserman into the house. Diana raced to see me. I gave her a head rub. She seemed jittery, and no wonder. The circus outside must've been driving her up the wall.

"It's all right, baby."

"What's your dog's name?"

"Diana." I put some kibble in her bowl then opened the fridge. "Beer? Juice? Water?"

"Water would be nice."

I handed her a bottle of Dasani and grabbed a Killian's for myself, then we settled in the living room.

"You mind if I text my fiancé?"

Wasserman's eyes narrowed. "About?"

"The insanity outside. I want to give him a heads-up to avoid it if possible. You can watch me text if you think I'm doing something nefarious."

"Go ahead." She waved it off, showing no interest in watching over my shoulder.

I sent a text to Conor. *Shit hit fan. Come in back way.*

Copy, he responded a moment later.

"So, what's new?" I asked her facetiously.

"I'm a detective with the Sex Crimes Unit now."

I nodded. "A step up from Property Crimes."

"Yes and no."

"Rough work, huh?"

She nodded. "Heartbreaking, especially when kids are involved."

I knew why she was here. I should have called Kirsten right then, but I trusted her.

"You're investigating that video that appears to show me talking dirty to that little girl. Only it's not me on that video. It's one of those deepfakes."

She took out a notebook and scribbled something down. "To create a deepfake, someone would need access to some powerful video software as well as the source material. A different video, possibly photos. Where would they get something like that?"

I thought about it. "I've been assigned to return Blair Marshall to custody."

"And who is she?"

I gave her the rundown. "When my team searched her house, Marshall's girlfriend, who works for DekaHedron Studios, took video of me and my team. I suspect she faked this video. She had the motive, means, and opportunity."

"Honestly, that makes more sense. You never struck me as a child molester. I will have our forensics team look into it."

I let out a loud sigh. "Thank you."

"What about that other footage of you getting arrested? Something that happened in Vegas?"

My chest tightened once again. I really didn't want to talk about it. Especially with a former colleague. At the same time, Wasserman had been a friend while I was on the force. And she was now working sex crimes. If anyone would understand what I'd been through, it would be her. I told her about Boyce's attempt to rape me.

"Have the Las Vegas police charged Boyce?"

"What do you think?" I locked eyes with her. "He's a famous TV star who likes to pretend he's a woke feminist guy. I'm just some transgender bounty hunter from out of state. You saw how out of it I was after he drugged me. They were ready to charge me with assault for defending myself."

A sly smile played across her face. "You really broke his wrist?"

"I don't like guys grabbing my ass without my permission. Had I been sober, I probably would have put him in a pinch hold. But the ketamine lowered my inhibitions. Just not in the way he intended."

"Good for you, girl."

Diana barked. I immediately went on high alert.

21

I heard the clack of the trapdoor lock in the coat closet and relaxed. Conor was coming in through the underground tunnel that ran from a tattoo studio on McDowell to our house.

"Daddy's home," I said to Diana.

"What's going on?" Wasserman asked, clearly concerned by my initial alarm.

Conor walked in and brushed some lint off his tight-fitting T-shirt. "That's what I'd like to know. What the bloody hell's going on outside? It's a fecking riot out there."

"Detective Rachel Wasserman, meet my fiancé, Conor Doyle. Rachel and I worked patrol together when I was on the force."

Wasserman shook his hand. "Pleased to meet you, Mr. Doyle. I didn't hear you come in."

"I slipped in the back." He peeked out the front window. "Now would someone care to explain the madness going on out there?"

I filled him in on WBW's attempts to make my life a

living hell. The doxing. The videos. The graffiti. And now the media frenzy.

When I was done, Conor turned to Wasserman. "I trust you'll be going after WBW for starting all this."

Wasserman looked apologetic. "I will have our forensics team examine the video that appears to portray Ballou as a sexual predator. My job is to confirm that it is a deepfake. If it is—"

"It is," I replied.

"Assuming it is, we will try to locate the source material to determine whether the child in the video was harmed by someone else."

"What about the harm to me?" I asked. "Someone doxed me. I'm getting harassing calls, texts, and emails. Someone defaced my door. And now I have a dangerous mob of bigots in front of my house, complete with media crews. Not to mention the fact that whoever created this fake video has defamed me."

"I can have patrol disperse the crowd. Not much we can do about the media so long as they stay off your property. As for the doxing and defamation, those are civil matters. You would have to handle that in court."

"Fine. When you disperse the crowd, could you please let them know it wasn't me in that video?"

"I'll see what I can do."

"Thanks, Wasserman." We stood.

She nodded. "I was disappointed when you quit the force. Rumor was that Lieutenant Goodman was going to partner us up. I was looking forward to it."

"I would have liked that too. But after getting suspended on a bogus complaint and then word getting around the squad that I was trans, it got to be too much. Even after PSB cleared me, the whole thing left a bitter taste in my mouth."

"I understand."

"Plus, as a bail enforcement agent, I don't have to wear a uniform, no departmental regulations, and no reports to fill out. I grab my fugitives, turn them in, and pick up a check." If only it were that easy.

"I'm glad you found your calling." She shook my hand. "Again, it was a pleasure to meet you, Mr. Doyle. Sorry it wasn't under better circumstances."

"Aye. Pleasure to meet ya as well, detective."

"Oh, and congratulations," she added as we walked her to the front door. "I hope you two have a lovely wedding."

"Thanks," I replied. "I'm sure we will, assuming this mob of angry villagers doesn't break out the pitchforks and torches."

"I'll see that they are sent on their way and don't disturb you any further."

Conor hugged me when Wasserman left. "How ya holding up, love?"

"Honestly, I don't know how much more of this bullshit I can stand. Bad enough that Sadie is threatening to pull this case from me and hand it to Leroy Drake. But now all this bullshit." I shook my head, feeling sick to my stomach. "And with the wedding in a few days..."

"Maybe you should let Drake have it. Sure, he's an eejit, but at least Marshall and her TERF Nazis would go after him instead of you. In a few days, we'll be flying out to the Keys, leaving all this shite behind us."

I shook my head. "Oh no. You don't understand these people. Now that they know I'm trans, they're going to keep coming after me like a pack of rabid dogs. They pretend they're these woke feminists, but in reality, they're no different than the wing nuts on the far right. Just a bunch of fucking bullies who get off on hurting people more vulnerable than them. And they are relentless. Me turning over this job to Drake won't stop them coming after me."

"Then we'll find Marshall and sue the shite out of whoever doxed you and created that dodgy video."

Outside, the crowd was slowly dispersing, though the news vans seemed to be going nowhere. I wondered how long I'd have to put up with their nonsense.

My phone rang. I was nervous about answering it until I saw it was Becca.

"Give me some good news. Please."

"I've talked with Kirsten. I am documenting all the calls coming into your phone that aren't in your contacts list. Also, the texts and emails. I'll send all the information to Kirsten, who will look into taking legal action. And those who are threatening violence, she's turning over to the feds."

"Are there a lot of those? Threatening violence, I mean?"

"More than a few, I'm afraid."

"Geez, these fucking people."

"Also, I've been looking at this deepfake. I gotta say, it's superb quality, technically speaking. But I've been doing some reverse image lookups from stills taken from the video."

"And?"

"I found the background source video of the little girl. It's from a low-budget indie movie released last year. In the original scene, a mom was talking with her daughter about their father. And she wasn't saying the awful things that were in WBW's sick deepfake version. They digitally replaced the woman's face with yours and used an AI-replicated version of your voice to change the dialogue."

"Fucking technology."

"I've let Kirsten know about my findings. She has a PR

person who will put together a public statement declaring the video a fake and providing a link toward the original footage from the movie."

"Geez, this shit is still going to cost me."

"No doubt. But there's nothing you can do but fight it. Hopefully, when it all shakes out, people will see them for that they are—a bunch of putas with nothing better to do than bully trans people."

"We'll see."

"Hang in there, chica. In a few days, you and your new hubby—geez, it sounds weird to say that—but you'll be headed to the Florida Keys for some tropical therapy."

"I'll talk to you soon."

Conor and I threw together some dinner and chilled in front of the TV. Periodically, I'd check outside to see if the news vans were still there. They were.

We were two-thirds through watching one of the *Taken* movies when I got an idea.

"Where ya going, love? It's getting to the best part. Liam Neeson's about to put the beatdown on the arseholes who took his daughter."

"I got an idea."

I stepped into my office and called Becca. "Hey, according to Blair Marshall's arrest report, someone in the Save Mart ladies' room recorded a video of the assault. I was wondering if there was a way to get ahold of that video."

"Hmm... that's tricky. Both Phoenix PD and the county attorney's office store their evidence in the cloud. But getting at it without authorization? Not so easy. Serious protocols in place. I've never tried to crack it because of the risks."

"You're saying you can't crack it?"

"No, I'm not saying that. But the chances of getting caught are higher than I'd like."

"Ugh, then don't. I was hoping to show the world that Marshall was the real threat to public safety. But I don't want to put you at risk."

"Although…" A glimmer of hope echoed in her voice.

"Although what?"

"Marshall's attorney would have received copies of everything as part of the discovery process."

"Meaning?"

"Meaning her attorney's system might be easier to crack. Do you know who's representing Marshall?"

I checked her bail application. "Lisa Thornton."

"Of Thornton, Booth, and Aguirre?"

"Yeah, how'd you know?"

She chuckled. "I installed their IT security system. And I left myself a back door. Just in case."

"Rebecca Maria Alvarez, I could kiss you."

"Promises, promises. I'll do a little digging and will be in touch. It may be tomorrow before I have anything. Okay?"

"It's cutting it close, but I'm willing. Thanks, bestie!"

I hung up, feeling a little better.

22

I didn't sleep well that night. Dreams of zombie mobs pounding on the windows and doors of our home. Only, in the dream, it wasn't the Bunker but a single-wide trailer, and the zombies were tearing their way in. I woke with my heart thundering in my chest.

Conor lay asleep beside me. Diana's eyes reflected the glow of a night-light from her bed nearby, apparently awakened by my restlessness.

I spent a long time listening to sounds. A creak in the roof. Bushes scratching on the windows in the night breeze. A year or so earlier, I discovered a homeless man had been living in my attic. Fortunately, he had only been there for a safe place to sleep and to occasionally steal my food. He was now a friend with a good job and a home of his own.

But now every unexplained noise seemed like a potential threat. I was dealing with a fugitive backed by a highly organized, tech-savvy group that would go to great lengths to protect her and destroy me. Who knew what they would try next? I didn't want to think about it, but I reminded myself that I needed to be ready for whatever they threw at me.

Dawn came eventually. Aside from the spray-painted slur on our front door, no further harm had been done to the Bunker. Most of the news trucks had moved on, though a couple lingered on the street. They were no doubt desperate for an interview with the transgender bounty hunter who'd broken the wrist of a much-adored TV actor and who had allegedly tried to seduce a child. I was about ready to give them a scoop. But I needed a few things first.

Conor and I avoided watching the news that morning. Last thing I needed to hear was some talking head waxing nonsensical about who I was and the rumors swirling about me. My mother called after I stepped out of the shower.

"Oh, sweetie, I saw the most awful news story about you. Please tell me it's not true."

"Mom, the video's a fake. I didn't try to seduce a child. You know me better than that."

"No, not that video. Of course I know that's a fake. I'm talking about the one of you being arrested for breaking Gerard Boyce's arm in Las Vegas."

I definitely didn't want to tell her Gerard Boyce had tried to rape me. While she wasn't an *Into the Black* fan, she loved a lot of the chick-flick movies Boyce had starred in. She, too, had fallen for his nice-guy facade. But I owed her an explanation of the situation.

"I didn't break his arm."

"Oh, thank the Lord Jesus." I could picture her crossing herself.

"I broke his wrist."

"Jenna Christine Ballou! How could you?"

"Mom, he tried to rape me. He invited me to his hotel room, claiming the cast of *Into the Black* would be there. But he was alone when I got there. He put ketamine in my drink."

"Why did the police arrest you and not him?"

"Because I hurt him before he hurt me. And he's a famous actor who gets special treatment. Especially in a place like Vegas."

"I never liked that city. Nothing but gambling, drinking, and people doing all kinds of awful things. I don't know why you let Juanita convince you to have your bachelorette party there."

"They have some good shows."

"Promise me you'll never go back there again."

"Mom, I have to go there sometimes to chase after fugitives." And I still wanted to go back to StoryCon next year unless they invited Boyce back.

"Speaking of which, why are those women saying such awful things about you?"

"Because their leader tried to murder a trans woman. When the judge revoked her bail, I was hired to pick her up. It's a distraction."

"I so wish you would find another line of work."

"You said the same thing when I was a cop."

"And you knew this wasn't any safer."

"This will all blow over, Mom. Trust me."

"But you're getting married."

"I'm well aware of that fact."

She sighed audibly. "I'm sorry. I let myself get so wound up, I didn't ask how you are doing. Are you okay, sweetie? Tell me the truth."

"I'm upset, angry, frustrated, and a little paranoid. But I'm functioning. I'm not drinking aside from one beer yesterday afternoon. I'm using all the tools Dad taught me to work through it all."

"Good. I love you, sweetheart. I missed you last Sunday. I don't like it when you miss our family brunch."

"I know. But I was on my bachelorette party weekend."

"Did you at least have fun with your friends?"

"I did. We had a fabulous dinner and went to see Cirque du Soleil."

"Oh, I love their shows. I suppose I won't see you this Sunday, either."

"No, we'll be flying out to the Keys. But you'll see plenty of me Saturday at the wedding."

She sighed loudly. "I... I simply can't believe it. My baby girl's finally getting married. I worried this day would never come." The emotion was evident in her voice. "You don't know how happy this makes me."

"I'm glad. I'm happy too. Gotta let you go. I have a fugitive to catch before Saturday."

At eight, Becca called. "I've got good news. A video has surfaced showing Blair Marshall assaulting LaTonya Garrett. It doesn't include the start of the confrontation, but clearly, Marshall is beating Garrett with an aluminum water bottle."

"Who took the video?"

"Another woman who was in the restroom. She didn't record the whole thing. I think she ran out, told Ciara what was happening, and called the police."

"Too bad she didn't intervene."

"True, but I also got surveillance footage from the store."

"Does it help?"

"It shows Marshall stalking Garrett through the store. In fact, Marshall looks both ways before entering the ladies' room, presumably checking to see if anyone was noticing what she was doing. I guess she didn't bother checking to see if anyone else was in there before she started beating Garrett to death."

I felt a surge of hope at last. "Awesome! That's what I've been looking for. Make me a copy. I'll meet you at the Hub in an hour."

"Will do. See you then."

"What's up, love?" Conor handed me a cup of coffee when I hung up.

"If Womyn Born Womyn wants to play hardball, well then I say, 'Fucking batter up, bitches.' I can play their game and win."

He gave me a worried look. "Oi! What're ya up to, Jinxie?"

"You'll see."

"Don't be stirring up more trouble with the TERFs, love. Catch your girl and leave the other stuff to your mate, Kirsten. Don't be starting a media war with those dodgy gals."

"They started it already with doxing me and putting out that bullshit video. I'm simply serving them up more of the same. I won't be intimidated by their transphobic bullshit."

He sighed. He knew me well enough to know that once I set my mind to something, there wasn't much he or anyone else could do to dissuade me.

23

I picked up coffees for Becca and me from the Tres Leches Cafe across the street from the Hub. She showed me the videos that she had gotten ahold of. Not only the store surveillance and the one the witness took on her phone but also the scene from the movie that Naomi Hoffman had used to create the deepfake.

I loaded them up onto the video-editing program on my laptop. While I wasn't an experienced editor, I could cobble together the videos into a coherent whole and do some recording of my own. And that was exactly what I did.

The final product wouldn't earn me a Peabody Award by any stretch. But it proved that Blair Marshall was a violent transphobe who took the law into her own hands and attacked an innocent transgender woman. It further proved, with the clip of the original indie movie, that the video that WBW had posted on social media was a fake, that I was not a sexual predator as they had claimed.

Finally, I explained that the video of me railing about how Gerard Boyce got what was coming to him resulted from an attempted date rape. I had hesitated about sharing that last part, but I felt I owed it to other women to know that he was indeed a predator. Because while StoryCon had banned him from future cons, other conventions might not.

I finished the video by pleading with viewers to contact me if they had any leads on the whereabouts of Blair Marshall. I promised a reward of a thousand dollars for information that led to her capture. It might not result in any viable leads, but it was worth a shot.

When I was done, I had Becca swing around to my side of the table and hit play.

"My name is Jenna Ballou, otherwise known as Jinx Ballou. I am a former Phoenix PD officer and have worked as a bail enforcement agent for over ten years. I have caught hundreds of fugitives, including Phillip Nelson, the Maryvale Arsonist who murdered eight people and destroyed more than a dozen homes. My team and I also helped stop the militant hate group White Nation from detonating multiple bombs in Phoenix that would have killed thousands."

I took a deep breath. *Got my bona fides out of the way,* I thought.

The video played the Save Mart security footage showing Marshall stalking Garrett through the store, followed by the recording of the assault.

While the recordings played, I continued my voice-over. "A month ago, Blaire Lynn Marshall was arrested and charged with aggravated assault after viciously assaulting a Black transgender woman in Save Mart who later died from her injuries. After being released on bond, Marshall violated the conditions of her bail agreement by threatening a witness. The judge revoked her bail, and I was hired by her bail bond agent to return her to custody."

The video cut back to me talking in front of my computer. "Unfortunately, Ms. Marshall, who is the head of the local chapter of Womyn Born Womyn, refused to surrender. Instead, she had members of her organization, which is recognized by the Southern Poverty Law Center as a transphobic hate group, assist her and prevent her from being returned to custody.

"Womyn Born Womyn has now attempted to discredit and harass me by sharing my personal contact information online in an illegal practice known as doxing and created a deepfake video that appears to portray me as a sexual predator. The truth is, they took the footage from a low-budget independent film." I showed a brief clip of the deep-fake, followed by a comparable clip from the indie film.

I cut to the video of me being handcuffed and hauled off by the Vegas cops. "They also accused me of attacking the actor Gerard Boyce at a hotel in Vegas and subsequently being arrested by the Las Vegas Metropolitan Police Department. What they failed to disclose is that I was, in fact, the victim.

"Gerard Boyce lured me to his hotel room under the premise that I would be attending a party with members of the cast of *Into the Black*. Shortly after I arrived, Boyce drugged me with ketamine and attempted to sexually assault me. In an act of self-defense, I fended off the attack by breaking his wrist. All charges against me were dropped by Las Vegas Metro. Boyce has since been banned from StoryCon and other sci-fi conferences."

I cut back to me on the video. "The hate group Womyn Born Womyn would have you believe that transgender women are men in dresses who want to infiltrate women's spaces in order to assault them. Nothing could be further from the truth. Transgender people are physically assaulted and murdered at a higher rate than almost any other demographic. So many of us are killed each year, overwhelmingly trans women of color, that we hold a Day of Remembrance each November 20. In 99.9% of violent crimes involving transgender people, the trans person is the victim, not the perpetrator. Blair Marshall's victim is only one of the most recent."

I cut the video to show Marshall's mug shot. Her hair was in disarray, her eyes seething with anger. I put text to the right of her photo saying Reward Offered. Below that, I included "For information leading to the arrest of Blair Lynn Marshall" along with the phone number of a burner I used occasionally and a new email I had set up for this purpose.

"If you know where the murderer Blair Marshall is hiding, please contact Ballou Fugitive Recovery. Please note, all harassing communications toward me will be prosecuted to the full extent of the law."

The video ended.

"Daaammmn, Jinxie. That is fucking awesome. Fight fire with fire. Or in this case, bullshit videos with authentic video. You show it to Kirsten yet?"

"Not yet. You're the first. I'm not even sure what to do with it now."

"Check with Kirsten in case she has any suggestions or legal concerns. Then I can send it out to my contacts. We'll make it go viral. That bitch Marshall won't have a chance."

My body felt like it was vibrating from the adrenaline coursing through my system. I honestly wasn't sure whether the video would help or hurt. In past years, I had occasionally used reward posters to get tips and leads. They worked about twenty percent of the time. Creating a reward video like this was a first. I hoped it helped me track down Marshall in the next day or so. I didn't want to go off on a weeklong honeymoon and leave Zahara and Rodeo to locate her on their own. Not that they weren't capable. But I wanted to be the one to snap the cuffs on Marshall. She and her TERF buddies had made it personal.

Thirty minutes after I sent it to Kirsten, she called me. "Jinxie, you are a genius. I love it. I will forward it to Elia Santiago, my crisis management person. She should get in touch with you soon to help it go viral and to handle media requests for interviews."

"Interviews? I have a fugitive to catch. I don't have time—"

"Jinx, listen to me. This video is a great way to turn the tables on Marshall. And the more publicity you can get, the more likely it is to work. I know you prefer more of a stealth approach for arresting fugitives, and far be it from me to tell you how to do your job, but you need to know that this fresh approach could work well for you. You could be the next Dog the Bounty Hunter. Ever considered getting a mullet?"

I ignored her lousy attempt at humor. "Okay, I'll consider doing some interviews. But my primary focus is putting this bitch behind bars. I have zero interest in becoming some reality TV star."

"A show on Discovery or A&E could make you some good money."

"I think I'll pass."

"I'll be in touch."

I called Rodeo and Zahara and asked them to meet me at the Hub. When they arrived, I filled them in on the video. "No idea if it will work, but I couldn't sit idle and let those psycho bitches ruin my life."

"You did the right thing," Zahara replied. "Good for you, girl, for being proactive and pushing back."

"What's the plan, boss?" Rodeo asked.

"Continue surveillance on Marshall's most frequent contacts over the past few weeks." I handed them each a separate list of addresses, keeping one for myself. I held up the burner phone. "Who knows if the tip line will yield any results, but I'll let you know if I catch a viable lead."

24

I drove back to Blair Marshall and Naomi Hoffman's street, parking a few houses down from the home they shared. I had an unobstructed view of the place but no idea if anyone was there. They had replaced the front door.

I got a text from Becca saying she'd posted the video on VidTube and had sent links to it to all of her social media followers, encouraging them to make it go viral.

The burner phone rang. "Ballou Fugitive Recovery."

A female voice shouted, "I fucking hate you, you goddamn faggot! If you don't leave Blair alone, I'll—"

I ended the call. *Great. Here we go again.*

I silenced the phone. Let the calls go to voicemail. I'd sort them out later.

I grew restless sitting in the Gray Ghost and took a walk around the house with my Taser in hand. On the front porch, Hoffman had mounted a small white security camera above the door. I gave it a wide berth, hoping not to trigger it. Didn't need to give Naomi Hoffman any more source material.

I circled the house and stepped through the gate into the back. An elaborate garden dominated the yard with beds of flowers, shrubs, and vegetables covered with a shade to filter the harsh desert sun.

The sliding glass door that Rodeo had shattered had been boarded up with plywood. I guessed those were a little harder to replace. No security camera mounted above it.

I returned to the front and peered through the living room window, out of range of the front-door camera.

The house was dark. I didn't get the impression either Hoffman or Marshall were home. Time to move on to the next house on my list.

I checked my burner phone when I climbed back into the Gray Ghost. In the past ten minutes, I'd received eight voicemail messages and twenty-seven emails. I scanned the subject lines. One was from Channel 7 News. Another from the *Arizona Republic*. A third from *Phoenix Living*. I'd deal with them later.

I checked a couple more houses on my list, knocking on the doors and ringing the doorbells. No one came to the door at either location. And there were no lights on inside. The only response I got was a cat who strolled back and forth across a window like a runway model.

I wondered if this was another fruitless effort. So much of my work fell under the 80-20 Rule. Eighty percent of my captures came from twenty percent of my effort. But I never knew which twenty percent that would be. So far, nothing had yielded anything but a couple of narrow escapes. Close didn't count in the world of bounty hunting.

While sitting in the Gray Ghost, I poured through the more recent documents Becca had sent me. She had searched the call logs for several of Marshall's WBW associates, but none of them showed any frequent calls to a number that could be a burner. I browsed through text messages and emails. None of them made any mention of Marshall or held any clues to her whereabouts. Most of it was praise for the deepfake video, which they treated as gospel. Also, a lot of trash-talking about how I was such a menace to society. A few had seen my response video and were calling my facts fake news.

Where the hell was this chick? Where would I hide if I were her? Most fugitives hid with friends or family. Marshall hadn't listed any family members on her bail bond application other than her girlfriend. And Becca had uncovered no living blood relatives in her research either. Neither she nor her girlfriend Naomi Hoffman owned any other properties other than their house. No cabins up in Prescott or time-shares in Lake Havasu.

I was flipping through bank statements for WBW when a large payment caught my attention. They had paid nine thousand dollars to PLC. The acronym seemed familiar, but I couldn't place it. My gut told me this was significant, though for the life of me, I didn't know why. A review of previous months' bank statements didn't reveal any similar payments.

I searched the internet for PLC and came up with a lot of hits but none that looked like an organization that a TERF group would send such a large payment to. There were a few political groups in Latin America that used the acronym. There was also a conservative group in Pennsylvania. Not likely.

I turned up a lesbian choral group in Phoenix. I ran a check on the choral group's website. They were a small nonprofit, but they were trans-inclusive. Didn't strike me as the type of group a transphobic organization would support.

The last potential match was the Patriots of Liberty

Caucus, an über-conservative political organization with strong ties to evangelical churches in the state. Anti-gay. Anti-choice. Pro-white, straight, religious patriarchy. Again, not likely an organization that a group of radical feminists would donate nine grand to. The transaction probably wouldn't lead me to Blair Marshall, but I filed it away in the back of my mind anyway.

My phone rang. It was Kirsten.

"What's up?" I asked.

"Jinx, have you heard from Elia Santiago, my crisis management person?"

"Um, I'm not sure. My phone is set to send all calls not in my contacts list straight to voicemail."

"She called me saying she's left three messages but hasn't heard back. You're not avoiding her, are you?"

"No, I've been busy trying to locate Marshall. What does she want, anyway?"

"To arrange some media interviews."

My gorge rose. The last media interview I did went horribly wrong. The story got me blackballed by most local bail bond agents. The reporter who interviewed me was later murdered by a sadistic gangster who dumped the body on my doorstep.

"Jinx, are you there?"

"Yes, I'm here. I'll call Elia back. Okay?"

"We're gonna beat this. You're going to catch Blair Marshall. And we're going to sue the pants off of those TERFs for defaming you with that deepfake video. They'll think twice before coming after our community again."

"We can only hope. I'll see you tomorrow night at the rehearsal."

"Looking forward to it, my dear."

I called Elia Santiago back. She had tentatively arranged for four interviews for tomorrow morning, two with local TV stations, one with the *Arizona Republic*, and one with MSNBC. I agreed and asked her to send me their phone numbers so I could put them in my contact list to avoid them being silenced along with the harassing phone calls I was getting.

I checked in with Rodeo and Zahara. Neither had seen any sign of Marshall. Since it was in the middle of a work-day, I sent them to question some of the senior volunteer members of the organization at their places of employment. Maybe humiliating them in front of their coworkers would get them to open up. Or at the very least send a clear message that we wouldn't let up until Marshall was back behind bars.

25

———

I drove to downtown Chandler and showed up at DekaHedron to talk to Naomi Hoffman.

I always loved this area. Great restaurants, cute art galleries, and boutiques selling interesting wares. The free parking in the garage was also a plus. Becca had originally worked out of a coworking space in the neighborhood before the Hub opened.

DekaHedron was housed in a brick storefront with a large metal sculpture featuring the company name and logo mounted above the door.

The interior had a similar industrial decor to the outside. Lots of glass, brick, and bare metal, not so much the framed prints on white-washed walls or stained wood.

A young woman with hair the color of green mold sat behind the glass reception desk.

When I explained I was looking for Naomi Hoffman, she insisted Hoffman was off-site at a shoot. I wasn't sure if she was lying, but forcing my way to her office wouldn't have accomplished anything. I told the receptionist to have Hoffman call me. That would send her the message.

I found Leslie Reinhardt, WBW's marketing materials coordinator, working at an office supply store. Despite me walking up in my armored vest and utility belt, she didn't recognize me until I told her I was looking for Marshall.

She blanched and whispered, "I don't know where she is. Please leave. I can't lose my job."

I got loud. "You're helping to hide an accused murderer, Ms. Reinhardt. We both know it. Why would you protect a murderer? Do you like helping to kill people?"

By the time her manager showed up and asked me to leave, Reinhardt was in tears, and the customers in the store had cleared out.

It was late afternoon when Becca called. "Any luck?"

"No sign of her anywhere. I suppose I should start going through the messages on the tip line and the email address."

"I've been looking through them. You've received more than a thousand emails."

"Shit. Mostly hate mail, I imagine."

"I created an algorithm to help sort the wheat from the chaff. You really don't want to read most of them. Like reading the comments section on a political opinion piece on the web. A lot of hateful idiotas who are fond of writing in all caps and not that great at spelling. Also, more than a few from creepy putos asking for nude photos."

"Figures."

"I forwarded the hate mail to Kirsten to handle any potential legal matters. Deleted the creepy solicitations. On the bright side, there were some that looked like potential leads. One in particular. I'll forward it to your regular email address."

My phone pinged, showing the received message. "Thanks, Becks. Don't know what I'd do without you. Talk to you soon."

The subject line of the forwarded email read "Former WBW member. Might help find Blair."

I opened up the email and read it.

~

Dear Ms. Ballou,

I saw your video. I'm sorry for the lies that WBW is telling about you and other trans people. I used to be a member of the group. I think I can help you find Blair. I want to help. Call me.

Tanisha Nolan

~

I stared at the email for no less than twenty minutes, trying to figure out if this was legit or possibly a setup. The last thing I needed was to let my fervor for arresting Blair lead me into a trap.

Finally, I dialed the number.

"Hello?" asked a female voice.

"Tanisha Nolan? This is Jinx Ballou. I got your email."

"Hey. Yes." There was a sadness in her voice. "I watched that video you posted. I'm... I'm sorry for what Womyn Born Womyn did. Trying to make you appear like a perv. It's not right."

"Thanks. You said you could help me find Blair Marshall."

"Yes. Could we meet?"

"Where?" This was the key. If she wanted to meet someplace private, I knew it'd be a setup. But if she were willing to meet in public, this could be a legit lead.

"How about L Street? Do you know it?" she suggested.

"I do."

L Street was a women's bar in central Phoenix, run by

my friends Izzie and Chelsea Quiñones. Chelsea was trans and wasn't shy about people knowing it. I'd seen her wife, Izzie, kick out patrons for making transphobic remarks. It wouldn't be a place where members of WBW would hang out.

"I can meet you there in an hour."

"See you there."

Izzie was a stocky woman in her late forties with purple hair that was shaved on the right side. She wore a softball shirt with the words L Street Sluggers on it.

A woman in a business suit sat at the bar. Her hair was in neat cornrows. I suspected it might be Tanisha Nolan.

"Jinxie!" Izzie said enthusiastically when she saw me. "How the hell are you?"

"Been a rough week." I sat on the stool next to the suit.

"Ah, that's too bad. What'll you have? On the house in celebration of your upcoming nuptials."

"Just some cranberry juice with a squeeze of lime."

"I see. Hitting the hard stuff." She tossed a glance at the suit then back at me. "You working?"

"Sort of."

She nodded and went to make my drink.

"Tanisha Nolan?" I asked the suit.

"Yes."

"Tell me why you're willing to help me arrest Blair Marshall."

"When I joined WBW several years ago, our mission was to protect women. I believed all the lies they told me. About how allowing trans woman into restrooms and locker rooms made us unsafe. That any man could claim to be trans and walk right in. I didn't think we were being transphobic. I didn't hate trans people. I didn't know any. But they convinced me that trans people were crazy fetishists who posed a threat to real women."

"Trans women are real women."

"I know. That's how they talked. When I was with them, I did and said a lot of horrible things, both online and off. I know I hurt a lot of innocent people."

"Why are you helping me now? What changed your mind about trans people?"

"A few months ago, I met this amazing woman. Her name is Stacie." She showed me a photo on her phone of her and another woman standing arm in arm. "After a couple of dates, she told me she was trans. I couldn't believe it at first. She wasn't like the stereotype, you know? She's shorter than me, has a feminine voice. There was nothing masculine about her."

"She's lucky," I said. "A lot of trans women don't pass as cisgender."

"I know. She explained that to me. But what really struck me was how sweet, gentle, and caring she was. Blair was always saying you could recognize trans women because no matter how good they looked, they had male energy. But Stacie isn't like that. She's more feminine than I am. She is truly a woman.

"That's when I realized that all of this stuff Blair and Elise and the others were saying was nothing but hate and bullshit. They claimed to be woke radical feminists who cared about women, but in reality, they were nothing but a bunch of bullies looking for someone to hurt and feel superior to."

"Where is Blair now?"

"Honestly, I'm not sure exactly."

Great. So this was a colossal waste of time. An opportunity for this ally to unburden her soul for being a shitty person to the trans community.

"You said you could help me," I said, allowing a certain amount of irritation to creep into my voice. Not so much that it would shut her down but enough to let her know this whole thing was looking like nothing but bullshit.

"I can. At least I think I can. I want Blair to pay for what she's done. And I think I can get close to her. But it will take a little time."

"I don't have time. The judge wants her in custody yesterday. And I'm getting married in about forty-four hours. I need to arrest her now."

"Elise and I were pretty close when I was a member. I can contact her tonight, tell her I was wrong for leaving and want to join the group again. If I can patch things with her, I can probably touch base with Blair."

"And then you tell me where she's hiding, right?"

"Right. I'll give you her location and let you do your thing."

"I suppose you're looking for a reward. I'm offering a thousand dollars for information that leads to her arrest. No arrest, no reward. Got it?"

"I don't need a reward. Knowing she's being held accountable is reward enough."

"Did you know the Garrett woman?"

"The woman Blair killed? No. Stacie thinks they might have met at a Phoenix Gender Alliance meeting. I sometimes go to the significant other meetings. They really opened my eyes."

I finished my drink. "I'm glad. Call me when you find Blair."

"I will." She smiled at me. "And congratulations on getting married. Where's the wedding?"

"Dragon Tree Gardens."

"Wow! That's a beautiful place. I've attended a birthday party there. It's like you're in a magical indoor forest. I wish you all the best."

"Thanks. I look forward to your call."

I waved to Izzie and took off.

Would she call? Maybe, maybe not.

On the way home, I checked in with Zahara. "Any luck?"

"Nope. I looked around at the places you gave me. No sign of her. How about you?"

"I may have a lead. A gal who used to be a member of Womyn Born Womyn but quit after she supposedly fell in love with a trans woman."

"You think she's legit?"

"Hard to tell. Says she and Elise used to be tight. Will try to speak with Marshall under the ruse of making amends to come back into the fold. We'll see what happens."

"Fingers crossed. I'll see you tomorrow."

"Will do."

I hung up and contacted Rodeo. He hadn't had any luck either. I headed home and nearly collided with a utility truck because my mind was preoccupied with finding Marshall.

"Focus, girl," I told myself. "You'll find her. No matter how clever they are, no matter how many people they have helping them, you always track them down."

I took a deep breath. "Almost always."

I hoped this wouldn't be the exception to the rule.

26

―――――

The next morning, I was sitting at my desk at the Hub, sorting through the potential leads that Becca had gleaned from the tip line and email address.

I returned some phone calls, made a list of locations where people had claimed to have seen Marshall. But none of the tipsters knew Marshall personally. And the sightings were all over the state and beyond, with some as far west as San Diego and as far east as Indiana. A few offered encouragement and support for trans rights. It was appreciated but didn't get me any closer to sending Marshall back to jail.

No word back from Tanisha Nolan either.

I was fixing a cup of coffee in the Hub's break room when a well-dressed man walked in. "Jenna Ballou?"

I turned and eyed him suspiciously. People rarely referred to me by my legal first name. "Yeah. Why?"

He handed me a piece of paper. "I'm a process server. These are your court papers from Clark County Superior Court. Good luck."

"Clark County? As in Nevada?" My stomach twisted. "What the hell's this about?"

"I don't look at them. I only serve them. The details are in there. Have a nice day."

He left, and I unfolded the papers. Gerard Boyce was suing me for lost income and pain and suffering for his broken wrist. "Motherfucker."

I called Kirsten right away. "He's suing me for thirty million dollars."

"I'm so sorry, Jinxie. You should be relaxing in anticipation of your big day tomorrow. Not worrying about fugitives or, God forbid, sexual predators like Gerard Boyce. I will talk with Priya Choudhry, the senior civil litigator in the firm."

"If you can get this asshole off my back and out of my life, I'd be very happy."

"Consider it done, sweetie. We'll see about filing a countersuit for Boyce's attempt to sexually assault you. I've been doing some digging. You are not the first he's tried this with. Some responses to your video were from women stating that Boyce raped them. I will also talk with the Clark County District Attorney. See if I can't prod him to file assault charges against Boyce. I'll let you know."

My heart ached for the women Boyce assaulted. "I hope we can make his life as miserable as mine is right now."

"I will certainly try."

I tossed my coffee in the sink and filled my mug with cold water from the dispenser instead. If I drank any more caffeine, I'd be at risk for going off on the next person who pissed me off.

I was about to tell Becca about the lawsuit when my phone rang. It was Sadie Levinson.

"Yeah?"

"Ms. Ballou, do you have Marshall in custody?"

"Not yet. But I have someone who knows her trying to get me a location."

"Don't bother. I've reassigned the job to Leroy Drake."

"What? Why?"

"I told you days ago that this was urgent. I can't wait any longer. You're getting married tomorrow."

"Tomorrow afternoon. I still have all of today and tomorrow morning."

"Ms. Ballou… Jinx, this isn't personal. I'll have other jobs for you. But the county attorney's office is riding my ass on this one. It can't wait."

"Fine." I hung up.

My phone showed a missed call from Channel 7. I checked the time. "Shit. I gotta do these fucking media interviews."

I rushed with my laptop to one of the meeting rooms and called back the anchor, a woman named Maddie Gillespie.

"Sorry I missed you. Been a crazy morning."

"No problem. I'll send you the link for the video interview."

"Video? Shit. Didn't realize it was going to be video as well." I was dressed in a black T-shirt with my company logo and hadn't bothered with any makeup. It would have to do.

"Well, we are a television station," Gillespie replied. As if I needed the reminder.

"Yeah, got it." I clicked the link she emailed me. I would have to look how I looked.

"Ready?" she asked me over the internet.

"As ready as I'll ever be."

"Okay, Jinx Ballou interview recording in three, two, one." Her face brightened suddenly. "I'm speaking today with bounty hunter Jenna 'Jinx' Ballou, who recently made news when a video she made went viral. Can you tell me about the video, Jinx?"

"A week and a half ago, I was assigned to return Blair Lynn Marshall to custody after the judge assigned to the case revoked her bail. Marshall is charged with murdering LaTonya Garrett, a Black transgender woman. Marshall is white, by the way.

"She violated her bail agreement by threatening a witness, who is also a Black trans woman. I'm offering a reward for information that leads to her capture." I figured I'd start with that, hoping it might foster more viable leads.

"According to your video, Marshall is a member of Womyn Born Womyn, an organization that describes itself as feminists working for the rights and safety of women and children."

"Let me be clear. WBW is not a feminist organization. They have only one goal—hurting transgender people, who are a threat to no one. The Southern Poverty Law Center has labeled them a transphobic hate group.

"Look on their website. Do they fight for equal pay for women? No. Anything about reinstating the Violence Against Women Act? Not a word. And what about protecting women's reproductive rights? Dead silence. They only spread harmful misinformation about trans people, which has led to more violence against our community.

"Additionally, they created a deepfake video that showed me trying to seduce a young girl. Only it wasn't me in the video. They took a segment from a film and used computer magic to make it look and sound like me saying horrible things. My attorney is already pursuing legal action against them."

"Actor Gerard Boyce, who stars in the popular sci-fi series *Into the Black*, has accused you of forcing your way into his Las Vegas hotel suite and breaking his wrist. How do you respond to these accusations?"

My pulse raced as my mind filled with explosive anger, accompanied by disjointed flashes of memory of that night. I took a deep breath to steady myself, not wanting to come across as a madwoman.

"Gerard Boyce invited me to his hotel room for what he promised would be a cast party. Turned out it was only him. He put ketamine in my drink and then tried to rape me. I defended myself. Since I posted my video, more women have come forward saying that he raped them. He is the criminal here. Not me."

"But you were arrested by Las Vegas police, were you not?"

"All charges against me were dropped."

"Well, thank you for taking time to speak with us today, Ms. Ballou. I understand you're getting married tomorrow?"

"Yes." I didn't bother to elaborate. The interview had been little more than an ambush.

"Congratulations. I wish you all the best." She paused. "And we're out. Thanks so much, Ms. Ballou."

After ending the connection without a word, I sat there fuming. I wanted to call Elia Santiago and tell her that doing these media interviews was a stupendously horrible idea. But I had another scheduled in fifteen minutes and was afraid that canceling at the last minute would make me look worse than I already did.

I used the time to clear my head, put on a little makeup, and strap on my body armor. I didn't know how it would look on camera, but it made me feel more in control.

The next two interviews with local press didn't go much better. But I had stopped caring. Their questions held the unspoken insinuation that it was inappropriate for a transgender woman to be pursuing Marshall, that I was biased. I assured them I went after other fugitives with the same fervor. But it felt like my answers fell flat.

One anchor brought up my quitting the police force years ago shortly after Phillip Nelson, the Maryvale Arsonist, filed a bogus complaint against me for police brutality. I reminded him that the Professional Standards Bureau dismissed the complaint as unfounded, and that Nelson was found guilty of eight counts of first-degree murder and more than a dozen counts of arson.

My interview with MSNBC went better. At least the anchor was better informed on the facts of the story and how trans people have been smeared by people like Blair Marshall. But by the end of it, I was emotionally wiped.

"Geez, Jinxie. You look like death warmed over," Becca said after it was over.

"I fucking hate doing media interviews."

She slid her chair over to my side of the table and leaned her head on my shoulder. "I'm sorry. It really isn't your day."

"Sure as hell isn't." I checked my phone for any calls I might have missed. Especially from Tanisha. But there was nothing from any of my contacts. Maybe Tanisha's attempt to integrate herself back into the fold of the TERF sisterhood was taking longer than expected. Or maybe Shiver and Marshall caught on to her scheme and told her to go to hell. Or maybe Tanisha was full of shit and had no intention of helping me.

My hopes to earn the twenty percent bounty had evaporated.

"I'm calling it a day. We're supposed to be at Dragon Tree Gardens for the rehearsal at seven. I'm going to go home and chill."

She kissed the side of my head. "Smart move. I'll see you there. Do I need to wear the bridesmaid dress?"

"Not to the rehearsal. But we're going out to eat at Dooley's Public House for dinner afterward."

"What kind of place is it?"

"Basically an upscale Irish pub, but they've got a great menu."

"Not like haggis or anything?"

I laughed despite the inky cloud filling my soul. "Oh yes. Everything they serve is haggis. Haggis salad, haggis soup, even a side of haggis fries with the haggis almandine."

She stuck out her tongue. "Bitch."

"No haggis, I promise. That's Scottish. Dooley's big entrees are shepherd's pie, beef stew, roast mutton, that kind of stuff. They have vegetarian items too. You should be okay."

"Thank Goddess. I was worried."

I grabbed my computer case, but Becca stopped me before I could head to the door. "One thing. I've been logging all the calls from your phone, and I've noticed an odd phenomenon."

"What's that?"

"When WBW first doxed you, nearly all the calls were from women. Presumably WBW's followers. But over the past twenty-four hours, more than half of the calls are from men."

"Is that significant?"

"The tone of the calls, especially from the men, have less of a rad feminist bent and more of an evangelical right-wing feel to them. Calls for you to burn in hell. Calling you a demon and an abomination in the eyes of God. Threatening to shoot you if they see you in a public restroom with their wives or daughters. A real white nationalist Jesus-gun-freak vibe. Less of the usual TERF rhetoric."

"Doesn't surprise me. Arizona's still a very red state. Now that the news is out, all the QAnon MAGA freaks are doing what they do best. Harass people."

She sat back, staring at her three display screens. "Maybe. But something's telling me something else is at play."

I felt it too. Something new was going on. "Well, if you figure it out, let me know. Otherwise, I'll see you at the rehearsal."

27

———————

When I arrived home, Conor texted me that his crew had captured a fugitive and were taking him to lockup. He would meet me at the rehearsal.

I really could have used his company but settled for taking Diana for a run and listening to an old Pink Trinkets album. Their intense punk musical style, combined with progressive, snarky lyrics, always put me in a better mood.

By the time I got back to the house, showered, and dressed, it was time to head to the rehearsal. The drive up the Piestewa Freeway was a rush-hour slog. Cranking up the tunes only eased my frustration a little. I reminded myself to take several deep breaths, but with the day's events replaying through my mind, it was impossible to relax.

After exiting onto Greenway Road, I turned down the winding driveway at Dragon Tree Gardens. The venue's namesake Socotra dragon trees that lined the road reminded me of a cross between gigantic mushrooms and ponderosa pine trees. I felt as if I was entering an entirely different world. An emotional weight slid off my shoulders.

The driveway emptied into a large gravel parking area surrounded by enormous greenhouses set among sprawling exotic gardens.

I parked next to my parents' Lexus. Instead of following the directions to Greenhouse 3, where the wedding would be held, I ventured onto one of the paths that snaked through the gardens.

The air was rich with the scents of life—verdant, earthy, fertile. One could almost believe that dragons and other magical creatures lurked among the exotic flowering plants and trees. The hummingbirds that flitted about could easily be mistaken for faeries.

Not even my failure to capture Blair Marshall or getting sued by Boyce could rob me of the sense of wonder that permeated the place.

"Wow," Becca said, startling me.

I hadn't heard her approach. "Yeah."

She gazed wide-eyed at the tropical paradise like a kid who had stepped into Willy Wonka's chocolate factory. "This is... wow. Can't believe you're getting married here."

"And in less than twenty-four hours."

She gripped my arms. Our eyes locked. The memories we'd shared for the past twenty years came flooding in, both the good and the bad but mostly the good.

"Been a long time, hermana."

"It has."

"We've been through a lot of mierda."

"Don't I know it."

Her eyes sparkled with tears. "You and Conor are such amazing people. I'm so immensely happy for you."

We hugged. "Thanks, bestie. I never would have made it without you."

"We ain't done yet. You becoming an old married lady does not absolve you of the responsibilities of being my best friend. I love Easton with all my heart, but you have a place in my heart they can never fill."

"Thanks."

"Hey, you two!" My brother Jake came strolling down the path. He was a few inches taller than me with a dark tan and a scruffy beard. "Heard there's gonna be a wedding here tomorrow."

I gave him a hug. "Is that so?"

"Missed you last Sunday. Sorry about what happened in Vegas."

I forced a shrug and tried to maintain a straight face. No need to bring the drama here. "Water under the bridge."

"Come on. Let's get this rehearsal over with. I'm starving."

The three of us walked arm in arm into Greenhouse 3. The sudden increase in humidity was startling. More paths wound through tropical gardens, filled with exotic plants I didn't know even existed. The air was heavy with the sweet aromas of flowers in bloom. We walked past a re-creation of a ruined Mayan temple and an artificial waterfall emptying into a pool that teamed with fish.

"Reminds me of the Yucatán," Becca said.

"No kidding."

We followed signs pointing toward where the wedding would be held. The path opened up to a large clearing. A white arched trellis draped with flowers stood at the far end, with rows of folding chairs already set up in anticipation of the big event.

Our wedding attendants were gathered in small groups at the edge of the clearing, gazing at the botanical wonders. Samantha West, the Unitarian minister, stood talking with Conor and my parents by the trellis. When my father saw me, he broke away and approached with outstretched arms.

"How you doing, cher?"

I put on a brave face. "Hanging in there."

"Yeah? I saw the interviews on Channel 7 and 11. You held your own. Good girl."

"Did I? I wasn't so sure."

"Absolutely. But all that's past. Be here now as you prepare for the next chapter of your life."

I nodded. "That's what I'm trying to do." There was more emotion in my voice than I intended. It was hard for me to hide things from him.

He kissed my forehead. "It's all going to work out, sugar. Trust the process."

"You always say that. I never have fully understood what this *process* is. Much less why I should trust it."

He chuckled. "You will."

Conor joined us and kissed me full on the lips. I didn't care who was watching. This was the rehearsal for our wedding. One could hardly hold a little PDA against me.

"Hello, love. Ya ready to do this thing?" he asked.

"Let's do this thing," I said as emotions threatened to choke off my words.

If there was one thing I was sure of, it was that Conor loved me. Even after I refused to run away with him to Mexico. When all was said and done, he'd come back to me. And I couldn't help but say yes to him.

The minister led us through the rehearsal. Gradually, my mind let go of all other concerns. I immersed myself in the joy and excitement of the moment. My long-held dream of marrying Conor was coming true. We each had earned a slew of scars, both physical and emotional, since we'd first met. But as my father often reminded me, scars were a sign of strength, not weakness. The challenges we had endured had strengthened our bond.

At the rehearsal dinner, we all seemed to let loose. The combination of the Irish pub's jubilant atmosphere, the amazing food, and the pub's house ale helped me submerse myself in the laughter and love of the people surrounding me.

Little did I know that this pink cloud of hope and love would soon evaporate.

28

When I woke the next morning, I found a note on Conor's pillow. For an instant, I feared the worst, that Conor had reconsidered and decided not to marry me. Because I was transgender. Because I hadn't wanted to run away with him to Mexico. Because he simply didn't love me.

I wasn't normally given to such paranoid, depressive thoughts, but with all the buildup to the wedding and all the shit going on in my professional life, it would follow that the worst would happen. But it hadn't.

～

My dearest Jinxie,

I know you're not much of a traditionalist, and ya consider superstitions to be nothing but rubbish.

However, being an Irishman, I'm not one to tempt fate when it can be avoided. Since they say it's bad luck for the groom to see the bride before the wedding, I sneaked out to hang with my mates for the morning.

Have fun being pampered with Becca and the gals. You deserve it. You are a goddess, my love. Strong, brilliant, and deadly. I can't wait to spend the rest of my life being known as Jinx Ballou's husband. See you soon.

Love,

Conor.

~

I bawled and laughed at the same time. I was tempted to go back through the information on Blair Marshall to see if brainstorming might reveal her location. But I closed my rolltop desk and went for a run with Diana.

While we wound throughout our labyrinthine neighborhood, I let my mind go blank, focusing on the cool morning breeze, the brilliant blue sky, and the fresh spring air.

Afterward, I took a long shower before meeting Becca, Easton, Zahara, Kirsten, and Juanita for brunch at Maisie's Southern Café, followed by getting our hair and nails done at Choices Salon in east Phoenix. By the time we were done, I hardly recognized myself. Everyone looked like a walking glamour-shot photo.

"Dayum, bitches," Juanita said, taking a photo of us with Sue Figueroa, the salon's owner, and her amazing team of stylists. "Those boys ain't gonna know what hit them when we walk through the doors."

We carefully piled into our vehicles and drove north to Dragon Tree. It was three hours before the wedding, and my heart was pounding. Despite my father's ever-present reminder to trust the process, I wanted everything to be perfect in a way I never had before. I wasn't normally such a sucker for the Disney-esque fantasy, but I was in full Cinderella mode emotionally. And for once, I let myself be.

Following the instructions from the night before, I led my bridal attendants to the garden's admin building, next to Greenhouse 1. It looked like a cross between my father's psychotherapy office and a church. My mother and Grand-Mère Marie were there with my wedding gown and the outfits for my attendants.

Juanita, Becca, Zahara, and Kirsten would wear lavender dresses. Easton would wear a white tux with a lavender vest and cummerbund. Easton had offered to wear a dress for the occasion, but I told them it was their choice. They chose the tux.

My mother helped me into my wedding gown—a white, strapless, A-line gown embellished with a floral lace applique bodice, more beads and sequins than an entire drag show, a tulle overlay, and a detachable train. The moment I had tried it on in the bridal shop, I knew it was the one. It was elegant, without being too fussy. Modern, but with an homage to the traditional.

My mother preferred one with ruffled sleeves and a less-revealing neckline, but I was firm on this one. And Juanita, my fairy drag mother, who had accompanied us to the bridal shop, firmly agreed that I was a vision in white. Sorry, Mom.

A half hour before showtime, I heard a distant rumble that one might have mistaken for a buffalo stampede if I hadn't heard it many times before. The Athena Sisterhood Motorcycle Club had ridden from Cortes County to see me get married. I wasn't sure how many, but I had issued them an open invitation.

"I have to go say hello," I told my mother.

She shook her head with a finality I had learned not to cross. "No! You might see Conor. It would be bad luck."

"I'll bring them here," Becca said.

My mother didn't look entirely pleased with that option

either. They were, more or less, a law-abiding motorcycle club. But my mother saw them as a bunch of female hoodlums who had brainwashed me into getting a motorcycle of my own.

Perhaps it was the fact that I had previously been hired to apprehend one of them who'd jumped bail. Or that doing so nearly got me killed. Again. But I reminded her they were there at my invitation.

Still, there was one member of the biker club I was nervous about seeing again.

Moments later, Becca walked in, followed by several leather-clad women. My stomach did the butterfly stroke the instant I saw the deep scars that crisscrossed Shea Stevens's face.

Her hair had grown out into a tousled but stylish mop. Under her Athena Sisterhood leather vest, she wore a white button-down shirt. For her, this was dressed up.

"Hey," I said shyly. A tinge of guilt cut into my chest. We had dated briefly before Conor returned to Phoenix, following his acquittal.

"Hey, yourself." She gave me a bear hug and a kiss on the cheek. "You look like a fairy princess."

"Thanks." My face grew hot. "Wasn't sure you'd come, considering."

She put a hand on mine. "Jinx, you did what anyone would do. You thought he was never coming back. And when he did, what was I going to do? Say no? He was your fiancé, for Chrissakes."

"So, you don't hate me?"

"What we had was fun. And I won't say it didn't hurt to see it end." Shea reached out to another woman who walked in. She was shorter, with dark features. Shea put an arm around her as I recognized her. "But it all worked out. I'd like you to meet my girlfriend, Toni Rios."

"We met." Toni shook my hand. "You were looking for Indigo."

"You're a detective with the Cortes County Sheriff's Office."

"Was. I retired. I'm a private detective now."

"Good to see you again." I recognized more familiar faces, including Shea's niece, Annie, and other members of the club. We exchanged greetings before they headed to the greenhouse.

Becca and my other attendants followed them out, leaving only my mother, grandmother, and me.

"Cher, you are a vision in white," Grand-Mère said. "I wondered if I would ever see this day."

"As did I," my mother added. "Now I expect to see some grandchildren before long."

"Yeah, well, that might be a little difficult," I said, facetiously. "Seeing as how I have no womb."

She slapped my arm. "There are always alternatives. You would make a great mother."

I scoffed. "I'm happy being the mother of a rambunctious golden retriever. Speaking of dogs, how is Guimauve?"

Grand-Mère Marie smiled. "Much better. She had an infected tooth. The veterinarian pulled it, and tout de suite, she is much better."

"I'm so glad, Grand-Mère."

"Merci." She clasped my hands. "I want to tell you something, boo. Papere and I were married nearly forty years before he passed. To the end, we were like two lovesick teenagers. Every time I saw his face, ooh la la," she said with a sigh, "my heart skipped a beat."

"He was a good man. You two had a perfect relationship."

"The secret to a successful marriage isn't being perfect,

cher. But we always looked for ways to bring joy to each other's day. A bon coeur, tous les jours. We made each other laugh. Every day. Don't wait for anniversaries or holidays, boo. Make every day a holiday."

"You told me the same thing when Edward and I got married," my mother said, putting an arm on each of our shoulders. The earnestness in her eyes was born from wisdom and experience. I found myself misting up.

"I learned so much growing up with you and Dad. You showed me what genuine love looks like. I believe Conor and I have it."

She dabbed the tear from my eye with a tissue, careful not to smudge my makeup. "I know you do. Now let's go."

"Allons," Grand-Mère echoed.

I followed them over to the entrance of the greenhouse where my father stood waiting in a white tuxedo. Inside, a string quartet from my mother's church played an instrumental version of Journey's "Don't Stop Believing" while our paired wedding attendants proceeded down the aisle. Juanita walked with Deez, Conor's second-in-command at Viper Fugitive Recovery. Kirsten entered with Tucky, one of Conor's friends from his days working for Dark Horse Security in Afghanistan. Rodeo was paired with Becca, Zahara with Jake, and Easton with Byrd, another member of Conor's crew.

Becca's nephew, Carlos, served as our ring bearer. He was dressed as Frodo Baggins from *The Lord of the Rings*. The idea sparked several months ago as a moment of punch-drunk silliness after a long day of pursuing a fugitive. But the more I considered it, the more it felt appropriate, if a bit goofy.

Conor was a fan of both Tolkien and the idea. My mother was less supportive, but since Conor and I were paying for our own wedding, she was overruled. Sometimes a little levity in such a solemn event is exactly what's called for. It certainly triggered ripples of laughter from our gathered guests.

The music paused. For a moment, I thought something had gone wrong until the quartet began playing Mendelssohn's "Wedding March." A fist of emotion hit me in the solar plexus. Excitement, joy, nervousness, disbelief, and hope. Probably more emotions than those, but they were the only ones I could identify at the moment.

"You ready, cher?" my father whispered in my ear.

"I'm ready." I looked at him on my right and my mother on my left. "Thank you both."

I stepped down the aisle with them at my side.

29

Walking down the aisle past a sea of familiar faces was like watching my life flash before my eyes. Family, some of whom I hadn't seen in years. Friends from as far back as middle school, others more recent, many from the Phoenix Gender Alliance, a dozen or so officers I'd served with at the Phoenix Police Department, and some from the local cosplay groups.

My sensei from the aikido dojo I used to attend. Coworkers and associates, including Sadie Levinson and other bail bond agents. I even caught a glimpse of Robert Rossellini, aka Conspiracy Bob. I'd arrested him so many times he almost felt like family.

Conor's mother, Siobhan O'Callaghan, sat in the front row next to Grand-Mère, having traveled all the way from Dublin. Her long thick hair was the same coppery shade as her son's, though heavily streaked with gray.

There were several unfamiliar faces I assumed were Conor's former comrades from Dark Horse Security. They shared a similar military physique and bearing.

And then my eyes met Conor's. He practically glowed in his white tux. The lavender cummerbund clashed a bit with his hair, but I didn't care. He was the most handsome man I'd laid eyes on. Seeing him standing there with anticipation in his eyes, I wanted to sprint toward him. But I reminded myself to breathe and take it slow.

When we reached the makeshift altar, my father kissed me, my mother hugged me, and they took their seats. I handed my bouquet to Becca.

The music subsided, and I clasped Conor's hand. He was shaking like a leaf. Or maybe I was. Or maybe we both were. I couldn't remember whether we were supposed to be holding hands yet or not. Oh well. I sure as hell wasn't letting go.

Samantha welcomed everyone and shared a brief history of marriage, the symbology of the rings, and blah, blah, blah. I didn't really listen. I was lost in Conor's emerald eyes and the freckles sprinkled across his ruddy face like cinnamon.

Samantha prompted me to say my vows, which I had written on a slip of paper tucked into my lace sleeve.

"Conor, I never told you this, but I fell in love with you the first time we met. Officer Garza and I had responded to a report of a shooting at Grumpy's Bar and Grill where you had stopped a gunfight between two rival gang members. Okay, maybe I first fell in love with your dog, Baskerville, but you were a close second."

Laughter rippled through the crowd, though my comedic timing was clumsy. Emotion turned my tongue into vulcanized rubber, and I stumbled over a few of the words.

"When we finally started dating, I realized that being with you meant I couldn't work for you. Too risky. It was a hard choice to make, but I have no regrets."

I spared a glance at Deez. The scar on his throat had faded, but I could still see it. He smiled back at me.

"And then there was the morning I thought I'd lost you forever. It was the worst day of my life. And I've had my share of bad days." I took a deep breath. "But then you appeared again on my doorstep. I could hardly believe it. You were a free man, alive and well. And after everything, when you could have started over anywhere else in the world, with any other woman in the world, you came back to me. And I'm..."

I couldn't speak. My throat constricted. Tears of sadness, relief, and joy streamed down my face as I relived that moment once again. "I'm so glad to be here, right now with you, to marry you, and to spend the rest of my life with you. I love you, Conor Timothy Doyle."

He was crying as well. He cleared his throat twice before he spoke. "Jinxie, I've never told ya this either. But I fancied ya the first time I laid eyes on ya too. Even though ya were pointing a gun at my head at the time. What can I say? I have a thing for women in uniform."

I laughed and had to blow my nose on a tissue Easton handed me.

"That day on the beach in Mexico, when ya refused to run away with me..." He shook his head. "That was the worst day of my life. I was shattered. Not that I blamed ya. It was selfish of me to ask ya to leave behind all these amazing people. I realized it was time to face my past."

He squeezed my hand. "By the grace o' God, I am here now, a free man thanks to some of my mates who helped me recover the life I thought I'd lost. And, darling, there's nowhere else on God's green earth that I'd rather be than in your arms. I can't believe ya took me back after all I put you through, but I'm bloody glad ya did. I'm overjoyed to be here with you now, in front of all our kin and mates to declare that I want to marry ya and spend the rest of my life with ya, to have and to hold and all that bollocks. I love ya, Jenna Christina Ballou."

We exchanged rings and said the "I dos."

Samantha said, "By the power of the state of Arizona, I declare you husband and wife. You may now..."

Shouting came from the entrance of the greenhouse. I turned, and a shiver of fear ran up my spine.

A horde of people flooded into the clearing shouting "Leave Blair alone!" and "Trannies are perverts!" They carried signs that read "Trannies Go to Hell," and "No Men in Dresses."

Most of them were women, but a fair number of their ranks were men.

I felt like I would puke. Or pass out. Or puke and then pass out. But I tamped it down as a surge of adrenaline and fury blazed through my system.

"Oh fuck no!" I kicked off my heels and struggled to detach the train from my dress. I wasn't letting these fuckers ruin my wedding.

Conor gripped my arm. "Let the cops handle it, love."

My former colleagues at the Phoenix PD jumped up, flashing their badges to confront the rabble. The members of the Athena Sisterhood also joined the fray. But the haters with their signs and their chants flooded in like an invading army, outnumbering the bikers and the cops three to one.

"I can't stand by while these assholes ruin my wedding." I ripped the train from my gown and rushed into the melee.

I spotted Mandy Hudson and charged her. She swung at me with her homemade sign, but I ripped it out of her hands and hit her squarely on the side of the head. I tossed the sign aside and threw Hudson to the ground, flipping her onto her belly.

Instinctively, I reached for my cuffs, which weren't

there. I was in a wedding gown for pizza's sake. Time to improvise.

She struggled to twist around onto her back, and I clocked her solidly on the nose. That seemed to stun her enough for me to pull the veil off my head and wrap five feet of tulle around her wrists.

"Stupid fucking bitch," I growled into her ear. "I'm going to make you and your pathetic TERF trolls sorry you walked in here. Didn't know I used to be a cop, huh? Or that I'm friends with a women's motorcycle gang?"

"We have to protect women," she muttered between sobs.

"You aren't protecting anyone." I shoved her hard into the wood chips that lined the paths of the greenhouse. "Trans people aren't a threat to anyone. You're the only threat here. You're the ones making everyone less safe."

"But the kids..."

My heart skipped a beat when two shots rang out. Like a murmuration of starlings, the violent wedding crashers bolted en masse from the greenhouse. For a split second, I spotted Elise Holbrook, unmistakable with her teal-blue side shave. She stood with a small pistol in her hand, staring at me with a surprised expression on her face. Mandy Hudson pulled her away toward the entrance. They vanished out the door, trailing their fellow bigots.

Sharp screams pierced the commotion of people rushing away. The shrill sound sliced through me like a katana. I recognized my mother's voice filled with horror and rushed toward her. She knelt over the body of someone in a white tux. I pushed my way to her and saw rosettes of blood spreading across my father's torso.

"Daddy!" I fell to my knees and applied pressure to the biggest wound. "Someone call medical!"

He opened his eyes and tried to speak, but it came out in gurgles.

"Don't speak, Daddy. You're gonna make it." I hoped.

My mother, who was a trauma nurse, snapped out of her anguish and shock enough to assist me in stopping the bleeding. He had two wounds to his chest, one of which bubbled, suggesting air and fluid were seeping into his pleural cavity, making it difficult for him to breathe. His eyes grew wide with panic.

"Medical's on the way." Detective Pierce Hardin stood over us with his phone to his ear. "How is he?"

"Two GSWs to the chest, perforated lung," my mother replied with clinical detachment. "I need a latex glove and some tape."

"Here's a first aid kit." Someone in a beige Dragon Tree polo shirt set it down in front of us.

"Do you have any kind of large-bore needle?" she asked.

"Uh yeah, we use them for root substrate testing."

"Get me one stat!" She took a latex glove from the kit, cut out the palm with scissors, and taped three sides of it over my father's wound, while I kept pressure on his other wound.

The Dragon Tree employee returned a moment later with a thick hypodermic needle. My mother inserted it into my father's chest. Air hissed from the needle. The panic in my father's face subsided, but then his eyes lost focus.

I squeezed his hand with all of my strength. "Daddy, no! Stay with us. Please, stay with us."

"He's gonna... he's gonna make it," my mother murmured, though I struggled to believe it.

Seconds ticked by at an agonizingly slow pace.

After what felt like hours, an emergency medical team arrived and took over. Conor lifted me to my feet, pulling me away so the medical team could do their work.

I stood there, bloody hands trembling. I felt cold and wondered if someone had cranked the AC in the greenhouse to full blast.

30

———

Conor drove me to Tatum Hills Medical Center and parked in the visitor lot for the Emergency Room. My gown was soaked in my father's blood now clotting into the lace.

"I know you can't go in," I said, recalling Conor's serious phobia of hospitals.

"I... I can." His face looked as pale as my father's. "I've been working with a therapist your da recommended."

I stared blankly at the entrance to the ER. "I'd understand if you didn't. After what happened to your sister Bernie..."

"Bernie's gone. I've made my peace with it. But your da's alive."

"We hope."

"He's a tough old Cajun. He'll make it. And I'll stick with ya, love, no matter how bloody bad my anxiety gets." He gripped my hand. "You're my wife, Jinxie. What kinda husband would I be if I couldn't stand by ya through this shite?"

I met his eyes. The chill I'd been feeling seemed to melt

away. I wasn't alone. I had him. And he was willing to suffer through his own past trauma to help me through mine now. "I love you, Conor."

He smiled with tears sparkling in his eyes. "I love ya too. Let's go in."

My mother and brother sat in the waiting room next to Grand-Mère and Conor's mom, Siobhan. Many of our friends, including bounty hunters, Phoenix PD officers, and members of the Athena Sisterhood spread out across the room, all with their eyes on me, the bloody bride. They parted to let me reach my family.

"What have they said?"

My mother shook her head, a crumpled tissue held to her lips. Her rosary hung from her other hand. Streaks and spatters of my father's blood marked her dress.

My brother sat beside her with a hand on her back. "He's in surgery. That's all we know."

Siobhan stood and put an arm around me. I'd never met the woman before today, but she already felt like family. "Don't ya worry, love. Your da seems made of solid stuff from what Conor tells me. I'm sure God'll help him pull through."

"Thanks." I didn't believe in God personally but appreciated the sentiment.

My mother stood up and took in a deep breath. "Jenna, I need to speak with you privately."

My insides trembled. I feared she was about to blame me for my father being shot. But she needn't have bothered. I already blamed myself. I brought this on. My choice of career. All the years I ignored my mother's pleas to find something less violent. It had nearly taken Conor's life. And now it looked likely to claim my father.

But the steely resoluteness in my mother's voice forced

me to obey. I followed her to a corner of the room, far from the ears of the others.

"I'm so sorry, Mom. I know this is my fault." The tears flowed unabated. "I should have listened to you."

"Quiet!" she snapped. "The blame for this violence rests solely on those awful people. Not you. They came after you because of who you are, not for anything that you've done."

Our eyes locked. I saw her fear but also a ferocity I knew lay in a mother's heart.

"Still..."

"Listen to me, Jenna. Did you see who shot him?"

"I think so." I remembered Elise Holbrook with her dark side-shave haircut, the gun in her hand, and a shocked expression on her face. I knew that look. It was the countenance of someone who realized they'd done the unthinkable—murdering an innocent person.

"I don't blame you for what happened, but I want you to make this right. Do you understand what I'm saying?"

"You mean..."

"You hunt people down for a living. I want you to hunt down this person. But I don't want you to turn her over to the police. Do. You. Understand?"

My mother's side of the family was Italian. But no one in the family was anything like the ridiculous stereotype of the Italian mafioso. The only criminal was my cousin Anthony Esposito, who went to prison for forging and selling LeRoy Neiman paintings. Otherwise, we were like any other American family.

But something in my mother's tone was straight out of a Martin Scorsese flick. She didn't want me to let the police handle this. And she didn't want me to arrest Holbrook. She wanted me to put her in the ground.

"Mom, I can't... the police."

"Fuck the police." My mother never cursed. Never. "You do this, Jenna. You make this right."

The weight of her anger felt like a boulder crushing my chest. I stared at the ficus in the corner. "Yes, Mama."

She grabbed my chin and forced me to meet her gaze. "Do this. Promise me."

"I promise. I will make this right."

She hugged me. All at once, she was no longer the scary mafiosa. She was my mother. At least I thought so.

When we returned to the group, Detective Hardin stepped forward with a woman in a dark suit. Hardin had been my field training officer when I joined the Phoenix Police Department. He now worked homicide.

"Ballou, this is Detective Carly Wong." He gestured to a woman in a suit next to him. "She will lead the investigation into your dad's shooting."

"I'm so sorry this happened, Ms. Ballou." Wong reached out to shake my hand but hesitated.

I looked down and saw mine covered in dried blood. "Sorry."

"No need to be sorry. Get yourself cleaned up and then let's talk."

"Yeah." I looked around and spotted a unisex restroom near the waiting room.

"Everything all right?" Conor appeared at my side while I shuffled toward the restroom.

I shrugged. I didn't want to tell him about the conversation with my mother.

"Sorry. Daft question under the circumstances."

"Just need to wash my hands." I looked down at my gown. "What am I going to do about all this?" I didn't want to be trudging about the hospital looking like something from a Tim Burton movie. Jinx Ballou as the *Corpse Bride*.

"I'll see what I can find in the gift shop."

"Okay."

I stepped into the restroom, locked the door. My knees buckled. I fell against the back wall and slid to the floor, sobbing uncontrollably for what felt like hours. Only the pounding on the door brought me out of the purgatory of my sorrow.

"Jinxie, you all right?" Becca's voice came through the door.

"Yeah. Be out in a minute." I grabbed the sink and pulled myself to my feet. Blood was streaked on my cheeks. My eyes looked hollow and lifeless. My hair was like cotton candy stained a ruddy black. I turned on the hot tap and washed as best I could, not even caring when the water became scalding. I kept rubbing my hands, muttering, "Out, damned spot!" It was a line from something I couldn't remember.

I scrubbed my face and attempted to get the blood out of my gown, but it only smeared more.

When I opened the door, Conor and Becca were there waiting for me.

"I'm so sorry, sweetie." Becca hugged me and offered me a pair of jeans. "I had these on earlier. They ought to fit."

"Thanks." She and I were roughly the same size. One of the many reasons people often mistook us for sisters.

"I got ya a shirt from the shop." Conor handed me a bag. "Get yourself changed."

I kissed him on the lips, and doing so made me feel a little more human. "Any word on how he's doing?"

They both shook their heads.

"I'll be right out."

I pulled off the gown, practically tearing out the seams as I did so. I stuffed the bloody mass of lace and sequins into the garbage bin, filling it to the brim. The T-shirt was a cheesy touristy shirt with Arizona written across the top and a stylized Kokopelli playing his flute below it. I didn't care. Better than the gown. Nor did I care that I had no bra, shoes, or socks.

Becca's jeans were a little loose in the hips but fit otherwise. They wouldn't be falling down.

I stepped out and walked with Becca and Conor back to the waiting room. Wong and Pierce beckoned me.

"I'll be back shortly," I told my new husband. "Gotta talk to the cops."

Kirsten stepped forward, still in her bridesmaid dress. "You want me with you?"

"Not a bad idea."

She and I followed the detectives to a room off one of the side corridors. The sign outside the door said something about consulting. Inside, there was a small laminate table and six brass upholstered chairs. A box of tissues sat at the far end of the table.

"I am so sorry that this happened to your father," Wong said. "And on your wedding of all days."

Hardin nodded his sympathies. "We've arrested several people already, but we need to hear from you about what may have led to this intrusion."

"Detectives, my client is not responsible for this mob's horrific acts of violence."

"Easy, counselor," Wong said. "We aren't suggesting she's responsible. We simply want to know what occurred and why."

I explained about being hired to locate Blair Marshall and about the various videos that I and WBW had posted to the internet. Wong and Hardin took notes on everything I said.

"The people who barged into your wedding, were they all members of this group, Womyn Born Womyn?" Wong asked.

"It all happened so fast. I'm obviously not a member, so I don't know their people on sight. But the signs they carried had the same slogans they often use. I saw men there too. I'm guessing they weren't WBW members. The group must have recruited other people to join them in harassing me. I didn't recognize them, though."

"We found one woman, an Amanda Hudson, hog-tied with what looked like a wedding veil. Was this your doing?" Hardin asked.

Kirsten and I exchanged a glance. "Detectives, my client would like to invoke her Fifth Amendment right."

"No, it's okay," I interjected, which earned me a concerned look from Kirsten. "Hudson attacked me with a sign. I defended myself and subdued her."

"Way to improvise." A wry smile spread across Wong's face. "Did you see who shot your father?"

"No," I lied, remembering my promise to my mother. The memory of Elise Holbrook holding the gun with the shocked expression on her face flashed in my mind. "I was grappling with Hudson. I heard the shots, and then the mob fled."

Wong and Hardin continued with their questions, asking for clarification about my pursuit of Marshall, if I knew of any WBW members who owned a firearm, or if any had used one against me to protect Marshall. I told them unequivocally no.

I still wasn't sure if I could really bring myself to murder Holbrook. If my father died, maybe I could. She wouldn't be the first person I'd killed. But never like this. Never in cold blood.

"How did they know where your wedding was being held?" Hardin asked. "Was it in the newspaper? Do they even publish wedding announcements anymore?"

I shook my head. "We chose to keep it quiet."

Tanisha Nolan came to mind. She had overheard me talking with Izzie about the wedding and asked where it was being held. And I'd not heard a word from her since that afternoon at L Street. Had the whole meeting with me been a ruse? The photo she showed me of her girlfriend could have been anyone. A stock photo. A social media contact. Even another member of WBW.

"I have no idea." Technically, it was the truth. I didn't feel like sharing my suspicions. If I was going to pursue Holbrook, I wanted to have a word with Nolan first. "Now I want some answers."

"Such as?" Wong sat with her hands folded, a lot of patient anticipation on her face.

"What kind of gun was my father shot with?"

"We don't have ballistics back, and even when we get it, we can't share that information this early in the investigation."

"Come on. I used to be a cop." I turned to my former training officer. "Hardin? Come on."

Hardin exchanged a glance with Wong, then asked, "Why do you need to know that?"

"He's my father. I want to know."

He grimaced. "We recovered three shell casings from a forty cal."

It was a common caliber. Didn't really tell me anything.

"You're sure you don't know who shot him?" Wong pressed.

"It was chaos. I was wrestling with Mandy Hudson like I said."

Wong stopped asking questions, and a silence settled in the room. This was an interrogation technique police often used when they believed an interview suspect was holding back information. People abhorred silence as much as nature abhorred a vacuum. It had a way of getting suspects and witnesses talking.

I sat there silent as the grave, even though the absence of conversation opened up the gates to the trauma of the wedding's horrific aftermath. I tried to focus my mind on the wedding procession, the exchange of vows, and Conor's handsome, rugged face. I found strength in those emerald eyes. The flecks of gold shone like fire. I clung to that emotion with all of my soul.

A knock on the door nearly sent me through the roof. Hardin got up and opened it. Conor stood there.

"He's out of surgery."

The weight of a thousand bulldozers rolled off my shoulder. The room grew less stuffy.

"We through?" I asked Wong.

"Yes, thank you for your time. I wish your father a speedy recovery."

I knew it probably wouldn't be the last time they would interview me over this. There were always more questions, more details to probe and rehash. The goal was to poke holes in a witness's story, even one who wasn't a suspect. It was important to establish a solid timeline of events. Memory of traumatic events was unreliable. People had a tendency to fill in the gaps or get the order of events confused.

I wondered if I had done the same. Had I really seen a gun in Holbrook's hand? Had I imagined it? She never struck me as a gun owner. But then again, this was Arizona. Many people were gun owners, regardless of political affiliation.

"How is he?" I asked Conor as we returned to the waiting room.

"Doc says he's stable," he replied. "He lost a fair amount of blood, but they think he'll pull through. He's recovering in the ICU. They'll let us know when we can see him. Shouldn't be long."

I hugged him, allowing myself to breathe for the first time in what felt like years.

We returned to where my family sat in the waiting room. My mother held my gaze for a split second, but it was enough to convey a clear message: remember your promise.

I nodded without a word.

31

———————

My mother and I were the only other ones in the room, as the hospital staff only permitted two visitors at a time for the time being.

The assortment of tubes, wires, and IV lines connected to my father's shattered body made him look like a cyborg. His pale face and arms were still spattered with blood.

He had always seemed invincible. Strong and resilient like the spindly sixty-foot Mexican fan palm trees that no monsoon storm could topple. And yet here he was, clinging to life, a fragile shell of his normal self. Seeing him like that felt like a blow to my soul. I gripped the bed railing to keep my knees from buckling.

"Edward," my mother whispered. "Please wake up."

His eyes fluttered then opened halfway. "Gia." The word was barely audible from his hoarse throat.

"I'm here, too, Daddy."

A faint smile formed on his face. "Cher." He took a deep breath and grimaced. "What?"

"You were shot," I said. "At the wedding."

"Wedding. My princess bride."

"Yes." My voice grew choked with tears.

"You're married?"

I nodded.

"I... can't remember."

"It's okay, Eddie," my mother assured him. "You're safe. Everyone's safe."

"So tired."

I wanted to say so much to him, but the grip of emotions felt like the tail of a facehugger from *Alien* wrapped around my throat, rendering me speechless.

"Get some rest, my love," my mother said.

He nodded slightly and closed his eyes. My mother glanced up at the vitals monitor, and I followed her gaze. His blood pressure was dangerously low. His heart kept throwing PVCs according to the EKG. But his blood-oxygen level was decent, hovering around ninety percent. He wasn't out of the woods, but there was reason to hope.

My mother put a hand on mine, and we returned to the ICU waiting room. Conor wrapped me in his arms.

"How is he?"

"He woke for a moment but went back to sleep. He doesn't remember anything."

"Can we see him?" Jake sat with his arm around Grand-Mère Marie. She looked frailer than she had a few hours earlier, as if she'd aged ten years in that time. Then again, who of us hadn't?

"Should be okay," my mother replied. "But he's going to need his rest."

Jake and Grand-Mère strode solemnly down the hall.

I looked around the room. "Where's Becca?"

"Easton took her home," Kirsten said. "They said she was out of spoons."

Hardly surprising. She'd been pushing herself this week, especially considering our crazy trip to Vegas the previous weekend. With her chronic fatigue, she should have been taking it easy. And then today.

Guilt over her flare-up compounded the guilt I felt about my father. I was again making the ones I loved miserable. I needed to make things right.

Everyone from Phoenix PD had also left. They had jobs to do. Not just my father's shooting or the attack on my wedding but other crimes as well.

Shea Stevens and a few other members of the Athena Sisterhood remained but kept their distance in the room. Perhaps afraid that if they touched me, I would shatter. They weren't entirely wrong about that. I felt as fragile as a soap bubble. At the same time, an ember of vengeance smoldered within me.

"How are you doing?" I asked Conor. I'd been so wrapped up in my own trauma, I'd forgotten he was dealing with his phobia and past traumas.

He put on a brave expression, but I could see the anxiety in his eyes. He had faced down the worst humanity had to offer, but hospitals brought back the horror of seeing his sister Bernie's shrapnel-riddled body in an Omagh hospital. "I'm managing."

"I need a shower," I told him.

I needed more than that. I needed to track down Blair Marshall, Tanisha Nolan, and Elise Holbrook. Marshall, I wanted in custody. I wanted answers from Nolan.

As for Holbrook, I was torn between turning her over to the authorities and exacting the revenge my mother and I both wanted. Holbrook didn't have any priors. Not even a speeding ticket. Model citizen. If she accepted a plea of aggravated assault, she might serve a few years. Might even get off with probation, with a good-enough lawyer. My mother would go crazy if that happened.

"Let's get you home," Conor whispered.

I approached my mother. "I'm going home to get cleaned up."

She looked hurt, as if I were abandoning her. "You're leaving? Now?"

"And to take care of that thing you asked of me."

"Of course. Yes. Go take care of things. Where's your gown?"

I shook my head, and she nodded in acknowledgement. Even if it hadn't been covered in my father's blood, it would forever be a reminder of what had happened today. This day that should have been the best day of my life.

"I love you, sweetheart." Tears sparkled in her eyes.

"Love you, too, Mama." I'd rarely called her that since childhood.

Conor took the most direct route out of the hospital, which was on the opposite side from the Emergency Room. But he wanted to get out of the building as quickly as possible, and I didn't blame him. When we passed through the sliding glass doors at the main entrance, Conor started gulping the warm spring air, as if he'd been holding his breath.

"You okay?" I put a hand on his back.

"I will be. You?"

I considered the tasks before me. "I will be."

"Suppose the Florida Keys are on hold."

"Yeah, sorry."

"Ya got nothing to be sorry for. This isn't your doing."

"Maybe it is. That video I made..."

"That video ya made was speaking truth to power. Those bloody cunts doxed ya and were spreading vicious lies. Ya did nothing that warranted what they did today."

"Maybe."

On the long drive home, I called Tanisha Nolan. It rang four times and rolled over to voicemail.

"Tanisha, this is..." A fury of emotion flooded through me while I fumbled for what to say. "I expected a call from you. Call me immediately when you get this."

The Billie Eilish song playing on the radio ended and was followed by a breaking news segment. At the first mention of the shooting, I turned off the radio. I didn't need to hear some bubble-headed news jockey tell me what he thought he knew about today's shocking events at a valley wedding involving—gasp—a transgender bride.

When we pulled up on our street, the news vans were back. Several blue-and-white patrol cars were also parked along the road. I almost told Conor to keep going and take me to a motel, but I would not let this bullshit take over my life.

At our driveway, a patrol officer stopped us. "Are you a resident here?"

"Aye, we live here." Conor showed the officer his license. "We're the couple whose bloody wedding was attacked."

The officer nodded and gestured for us to proceed. While Conor drove into the garage, I saw the camera crews emerge from their news vehicles and swarm toward the driveway. Fortunately, the patrol officer herded them back.

When the garage door thumped closed behind us, leaving us in the dim aura of the overhead light, I finally felt I could breathe.

Diana was more excitable than usual when we stepped into the house. Clearly the rabble outside was making her anxious. Under normal conditions, I would take her for a run to work off the excess energy, but even if I hadn't been wrecked from the day's tragic events, I wouldn't have tried to run the gauntlet of the protestors and media.

I sat down on the living room couch and hugged her. It seemed to make both of us feel a little better.

"I have to find Tanisha Nolan."

"Who's she?"

I told him. He cradled my face. "Jinxie, my precious, beautiful bride, let the constabulary do their job. They'll sort this out."

"I still need to find Blair Marshall. Tanisha Nolan was supposed to track her down."

"The Marshall job's been reassigned. Ya told me yourself. Let Leroy Drake deal with her."

"I don't care who Sadie Levinson reassigned the case to. This is personal now."

"All the more reason to let Drake handle it. You're too bloody close to it."

"Drake is an idiot."

"Aye, he is. But that's Sadie's problem now."

"I can't let it go, Conor. You don't understand. This bitch attacked my community. And now she and her TERF friends have ruined my wedding. Her fucking cousin tried to murder my father."

"Trust me, love. I get it. I may not be trans, but I remember all too well what that shite felt like growing up north of the wall. How the loyalists treated us Catholics. How that bitch Thatcher turned a blind eye to what was happening, leaving us little choice but to fight back. And I know what it cost us, what it cost me and my family when I did."

The hurt in his eyes was palpable. I could see the frightened teenager, aghast at his part in the deadly explosion.

"I'm not looking to kill Nolan. Or Marshall." I still hadn't decided what to do about Holbrook.

"Aye, but this is how things turn out. Let it go. Your mate Hardin and Detective Wong will find Holbrook and her dodgy bunch. We need to be there for your father and your family. Your ma needs you there. Take a shower, put on some decent clothes, and we'll head back. I'll take my anxiety meds. We'll get through it together."

I grasped his hands. He was right. His history wasn't entirely like my current situation, but there was a lot of wisdom in what he was sharing. Things were bad enough. I didn't need to make them worse. Let Marshall be Drake's problem. Let Hardin and Wong deal with the TERFs.

"Okay. Let me take a shower."

"Ya want some company?" A devilish twinkle appeared in his eyes.

"Normally, I would say yes, but right now, I need to decompress alone."

"Of course, love."

I pulled off the touristy shirt and borrowed jeans and stepped into the steaming shower. As my tense muscles loosened, so did the flood of emotions. I no longer tried to hold them back. My father had taught me years earlier that it was important to allow ourselves to feel whatever was coming up, no matter how scary those emotions seemed. Keeping them bottled up was a recipe for disaster.

I sobbed, screamed, pleaded with a God I didn't believe in, and screamed some more until my soul was empty, the water cold, and my fingers pruney. I was exhausted, physically and mentally, but I felt a little better.

I put on some clean clothes and sat on our bed staring at the wall, trying to be in the moment.

"Breathe in love," my father would say. "Breathe out negativity."

I should leave the investigation of the shooting to the police. I should leave catching Blair Marshall to that loser Leroy Drake. I should return to the hospital and sit vigil in the ICU while my father recovered.

I had told Conor I would do all these things. But I couldn't face my mother until I had made this right. Until

Blair Marshall, Elise Holbrook, and perhaps Tanisha Nolan had been held accountable.

The muffled television drifted in from the living room. Shouts and cheers. I guessed Conor was watching a soccer match.

I crept into our home office and opened my laptop. I wanted to run a quick check of things.

32

———

I ran Tanisha Nolan's name through the SkipTrakkr database. It pulled up recent addresses, work history, phone numbers, criminal background, and a credit report.

She lived in an apartment on Thomas Road west of the Piestewa Freeway and had been there for six years. She'd worked for the 16th Street Pawn & Jewelry, between Thomas and Indian School Road for less than a year. Previous jobs included working retail at a dress shop, now closed, and a sporting goods store.

No criminal record, and she didn't have any outstanding debts other than a two-grand bill with a hospital chain for which she was current in her payments.

I called her phone again, and again, it rolled over to voicemail. Didn't bother leaving a message. Maybe she was at work.

It was a few minutes past seven o'clock in the evening. According to the pawnshop's website, they were open until eight. I dialed the number. A guy with a gruff voice answered.

"Hi, I'm looking for Tanisha. She was helping me with an antique bracelet I pawned last week. Is she there?"

"You're looking for Tanisha? That makes two of us. Damn girl didn't come in today. What's your ticket number? I can help ya."

"That's okay. I'll try her later. Thanks."

I hung up and considered the possibilities. Maybe she blew off work to crash my wedding. I didn't recall seeing her there, but there must have been several dozen uninvited guests. Maybe one of the cops had arrested her or was holding her for questioning. Or maybe she was trapped under something heavy like a refrigerator. Or a guilty conscience.

I copied her address and her MVD photo onto my phone and began suiting up. Body armor. Ruger in the pancake holster. A backup revolver in an ankle holster. No Taser. Flashlight. Handcuffs. Extra mags for the Ruger. A speedloader for the revolver. A nondescript baseball cap to keep from being too recognizable.

Conor walked in and froze. "Jinx. What're ya doing, love?"

"Tanisha Nolan never called me back. Didn't show up to work. I'm going to see if she's at her condo."

"You look like you're going into combat."

"After today, I'm not taking any chances."

"Thought we were going back to hospital for your da."

"I know. But I need some answers." I didn't know how to explain it. "I have to find Nolan."

He crossed his arms and studied me for a moment before saying, "You're daft, Jinxie. Absolutely mental. But if this is what ya feel ya have to do, then by God, I'll be right by your side. Gimme a moment to gear up."

Fifteen minutes later, he was ready. We drove past the growing mob of media vans and protesters in Conor's

Charger. My mind was a muddled mess as we cruised through the growing dark to Nolan's apartment.

The complex was small and had a neglected look to it, as did the vehicles in the lot. Finding the building was easy enough. Her apartment was on the ground floor, tucked underneath a stairway.

"Ya sure about this, love?" Conor asked.

"No," I confessed. "But my father always told me that when I was lost and unsure what to do, simply do the next best thing. That's what I'm doing."

I pounded on the door and rang the bell a couple of times. After a few minutes, a skinny woman with unkempt hair and a husky voice answered the door. "Yeah? What you want?"

"I'm looking for Tanisha."

"Yeah?" She put a hand on her hip.

"Yeah. She here?"

"I ain't seen her."

"But she does live here."

"Yeah, she live here." Finally, a straight answer.

"Do you know where she is?"

"Why? She in some kinda trouble?"

"She was supposed to call me with some information. I never heard from her."

"Who you is?"

"Someone who's working with her on something. Where is she?"

"You the poh-lice?"

"Look, lady. Answer our bloody questions. Where the feck is she?" Conor sounded as exasperated as I felt.

"Listen to you with your funny accent. Where you from?"

I stepped into the woman's space. "Where the hell is Tanisha?"

"How the hell I supposed to know?"

I remembered the story Tanisha told me at L Street. "You Stacie?"

"How the fuck you know that?"

"She mentioned you when she and I met at L Street. You're trans, right?"

She eyed me warily but said nothing.

"Listen, it's cool. I'm trans too. She was trying to help me find the woman who murdered LaTonya Garrett."

"You trans?" She sounded skeptical. "Don't sound trans."

"I transitioned young. I had a supportive family."

"Lucky you." An awkward silence settled between us.

"Look, I don't know where she at. She said she was looking for that ho Blair Marshall. Her and her little cult of White-ass, trans-hatin' bitches. Guess you's the one she was doing that for. But I ain't seen her since yesterday. Ain't been answering her phone." Her eyes teared up. "Wondering if maybe she hooked back up again with them, you know?"

"Do you have the FamFinder app?" It was a long shot. FamFinder was an app pitched to parents of kids with phones and to people who suspected their partners of cheating.

Stacie appeared to consider my question, and her face brightened. "Yeah, I do. Hold on."

She vanished into the apartment and reappeared with her phone. "I installed it on our phones when I found out her ex got hired at the pawnshop." She opened the app. "What the hell?"

"You find her?"

"Some place on Flower Pot Road. Middle of fucking nowhere. Way north of town."

She read off the exact coordinates. I pulled them up on

a map on my phone. It looked like a small rectangular building from the satellite photo. Maybe a trailer.

"Up toward Camp Verde," Conor noted.

Stacie shook her head. "What the hell she doing way up there?"

"If I had to guess, I think she's meeting with Blair Marshall." I turned to Conor. "Let's head up there. Maybe we can finally nail this bitch."

"And you tell that girlfriend of mine to call me and get her Black ass back here, you read me?"

"I'll tell her."

We piled back into the Charger and took the Piestewa Freeway north to the Loop 101 and around to I-17 north out of the city. As the lights of Phoenix vanished behind us, I stared out at the pitch-black desert. The Pink Trinkets' album *Re-Sisters* played on the stereo. Conor must have put it on to cheer me up, but it didn't help. Like trying to fill up the Grand Canyon with an eyedropper.

"So, we find this Tanisha Nolan and then what?" Conor asked.

"I'm hoping this place is where Blair Marshall's been hiding. I arrest Marshall, turn her in, get paid."

"Aye. And is that where it ends with you?" His question was loaded with implication.

"Elise Holbrook shot my father. She has to answer for that."

"Answer how?"

When I didn't answer, he pressed on. "Let the cops go after Holbrook."

"They don't know she shot him. I didn't tell them."

"Why the bloody hell not? Are ya daft?"

"I don't know. Maybe. I think a little payback's in order."

"Jinx, I understand your anger. But ya can't do that. Tell

the coppers what ya know. What would your ma say if you murdered Elise Holbrook?"

"She's the one who told me to do it."

"Oi! Now I know you're mad. I've known your ma for ten years. She's a devout Catholic and a trauma nurse to boot. She'd never—"

"She did, Conor."

"Jesus fecking Christ. You're all mad, the lot of ya. This isn't *Sons of Anarchy* or any of that blarney. You murder Elise Holbrook, then you're the one spending the rest of your life in the slam. It's not worth it, love. We just got married, for Chrissakes! We've got a whole life ahead of us. Don't blow it on some revenge killing."

"Can we talk about something else?"

"Fine. We'll show up at this trailer and see what we got. But know one thing, Jenna Christine Ballou. I love you. I want you to be happy above all things. And it tears me up to see ya go down this path. I know you like to play fast and loose with how you and Becks skip trace fugitives. But this is a whole other level."

I didn't respond. He was right. Killing Holbrook wouldn't solve anything. And it would only strengthen WBW's claim that trans people were violent and dangerous to women. And yet my mother's words echoed in my soul. *"Make it right."*

By the time we pulled off the highway, I was nodding off. The sound of gravel under the tires roused me from my stupor. Everything outside of the glare of the high beams was pitch-black. The car bounced around on the hilly, unpaved road. According to the GPS, we were way off the beaten path.

Opening the window brought in cool night air, along with dust kicked up by the front tires. It helped to wake me up and get my mind in game mode.

Eventually we spotted the trailer parked in a pocket carved out of the hillside. A single car sat parked in the surrounding dirt lot. A quick check of the plate confirmed it belonged to Tanisha Nolan.

Surprisingly, I still had a cell signal. Only a bar or two but enough in case we needed to call for backup or I needed to send something to Becca.

"Guess this is it." I pulled an LED flashlight off my utility belt. "That's Nolan's car."

"Aye. No lights on inside. Not a good sign."

"Yeah, I want to look around before we try to make entry."

"Copy that. Watch your six. I'll grab the ram and cover the front."

With my flashlight's blue-white beam guiding me, I walked the perimeter around the trailer. It was a typical single-wide mobile home. From the layer of desert dust on the aluminum siding, I guessed it had been here for some time. On the back side, I found a metal plate. I rubbed off a layer of dirt, took a photo, and sent it to Becca.

"Ya ready, love?" Conor asked when I got back to the front door.

"Yeah, let's do this."

A splash of red on the outside wall beside the door caught my eye. I shone my light on it.

"Conor, blood." I could make out the smeared outline of fingers.

"Aye," he said grimly. "Best glove up."

We each slipped on latex gloves, not wanting to contaminate what could be a crime scene. And certainly not wanting to leave behind any fingerprints of our own.

He gave the door a good pounding with his fists. "Bail enforcement! Open the door."

I checked to see if the door was locked. It was.

Conor hefted the battering ram and drove it into the flimsy aluminum door. It buckled and came off the hinges. I pulled it all the way open and aimed the flashlight inside, propped atop my Ruger, finger on the trigger.

"Bail enforcement!" I shouted. "Everyone down on the floor."

The only person inside was already on the living room floor, blood pooling around her. I recognized her cornrows immediately. Tanisha Nolan.

"Shit."

33

"Tanisha?" I knelt down and placed a couple of fingers on her neck. Even through the latex glove, I could detect a faint pulse.

She was bleeding from two wounds in her abdomen. I grabbed a towel from the kitchen area and applied pressure. A sharp cry of pain escaped her throat.

"I'll call 911," Conor said, stepping outside to get a better cell signal.

"Hang in there, Tanisha. Help's on the way."

The moments ticked by slowly. I monitored her breathing, checking her pulse periodically. She'd lost a lot of blood. I wasn't sure how she was still alive at this point. Memories of trying to save my father hammered at my psyche. I tried to wall them off and focus on the situation at hand, but still, the emotions of panic and despair seeped through.

"Medical's on its way," Conor said when he stepped back in. "How is she?"

"Alive for the moment. Can you come put pressure on the wound?"

He gave me a funny look but knelt down and took over, holding the towel against Tanisha's belly.

"What are ya doing, love?"

"I want to poke around a bit before the cops get here."

"Jinxie, this caravan's a bloody crime scene." His tone had a warning in it.

I held up a hand. "I won't touch anything. I'm just looking."

I washed the blood off my gloved hands in the sink and swapped out the soiled gloves for fresh ones, putting the used ones in my pocket. I then used my phone to take photos of everything in the trailer that could point to Marshall or what had occurred here.

A mobile phone lay on the carpet next to the pantry cabinet, the screen cracked from what appeared to be two distinct impact points. I guessed someone had deliberately tried to destroy it. A few empty frozen dinner packages were in the trash beside the kitchenette. In the sink, I found dirty dishes. Someone had been living here for a couple of days at least.

On the inside door of the pantry, I found a piece of paper with a serial number and a lot of fine print. I took a photo.

A glint of metal underneath the kitchen table caught my eye. I shone my flashlight on it. Brass. With a pen from my pocket, I retrieved one of several spent bullet cartridges. It was a forty caliber like the one used on my father. Had Holbrook been here? Did she shoot Nolan as well as my father? I replaced it where I found it.

The bed was unmade in the bedroom. A few empty hangers hung in the small closet. The dresser drawers were empty. In the bathroom, a box for teal-blue hair dye and an empty prescription bottle lay in the wastebasket. The hair dye was further proof that Holbrook had been here with her cousin. The prescription was for Wellbutrin, an antidepressant. Blair Marshall's name was on the label. She had been here too. I put it back.

As I did so, I spotted a business card that had fallen in the corner behind the wastebasket. I picked it up. Josiah Faulkner, Chairman for the Patriots of Liberty Caucus. There was a phone number and a P.O. box printed on the front. I flipped it over and found a physical address handwritten on the back. I pocketed the card.

"How is she?" I asked Conor.

"Not good. She's lost a shiteload of blood."

Her breathing was rapid and shallow. Her face was ashen. The thought that I sent her into danger left me nauseated. Had my calling her tipped off Marshall and Holbrook that Tanisha was helping me?

"Ya find anything?"

"A spent forty-caliber cartridge, same as the one Holbrook used to shoot my father. An empty box for hair color, the same teal blue Holbrook uses. And a prescription bottle for an antidepressant with Marshall's name on it."

"You think both Holbrook and Marshall were here?"

"My guess is that Marshall has been hiding out here. Maybe Holbrook brought Nolan up to meet with her. They must have figured out she was working with me and shot her."

"No wonder you couldn't find her. You left everything where you found it, I hope."

"Everything but this." I showed him the business card.

"Patriots of Liberty Caucus? They're those far-rightwing plonkers who're lobbying to make life miserable for queer people? What's Marshall doing with that lot?"

"That's what I'd like to know. Maybe the Patriots of Liberty are WBW's next target. Won't hear me complain if they are."

Twenty minutes later, the faint wail of sirens pierced the quiet desert night. I stepped out of the trailer as two cruisers from the Yavapai County Sheriff's Office pulled up. An ambulance appeared out of the cloud of dust kicked up by the cars.

"She's in there!" I shouted. "African American female with two GSWs."

The deputies pointed their weapons at me, and I raised my hands. "I'm bail enforcement. She'd already been shot when we found her. The shooters are long gone."

They disarmed us and asked why we were there. I explained that we'd been looking for Tanisha, who had been helping us locate a fugitive wanted for attempted murder. The deputies questioned Conor and me about our involvement in the case, while the paramedics went to work on Tanisha. Fifteen minutes into the interview, we had to stop because an Air Med helicopter landed on the far side of the gravel parking lot, forcing us to take cover from the blast of dust and gravel and making all conversation impossible.

The paramedics rushed Tanisha to the helicopter, which took off moments later, headed north.

I was happy to get the hell away from there when they finally returned our weapons and cut us loose thirty minutes later. Even with the short time I spent in the trailer, I could still smell Tanisha's blood in my nose, melding with the memories of my father getting shot. I had too much blood on my hands from this case. And I was no closer to bringing in Marshall. Further, in fact, since I was technically off the case.

On the way back to Phoenix, I called Stacie.

"Yeah?"

"Stacie, it's Jinx Ballou. We found Tanisha."

"Y-yeah? Where she at? Is she okay? Why ain't she called?" The panic in her voice was palpable.

"She's hurt. I think a member of WBW shot her."

"No, no, no, no. She can't be dead."

"She's still alive. At least she was when the paramedics showed up. They flew her to the Flagstaff Regional Hospital trauma center."

"Why would they shoot her? She used to be a member. Is it because of me?"

"I-I don't know why." I felt that I was the one responsible but couldn't bring myself to say it. "The Yavapai County Sheriff's Office is investigating. They'll probably be in touch and can answer more than I can."

I could hear her sobbing on the other end of the line. I was about to say something when the call disconnected.

It was all I could do not to throw up from a combination of grief, anger, and frustration. I opened the window as we drove south on the I-17.

When we turned onto the Loop 101, I called my mother. "How's Dad?"

There wasn't an immediate response.

"Mama, how's Daddy?"

"He's in a coma. They think he had a stroke. They're trying to save him but..."

Fuck, fuck, fuck! "We're on our way," I said, trying not to completely lose it. "Should be there in about thirty, forty minutes."

"You do as I ask?"

"I'm working on it, Mama. I've got some leads."

Again, she said nothing.

"I'll be there shortly." I hung up. I felt numb. "My father had a stroke. He's in a coma."

"Oh, Jinxie, I am so sorry."

"My mother... it's like I don't even know her. She wants me to kill Elise Holbrook for shooting my dad."

"I still don't believe it. She said that specifically?"

"No, not specifically. She told me to take care of it. It was the way she said it. Like a character from *The Godfather*. It was spooky."

"People react to grief in strange ways sometimes. She's angry and grieving. Someone hurt the man she loves, and she wants to strike back. And she sees you as this instrument of justice. She's trying to make sense of an upside-down world, love. She's acting in a way that's one-hundred-eighty degrees off her usual self. It doesn't mean you have to do what she's asking of you. It won't bring him out of the coma. It won't undo the damage. And if you did it, she'd wish you hadn't. You know her."

"What the hell am I supposed to do, Conor? These crazy bitches from WBW are out of control. First, they murdered LaTonya Garrett. Then they doxed me and made everyone think I'm a pedophile. Then they crashed my wedding and shot my dad. Now they shot Tanisha Nolan. How do I stop them? I feel like I'm trying to hold back a storm surge even as it keeps flooding past me."

He gripped my hand and squeezed it tenderly, keeping his eyes on the road, stealing glances every once in a while. "I don't have the foggiest how to stop them. But maybe the authorities can. The Yavapai Sheriff's Office is looking into their shooting Nolan. Wong and Harden are investigating your dad's shooting. And Kirsten is pursuing the doxing and the deepfake video. They have far more resources than the two of us. Let them handle it for now."

"And what about Blair Marshall?"

"Leroy Drake's assigned to the case. You're off. We need to be there for your father. That's our primary responsibility."

"I can't walk away from it."

"Ya can, love. Trust me. It's probably best if you do. Sometimes you gotta step outta the ring for a while. Recover your wits. Let it be someone else's fight."

I considered it for a while, watching the glow of the taillights in front of us. "Perhaps you're right. I just need to make one more phone call." I took out my phone. "Detective Wong? Jinx Ballou."

"Ms. Ballou. How's your father?"

"In a coma."

"Oh, I am so sorry."

"I'm calling because I remembered something. Not sure how I forgot." I paused, trying to figure out how best to phrase it. I didn't want her to know I had intentionally withheld information before. "When the crowd was rushing out of the greenhouse, I saw Elise Holbrook holding a gun. She's the assistant director of Womyn Born Womyn and Blair Marshall's cousin."

"That's good, Jinx. That helps. We've been reviewing the footage from your wedding videographer. We'd like you to stop by the precinct, perhaps tomorrow if you can, and help us identify some of the people trespassing at your wedding."

"Okay. There's one other thing." I told Wong about Tanisha in the mobile home. "I believe the two shootings are connected."

"We'll reach out to the Yavapai County Sheriff's Office. In the meantime, get some sleep."

"Thanks, detective. I'll try."

When I arrived back at the ICU, I was beyond exhausted. My mother was asleep on one of the waiting room couches. My brother sat reading a magazine, a cup of coffee in his hand. Grand-Mère and Siobhan had sat vigil in Dad's room until Rodeo had taken them back to their motels. All other friends and family had gone home.

"How's Dad?" I asked.

"Still in a coma. Where were you?" he whispered tersely.

"Trying to find some answers."

"You should have been here. Mom needs you."

"I'm sorry. You might have noticed it's been a shitty day for us too. It was our wedding that those fuckers ruined, after all."

Jake's expression softened. He looked at Conor and back to me. "Yeah, sorry. It felt like you were avoiding being here."

"We're not." I leaned close to Conor. His body was tense, but he seemed to be managing his traumatic fear of hospitals.

"I'm glad you're married. That's something at least."

"Thanks, mate." Conor clapped Jake on the shoulder.

"How come your mother keeps calling you Liam?"

Conor blushed. "Ah, that. It was my name back when I lived in Ireland. 'Liam O'Callaghan.' Changed it when I started a new life."

Jake nodded. He knew the story. "Right. Got it."

"Take your mum home and get some sleep, brother," Conor offered. "We'll keep vigil for the night."

"Yeah," I agreed. "Seems only right."

Jake regarded our mother. Asleep, she looked like her usual self. Not the vengeful mafiosa hungry for payback.

"I hate to wake her. And I just had a cup of terrible coffee. I'll be up for hours. You two might as well go home. You can relieve us in the morning. After all, you all should be on your honeymoon."

I hugged my brother and kissed him on the cheek. "Call me if anything changes."

"Will do."

On the drive home, I pulled the business card out that I'd found in the mobile home. How was WBW connected to this far-right-wing political organization? Were the Patriots of Liberty their next target? Or a new unlikely ally? Despite their obsessive hate against trans people, Blair Marshall's organization claimed to be a radical feminist group. Not a lot in common with the patriarchal Patriots of Liberty Caucus. But as the saying goes, politics makes for strange bedfellows.

34

The street was quiet when we got home. The media circus and protestors had gone. Diane was excited to see us and clearly needed to go for a run.

"Oh, baby." I held her face in my hands. She was my golden-furred angel. "I don't have the energy to run right now."

"I'll take her," Conor replied. "The exercise would do me some good."

I clasped his hand. "Thank you."

His smile lit up my heart. "Anything for you, love."

When he returned thirty minutes later, I was half-dozing in bed, still in my clothes, body beyond exhaustion, mind numb. He lay beside me and met my gaze.

"Hey, wife."

"Hey." It was all I could manage. Not even a "Hey, husband."

"All this rubbish will sort itself out."

"I should have become a lawyer."

"Why?"

"None of this would have ever happened. We would have had a normal, happy wedding. My father and Tanisha would be safe."

"Aye. And perhaps we never would've met. Never fallen in love. Never stopped White Nation from blowing up Phoenix City Hall and the stadium. You never would've brought the man who nearly beat you to death to justice. And Blair Marshall would still have murdered LaTonya Garrett."

Everything he said was true. But it didn't stem the tide of guilt that flooded my consciousness.

"I'm so sorry all this happened on our wedding day." I burst into sobs and felt his powerful arms pull me to his warm body. His normally sexy scent was overpowered by the memory of the smell of blood in the trailer and at our wedding.

Despite it being our wedding night, Conor and I were both too exhausted to bother with sex. And yet, I woke frequently in the night with a sense that someone was breaking into the Bunker. Twice I got up and checked all the doors and windows. Even the trapdoor to the tunnel.

In the wee hours of the night, Diana jumped onto the bed and snuggled up between us. Perhaps she sensed we needed a little extra doggy comfort. I wasn't complaining. She had seen me through worse times than this.

When I rose the next morning, I called my brother. "Any news?"

"No change." He sounded nearly dead from exhaustion.

"How's Mom?"

"Quiet."

"Detective Wong asked me to come in and look at some video from the wedding. Hoping I can identify some suspects."

"How long will that take?"

"Not long, I hope. I'll get to the hospital as soon as I can."

I hung up and wandered into the kitchen to make coffee and throw together some breakfast. On any other Sunday morning, I'd be at my parent's place for brunch. It was a family tradition, and attendance was all but mandatory without a good excuse.

There'd been a time recently when I made a lot of excuses for not showing up. I was strung out with grief, alcohol, and weed to avoid dealing with my shit. Now I wanted to kick myself for missing all of those moments with my dad. Him humming some zydeco tune while cooking omelets or crêpes. Calling me cher and his little warrior girl. I might not get another brunch with him. It made me so sad.

I was turning over all the shit with WBW to the cops. Let Leroy Drake find Blair Marshall if he could. Maybe they'd make his life as miserable as they'd made mine. And Kirsten could handle the legal issues over the doxing and the deepfake video, as well as this bullshit with Gerard Boyce.

At nine o'clock, Conor and I showed at Phoenix PD's Violent Crimes Bureau.

Detective Wong shook our hands. "I'm so sorry to ask you to come back in, but I need your help identifying anyone from the video that wasn't invited to your wedding."

"Whatever we can do to help," I replied.

"How's your dad?"

I shook my head.

"We're still hoping he'll recover," Conor replied.

She led us to an interview room where a laptop had been set up. She inserted a thumb drive into the USB port. A video appeared on the screen showing Conor and me at the altar making googly eyes at each other. Voices began shouting in the background. Samantha, the minister, grimaced as she was declaring us husband and wife. The camera panned around in a disorienting way and refocused on the crowd of people flooding in.

Wong paused the video. "Do you recognize anyone here?"

The crowd of faces were too distant. "Kind of hard to make out anyone in this shot."

Wong hit play again. It made me sick to watch the chaos unfolding on the screen, knowing what was coming.

And then I recognized a face. "There!" I pointed. "That's Leslie Reinhardt."

Wong paused the video. "Who's she?"

"Womyn Born Womyn's marketing materials coordinator."

"Anyone else you recognize?" Wong asked.

"Not yet. Keep playing the video."

The chaos continued, and the camera zoomed in on some faces. I recognized members of WBW I had researched. "That's Mandy Hudson, another WBW member. She's the one I hog-tied. The blonde is Ashley Carroll, their volunteer coordinator. The woman carrying the sign there is Nicci Fiorello. Not sure what her title is. Those three prevented me from apprehending Blair Marshall before the wedding."

"What about the men?"

I studied their faces. "Some look vaguely familiar, but I don't their names. Wait, I know him." I pointed to a tall man wearing a blue polo shirt. His hair was cut in a conservative style. "That's Josiah Faulkner, chairman for the Patriots of Liberty Caucus. I think the two organizations are working together."

I opted not to mention finding his business card in the trailer where Tanisha Nolan was shot. For the life of me, I had no idea why WBW would be working with the extreme right-wing lobbying group.

I studied the screen further and recognized two bald, muscular men with a new-Nazi vibe. "Those two guys. They're members of White Nation, the group responsible for the Piestewa Freeway bombing. I don't know their names, but I recognize them from when I was pursuing one of their members a few years back."

"I thought Womyn Born Womyn was a liberal feminist group," Wong said. "What are they doing with members of White Nation and the Patriots of Liberty?"

"Beats the hell outta me."

Wong made some notes and continued playing the video.

"There." I pointed to the screen. "Stop."

Holbrook appeared on the right side of the screen, pushing past one of her cohorts with her arm raised. She held a pistol in her hand. On the other side of the screen, I was grappling with Mandy Hudson. From this angle, Holbrook appeared to be aiming at me.

"Who is that?" Wong asked.

"Elise Holbrook. She's acting director for WBW since Marshall went on the lam. Also, her cousin. Go ahead and play it."

"Hold up," Conor cautioned. "Jinxie, you don't need to watch this."

I took a deep breath and let it out. "Yes, I do." I nodded to Wong.

On screen, Elise fired off two shots. The shock and fear rippled through the crowd like the pressure wave from an explosion. Everyone stopped for a fraction of a second, then the mob of wedding crashers fled en masse. Holbrook stood there for a moment, a shocked look on her face, before Hudson grabbed her arm and pulled her away.

"Oi! I think that's bloody well enough." Conor clicked the pause button on the screen. "I think ya got your bloody ID."

"I'm so sorry to put you through this again." Wong put a hand on my shoulder and offered me a tissue.

I realized I was sobbing so hard that I could barely breathe.

"We'll pick up Holbrook and bring her in for questioning. Thank you both for coming in."

I sat there, feeling pulled in all directions. I wasn't even sure what I was feeling. All the anger, hurt, humiliation, and fear were so intertwined it felt like a boulder sitting on my chest. Added to that, my mind was trying to make sense of why a so-called feminist group like Womyn Born Womyn would align themselves with far-right hate groups like the Patriots of Liberty Caucus and White Nation.

"Come on, love. Let's go see your da." Conor helped me to my feet, and we followed Wong out of VCB to the elevators.

"We'll do everything we can to see that justice is done," Wong said.

I nodded. "Did you talk to the Yavapai Sheriff's office?"

"We did. Tanisha Nolan's still clinging to life, thanks to you two. Good job on that. We'll be collaborating with them on these related cases."

"Good."

"We'll be keeping your father in our prayers." She smiled at us and then returned to the VCB.

I was so deep in thought that I nearly jumped out of my skin when the elevator dinged, and the doors opened.

35

When we walked arm in arm through the main entrance of the hospital, I felt Conor tense. He hadn't completely gotten over his hospital phobia, but he was here to support me. I was grateful beyond words for that. This was what love looked like, and I was immensely moved.

My friends and family filled the ICU waiting room, Becca and Easton huddled together with Rodeo, Zahara, and Juanita. Siobhan and Grand-Mère Marie sat together in a corner and appeared to have formed a bond of sorts. A few members of the Athena Sisterhood, including my ex Shea Stevens and her girlfriend Toni, were there as well.

Becca rushed up to me with Easton not far behind, crushing me in a group hug.

"How is he?" I asked.

"Your mom and Jake are in there with him now," Becca replied. "He's in what they're calling a semiconscious state. The doctors haven't said much, except he's out of the coma. They're cautiously optimistic he'll recover. They just don't know to what extent or how long it may take."

The weight on my chest eased a fraction, but I knew my father wasn't out of the woods.

"I'd like to see him."

"Tell the nurse," Easton replied. "She'll let you in."

Conor and I walked through the double doors into the ICU ward and approached the nurse's station. "I'm here to see my father." I gave the woman behind the desk our names.

"Your mother and brother are in there with him now. Only two people allowed in at a time. But I'll let them know you're here." She stood up and went into my father's room.

A moment later, she returned with my mom and Jake in tow. The four of us embraced without a word. I had half expected a snarky response from Jake, but he remained silent.

"Can I see him?" I asked my mother.

She nodded. "Come with me."

I had wanted to go in with Conor. I glanced at him, but he nodded, indicating I should follow her.

My father's face had more color than the last time I'd seen him. He was still hooked up to a thousand tubes and wires, including the ventilator pumping oxygen directly into his lungs. A bag of saline had replaced the pint of blood dripping into his arm. His color had improved.

"Daddy?" My voice was barely even a squeak. I clasped his hand. He squeezed back. His eyelids fluttered but remained closed. "It's me, Jenna."

Another squeeze, this one a fraction longer. Or so it seemed. I didn't know what else to say, so I sat in the chair holding his hand.

"Father Martin was here," my mother whispered, pulling up another chair.

"Yeah?"

"I told him what I asked you to do."

"You told him?" I was incredulous. A priest couldn't report a previously committed crime to the police but would be compelled to report someone who intended to commit a serious crime in the future. Especially murder.

"Jenna, it was wrong of me. I was so, so angry. So afraid." Her face contorted in anguish. "You haven't... have you?"

I let out a deep breath. "No, not yet."

"Don't. I should never have asked you. If they arrested you for... I could never live with myself."

I put an arm over her shoulder despite the emotional whiplash I was feeling. I still wanted to blow Elise Holbrook's fucking head off. But for now, I'd let the cops deal with it. At least my mother was behaving as her normal compassionate self and not some horrible Italian stereotype.

"I gave the cops the name of the woman who shot him. The videographer recorded it."

"Then we'll let them handle it." Again, there was iron in my mother's words.

I nodded.

I spent the rest of the day taking turns with my family spending time in my father's room and the rest of the time surrounded by my friends and family in the waiting room. It wasn't how I had dreamed of spending the day after my wedding. We should have been flying to Key West, complaining about cramped seats, lousy airline food, and the brutal Floridian humidity, swatting mosquitos the size of vultures, getting sunburned, and drinking Bahama Mamas and Rum Runners until we puked.

Instead, I was being reminded in a harsh but meaningful way how truly blessed I was to be surrounded by so many caring people.

Conor and I spent all night Sunday in my father's room,

allowing my mother to go home and sleep under the watchful eye of my brother.

I drifted in and out of sleep myself, sitting by my father's bedside. His condition remained unchanged. Not fully opening his eyes, much less speaking. But he would squeeze my hand when I spoke to him. A nurse suggested it might be a reflex. But I still felt he was responding and trying to communicate, if only to let me know he heard me.

My mind drifted to what I was going to do now. While I no longer planned to take vengeance on Holbrook, I still wanted to arrest Marshall, whether or not I got paid for it.

A news search for Blair Marshall's name didn't turn up anything, so it appeared that Drake had not yet apprehended her.

Sadie must be shitting bricks, I thought. *If Marshall isn't arrested soon, Sadie will have to pony up the entire amount of the bail.*

At six o'clock on Monday morning, I woke to the sound of my father trying to clear his throat. "Daddy?"

His eyes were wide with panic. He was making panicked sounds and reaching for the ventilator.

"Hold on, Daddy. You're on a ventilator. It's okay. Just relax. It'll help you breathe." I pressed the nurse call button then grasped his hands.

His eyes locked onto mine and appeared to calm somewhat. "It's me, Dad. It's Jenna. You're okay. Just breathe."

He nodded ever so slightly, but I could still see the alarm in his eyes.

A nurse came in and saw that he was awake. "Okay, we're going to run a spontaneous breathing test to see if we can wean him off the ventilator."

"How long will that take?"

"At minimum, thirty minutes."

Again, I caught alarm in my father's face. "Can't you

hurry it up? He doesn't like the tube being down his throat."

"We have to make sure he's strong enough to breathe on his own. Let's see how he does."

I squeezed his hand. "Hang in there. You'll get through this. Trust the process. I'll be right here."

This reversal of roles felt weird. Usually, he was coaching me through a panicked situation.

Conor showed up with coffee a moment later.

For the next half hour, I told my father about all the things that Conor and I were going to do once he was out of the hospital and could reschedule our honeymoon to the Keys. Scuba diving. Deep-sea fishing. Watching the sunsets from the deck of the motel in Key West. Touring the Hemingway House and the Mel Fisher exhibit. Taking a ferry to the Dry Tortugas.

Periodically, I glanced at the screen monitoring his breathing. No alarms as far as I could see, but I did not know what I was looking at.

Shortly after the screen beeped to indicate the test was complete, the nurse returned. "Good news, Mr. Ballou. You passed your SBT. We can take you off the ventilator." She turned to Conor and me. "You two will need to step out of the room for a minute."

We did as she asked. Jake, my mother, and grandmother walked into the unit from the waiting room.

"What's happening?" he asked.

"He's awake. Fully awake. They're taking him off the ventilator as we speak."

My mother burst into tears of gratitude and crossed herself. "Thank you, Lord. Thank you, Mary."

"It's progress," Conor said.

"Yeah." I realized I was breathing easier as well. "How are you doing?"

He gazed around at the ICU unit. "Didn't sleep much. All the dings and beeps and alarms, it's a bloody wonder anyone gets better here. But all things considered, I'm managing."

"Thanks for being here," my mother said to him.

"Don't be daft, Mrs. B. Where else would I be at a time like this but with my wife and her family?"

36
___

We spent the next hour or so sitting with my father. The nurses lifted the two-person limit so that Grand-Mère Marie, Jake, Rodeo, and my mother could sit with us.

My father's voice was hoarse, and he limited his speaking to a few words at a time. Cognitively, he seemed to be his old self, joking around with us. He couldn't remember anything after getting dressed for the wedding, and that made him sad.

"The important thing is that we're married." I pulled Conor closer. He kissed my temple.

"Yes. So happy." My father turned to Jake with a wry smile. "You're next."

Jake and Rodeo had been dating for a while. And Rodeo's daughter, Gwyneth, really liked Jake. But so far, there had been no talk of weddings.

"Tired," my dad said after a while.

"Okay," my mother said. "Everyone else out. He needs sleep."

I wanted to protest. Now that he was awake, I wanted to

spend every minute with him. But she was right. He had a long recovery ahead of him and needed to rest.

When we reconvened in the waiting room, I gathered Zahara, Conor, Becca, and Rodeo together. "I know Assurity Bail Bonds reassigned the Marshall case to Leroy Drake, but last I heard, she was still unaccounted for. I want to find her. No guarantee we will get paid if we do, but if you're willing, I could use some help."

"What about Elise Holbrook?" Becca asked.

"Last I heard, the Phoenix PD and the Yavapai County Sheriff's Office were looking for her in connection to shooting my father and Tanisha Nolan. Much as I'd like to kick her soft butch ass for shooting my father and ruining my wedding, I'm leaving that to the cops. Also, for reasons I can't explain, Womyn Born Womyn appears to have joined forces with the Patriots of Liberty Caucus and White Nation."

"I'm in," Zahara said. "Those crazy women have done enough. Time they learn their actions have consequences."

"We're all in," Rodeo added. "What's the plan? Where do you think Marshall's hanging out?"

"I might have some insight." Becca held up her laptop bag. "I've been monitoring text messages between a few key members of WBW. I think I got something."

She pulled out her laptop and set it down on an end table. After a long series of keystrokes and clicks on the track pad, she showed us the screen. It revealed a conversation between three people, one of whom was Mandy Hudson.

One person in the conversation asked when they would meet to finalize the details. No name was listed. Only a phone number.

Hudson responded, *We can be at your office at 2 p.m.*

I'll B there 2. Must get this passed, replied a third person whose ID was a five-digit number.

The initiator of the conversation, the one with the phone number, confirmed that the time and place were agreeable.

"So Hudson's talking with two people about a meeting." Zahara shrugged. "What does that tell us about where Marshall is?"

"Who's she talking to?" I asked.

Becca replied, "The phone number belongs to a Joshua Faulkner, director of—"

"The Patriots of Liberty Caucus." I pulled the business card from my wallet. "I found this in the trailer where Tanisha Nolan was shot."

"Which I've learned belongs to Naomi Hoffman," she continued.

"Why didn't this turn up before now?"

"It's technically listed in Hoffman's parents' names, both deceased. She never updated the title with the MVD. HUD has it listed under the original purchaser from twenty years ago, no connection with Hoffman or her folks."

"And this other person on the text conversation?" asked Rodeo. "What's with the five-digit number?"

"They're using an anonymous texting app," Becca explained. "I tried to get an ID, but no luck so far. But if I had to guess, it's possibly Blair Marshall. Why else go to the trouble of using an anonymous texting app?"

"So Hudson and possibly Marshall are meeting with Joshua Faulkner about finalizing the details on something. But what?" Then it hit me. "They're working on some sort of anti-trans legislation."

"Politics makes for strange bedmates," Conor added.

"It's nine o'clock now. Let's stake out the PLC office

starting at one." I turned to Becca. "Be on standby with your computer in case I need you to check something."

"Will do. We'll get her." Becca hugged me.

We all high-fived each other. Perhaps it was premature, but at least we had a solid lead.

"I'm so glad your dad's doing better," Zahara said.

Rodeo added, "Me too. He's a good man."

"Thanks, everyone."

Conor and I checked in on my father periodically for a couple more hours then drove home so I could catch a quick nap, shower, and gear up.

The PLC office was downtown on Madison Street, near the Arizona legislature complex. I parked the Gray Ghost in the parking lot next door. Conor sat in his Charger across the street. Rodeo was one building down from him in his Miata. And Zahara watched from a bus stop in front of the PLC. We had agreed to connect via radio ahead of time.

"Pack Leader to pack. Check in."

"Copy, Pack Leader. Coyote One checking in," Rodeo replied.

"Coyote Two here," Zahara chimed in.

"Not sure if I'm Coyote Three or Viper One," Conor said. "But I'm here with eyes peeled."

It was a quarter after one. If Hudson and the mystery guest were on schedule, we would catch them going in. I crossed my fingers that it would be Marshall and not some other member of WBW.

Stakeouts were a whole lot of boring, occasionally followed by white-knuckle excitement and hopefully a capture. It helped to have someone in the car with you. But after losing Marshall not once but twice, I wanted to have as many vehicles as we could for the chase, if there was one. She would not escape from me a third time.

It was tempting to start a conversation over the radio,

but I kept the channel clear for when things started to happen.

I pulled up Deap Vally's *Femejism* album on the sound system and followed it with the Pink Trinkets' *TERF Whores* album.

"Pack Leader here. It's two o'clock," I said over the radio. "Keep your eyes peeled."

We continued to wait. And wait. Two fifteen came and went.

At two thirty, I was growing impatient. Had they gone in a back entrance? Had they canceled the meeting?

"Coyote Two to Pack Leader, what's the deal?"

"Let me check in with our little bird. See if she's heard anything." I called Becca. "Hey, no sign of anyone coming in or out of Patriots of Liberty's HQ."

"Hold on. Easton and I just got back to the Hub from lunch." A moment later, she added, "Oh my gourd! Looks like they moved up the meeting time to one. Jinxie, I'm so sorry I missed that."

"No worries. Keep an ear to the ground. Let me know if anything else of interest pops up."

"Will do. Good hunting, hermana."

"Thanks." I hung up. "Pack Leader to Coyote Pack. They moved meeting up to one. We must've just missed them coming in."

"Coyote One, copy that, Pack Leader. What now?"

"We wait. They gotta come out sometime."

We continued to sit and watch. Traffic on the street gradually increased as we approached rush hour.

At three, a couple of familiar faces appeared. I grabbed my phone and caught it on video. Capturing members of WBW coming out of PLC's office on video might prove useful in the future. Just before they reached their cars, I called on the radio.

"Pack Leader to Pack. Move in. Let's take these bitches down."

I pulled out onto the street and into the lot that PLC used, stopping right behind the Volvo that Mandy Hudson was driving. She laid on the horn, but I got out with my Ruger drawn. Rodeo, Conor, and Zahara all pulled in, boxing them in on all sides. Carefully, I hustled around to the passenger side where a woman wearing a large hat and dark round sunglasses sat.

"Get out of the car!" I shouted. "On the ground, hands behind your head."

"You're not a cop!" said the woman in the hat through the closed window. "You can't arrest me."

"Watch me." I tried the door, but it was locked. "Open the fucking door. Now!"

She stared at me. Defiant.

With the butt of his pistol, Conor shattered the window. "She said get the feck out!"

Hat Lady gasped. "Hey! You can't do that."

Conor reached in, unlatched the door. I dragged her out and pulled off her hat and shades. It was Elise Holbrook. A thrill of satisfaction lanced through me as I put her on the ground and cuffed her.

37

"I called the cops!" Mandy shouted while Zahara and Rodeo pulled her from the driver's side and turned off the engine.

"Good. Saved us the trouble," Rodeo replied. The rest of my team laughed.

"Fucking bitch." I kicked her in the side, hard enough to make her grunt in pain. My finger rested on the trigger, the back of her head squarely lined up in my sights.

"Easy, love." Conor put a hand on my shoulder. "She'll pay for her crimes. I'm calling the cops now."

"She tried to kill me. Damn near killed my dad. Ruined my wedding. Probably shot Tanisha Nolan as well."

"It wasn't me. I didn't do none of that."

"I saw you, bitch. It's on video. Don't even try denying it. Did you think you could shoot my father at my own wedding and get away with it? Ever hear of a wedding videographer? Dumb fucking bitch."

"I wasn't at your wedding. I was out of town all weekend."

"Oh, really? Where?"

"Tucson. At a planning meeting for the Southern Arizona Pride Festival. I'm on the organizing committee. We met from ten in the morning until five o'clock at night on Saturday and Sunday. I've got witnesses."

"Bullshit. I saw you! And the cops know it was you. We got it on video. You stick out a little with that goddamn green hair."

Spectators had gathered around and were recording us with their cell phones. Everyone wanted to show how they were at an exciting event and have their video go viral. Everyone wanted to be a star for fifteen seconds. I didn't care. Let them gawk. I was in the right. So long as I didn't blow the bitch's head off. Probably a good thing they were there.

"Hey! Leave them alone." Joshua Faulkner, lobbyist for the fascist wing nuts, approached in his fancy suit.

"Back off, jackass," I warned him. "This doesn't concern you."

More men in dress shirts and ties approached. Some looked fairly buff. One with an ex-military bearing drew a pistol and pointed at me. "He said to leave them alone."

Conor aimed his at our armed visitor. "Put it down, mate. Or you'll wish you did."

Rodeo and Zahara appeared on his other side, weapons drawn.

The quick burst of a police siren made me jump. It was a miracle no one accidentally pulled a trigger. In a matter of seconds, the lot filled with four blue-and-white squad cars.

"Police! Drop your weapons! Down on the ground! Do it now!" a female patrol officer shouted. Several of her fellow officers echoed the commands.

I carefully lowered my weapon and knelt down on the sidewalk. "Officer, I am a bail enforcement agent. This woman is wanted by Phoenix PD for attempted murder."

"It's a lie," Holbrook whined. "She's making this shit up. She's a bounty hunter."

The officers seized our weapons and separated us, sticking me and Zahara in the back of a patrol car, while more cruisers filled the lot, blocking all exits.

"Well, that went well," I said sarcastically.

"At least you caught Holbrook," Zahara replied. "She won't be able to hurt anyone else."

"Yeah." But a nagging thought in the back of my brain was telling me it wasn't over. Holbrook almost sounded convincing with her bogus alibi. I hoped the cops saw through it.

After a half hour, the air in the back of the cruiser was getting stuffy. Finally, Detective Wong appeared and let us out.

"Sorry about holding you," she said. "Situations like this..."

"Not a problem," I said solemnly. As a former cop, I knew the drill.

"How did you know Holbrook would be here?" She had her pad out to take notes.

"We didn't. We had a lead that told us members of Womyn Born Womyn were meeting with the Patriots of Liberty. I was hoping Blair Marshall would be among them. Just our luck it was Holbrook instead."

"Any idea why they were meeting with the Patriots of Liberty Caucus? Seems like an odd pairing, don't you think?"

"You'd have to ask them."

"How's your father?"

"Better."

"Glad to hear it." She shook my hand. "I hope he has a speedy and full recovery."

"Thanks. You arresting Holbrook?"

"Yep. We arrested Hudson yesterday. Charged her with trespass and assault. Apparently, she already got bailed out, as did several others." She shrugged. "What can you do?"

I stared out at the sea of vehicles crowded into the parking lot like herring in a barrel. "Well, if they miss their court date, maybe I'll have the pleasure of dragging them all back to jail."

"Good luck. You should be free to leave shortly."

While we waited, I considered our next move. So far, my offers of a reward weren't yielding much. Tracking phones and text messages weren't turning up anything productive either. I needed a change of strategy.

If I could only find some leverage to get one of them to turn on Marshall. This bizarre alliance with the Patriots of Liberty and White Nation might be the wedge issue to do it. But I had to find the right person to target.

38

———

Rush hour was in full force by the time Phoenix PD allowed us to leave. At least the weather was pleasant. Not a hundred twenty degrees, though those days weren't far off. During the previous summer, Phoenix's monsoon season was more of a non-soon. We broke the record for the most days over a hundred, over a hundred ten, and over a hundred fifteen, with record-breaking temps well into November. I hoped the approaching summer would be cooler but wasn't holding my breath.

We stopped at the Bunker to take Diana for a run and to change out of our gear before heading on to the hospital. I was tired but figured the workout would help me burn off the flurry of emotions inside me.

When I returned home, Conor had showered and smelled really good. I wanted him to take me to bed and fuck my brains out. But I needed to get to the hospital to check on my dad.

We ran through the Jack in the Box drive-through on the way. After I inhaled my burger and more than half the curly fries, I hand-fed Conor his so he could keep his hands on the wheel and eyes on the road. I made a teasing game of it, like some newlyweds did with the first slice of wedding cake. Our own cake had been trashed in the riot.

By the time we reached the hospital, I was feeling a little more invigorated. The protein kick of the Ultimate Cheeseburger, combined with the carb load from the fries and the caffeine in the soda, didn't hurt. Sometimes you needed a little fast food to make things better.

"Hey, there's my hero," my father said when we walked into his room in the ICU. He looked a bit more like himself. More energy in his face.

"Mom's the real hero. She did that whole trick with the needle in the sucking chest wound." I shivered at the memory. Seeing my father so close to death had shifted the world under my feet.

"A little birdie told me you arrested the woman who shot me."

I looked at Conor, who shrugged. "Don't look at me."

"Rodeo called me," Jake confessed. "Told me about the stakeout downtown. Pretty intense from what I hear."

"It was no big deal," I said, catching a worried glance from my mother. "We caught her coming out of a meeting she was attending. Phoenix PD did the actually arresting."

"Aw, that's just the paperwork, cher. Catching her, that's the hero bit."

"Thanks, Dad."

Even my mother seemed pleased with the situation. "Much as your work worries me, I am glad you handled the situation the way you did." She gave me a knowing look.

I didn't have the heart to tell them it had been a fluke, that I'd actually been hoping to nab her cousin, Blair Marshall.

Conor and I spent the evening with my dad so that Jake

and my mom could go home and relax. They promised to return in the morning.

We watched old reruns of *Law & Order* on the TV while my father drifted in and out of sleep. At one point, he shared embarrassing stories from my youth, which Conor found amusing. I helped him eat his dinner, which was basically chicken broth and Jell-O. Though he didn't mention it, I could tell the impact the stroke had had on his fine motor skills frustrated him.

"Jenna, sweetie, you and Conor should go home and get some rest," my father said when he'd had enough. "I got plenty of nurses here to keep me company."

"We can stay, Daddy. It's no problem," I replied between yawns.

"No, cher. You two deserve some couple time."

Conor put a hand on my shoulder but said nothing.

I was afraid to leave him. Afraid something might happen. "You sure you'll be okay?"

"Be better if they'd let me have some real food. This clear liquid diet is for the birds. Could use some good old country cooking. But I'll be fine, Jenna. Go on now."

"Maybe we can stop by Maisie's Southern Café on our way over tomorrow."

"Ooh, sweets, now you're singing my tune. Some of them fried green tomatoes and pimento cheese would really hit the spot. And a quart of their sweet tea."

"You got it, Daddy." I hugged him awkwardly, trying not to pull on any of the monitor leads or IV lines.

"Y'all get yourself some sleep, ya hear?"

"We'll do that, Edward," Conor replied.

"And you keep my baby safe, young man."

"Aye, sir. That I promise."

When we got home, Conor and I made love, despite being mentally and physically exhausted. I did it for him, having felt like I'd been neglecting him at a time we should have been screwing like rabbits. But honestly, it did me some good. Conor had always been a generous lover, and tonight was no different. Afterward, I slept like a stone.

The next morning, Becca texted me, *No new leads on Marshall. FYI new anti-trans bill in AZ Senate. Has WBW fingerprints all over it.*

She sent a link to a news article that outlined the proposed bill. It criminalized doctors who prescribed hormone blockers and cross-sex hormones for trans youth. It allowed medical personnel to refuse to treat trans patients, even for basic healthcare. And it required trans people to use public restrooms based on their assigned sex at birth.

I felt sick. After twenty years of living as my true self, I had thought things were improving for the trans community. But the vindictive cruelty of this horrific bill was chilling.

The news article credited the Patriots of Liberty and an unnamed women's nonprofit for crafting the bill for the GOP legislators. Womyn Born Womyn. It had to be them, despite the Patriots of Liberty lobbying a year earlier for a bill that created ridiculous hurdles for women seeking abortions and another bill that allowed anyone charged but found not guilty of rape to sue his accusers.

I recalled the nine-thousand-dollar payment on WBW's bank statement to the PLC, the Patriots of Liberty Caucus. What feminist group would give nine grand to an anti-LGBT, sexist hate group? Surely there were members of Womyn Born Womyn who opposed allying themselves with the PLC. Someone with enough sense to realize that their absurd hatred of trans people was ultimately hurting women.

I dove deep into the background of WBW's major players, looking for a weak link. Social media feeds were a treasure trove of information, helping me refine the profiles I had created. Many were myopically focused on oppressing transgender people in every way possible. No mention of any other feminist issue.

But a few posted about reproductive rights, equal pay, and representation. Among this latter group was none other than Naomi Hoffman, which struck me as odd considering Blair Marshall was her girlfriend. Maybe this was my in.

Did Hoffman know about WBW's alliance with the PLC or the nine-grand payout? Surely she must. But if I could convince her that her girlfriend was throwing women under the bus, maybe she would give Blair up.

According to DekaHedron's social media, Hoffman had finished overseeing a video shoot for a local casino's media campaign. I had a hunch she would be in the office for the next few weeks managing the postproduction.

As I was formulating a strategy, Sadie Levinson called.

"Ms. Ballou, are you still pursuing Blair Marshall?"

"You assigned the case to Drake."

"Don't give me any mishegas. Answer the question."

"I've been trying to figure out who shot my father."

"Word on the street is you helped apprehend Elise Holbrook, the one charged in the shooting."

I didn't know how she knew that, but she had connections in the Phoenix PD and was a resourceful woman.

"That's true."

"Are you also still trying to apprehend Marshall?" The tone of her voice suggested she knew the answer to the question.

"Why?"

"Because Drake has bubkes. Do you have any leads?"

"You want me to give him my leads? After you took me off the case?"

"I will put you back on. If you have any leads. And don't lie to me."

I explained my goal of turning Hoffman or possibly another member of WBW over their alliance with Patriots of Liberty.

"You really think this will work?" she asked.

"No guarantees. It's a strategy. But it's all I've got."

"It sounds reasonable. And it's all I've got too. Drake's off the case. You're on. But I need this now."

"You got it, boss."

I called Zahara and Rodeo and asked them to meet me at DekaHedron at ten.

Conor walked in with two cups of coffee and set one down for me on my rolltop desk while I was packing away my laptop. He was dressed in an old T-shirt and sweatpants. Nevertheless, a rush of endorphins flooded through me at the sight of him. I took the offered cup. "Morning, handsome. Thanks for the cuppa."

"You're welcome, love." He hugged me and sat down on the bed next to me. "Where ya headed?"

I felt a pang of guilt. I should've been on my honeymoon with this beautiful man. And failing that, I should have been at my father's side, feeding him Southern treats that were not approved by his doctor.

"I'm hoping to get Naomi Hoffman to flip on her girlfriend. Care to join us?"

"My mum wanted me to show her round the city. Can I convince you to postpone your crusade against Marshall and her violent band of TERFs for a day? She'd really like to get to know her new daughter-in-law."

The pangs of guilt doubled. "I... I can't. Sadie reassigned me to the case. Honestly, it's not even about the bounty anymore. The TERFs declared war on my community. I brought down Elise Holbrook for shooting my father. I'm going to apprehend Marshall for killing LaTonya."

He leaned in and kissed me deeply. His face was scruffy and scratchy, which I normally hated. Kissing a guy with a scruffy face felt like rubbing my face with coarse sandpaper. But this morning, I didn't mind. It stirred something deep inside, making me feel safe and confident.

"I understand, love," he said when we parted lips.

"I'm sorry. We should be in the Keys getting sunburned and drinking cocktails."

"Ah, don't ya worry. We can get sunburned and drink cocktails any time. You have to do this. I understand. But don't forget who you are."

"Forget who I am? Why would—"

He locked eyes with me. "Arrest her. But don't turn vigilante. You've killed people before in self-defense. You know what a burden it is to live with. Don't make that burden worse."

I knew what he was saying. Some things can never be undone.

"I promise you I will do everything I can to bring her in alive so she can spend the rest of her life behind bars."

"And bring yourself and your team home alive too."

I stood and hugged him. "I will."

When he released me, he smiled that goofy grin of his. "Good hunting, love."

39

I drove east to the Chandler area and met up with Zahara and Rodeo in front of the parking garage across from DekaHedron. We were all in full gear. I had debated whether to put a Taser in my primary holster or to go with my Ruger. But since our goal was to capture, not kill, I went with the Taser, as did my associates.

"What's the game plan?" Rodeo asked.

"I'm hoping to get Hoffman to flip. I don't think she's too keen on Marshall's collaboration with the enemy."

"Namely, the Patriots of Liberty," Zahara added. "Did you hear—"

"About the new anti-trans bill?" I finished. "Yeah. It fucking sucks."

"Wasn't Hoffman responsible for the deepfake video of you?" Rodeo asked.

"Most likely. But if her social media posts are to be believed, she's more mainstream feminist. She's got a lot of posts about gay rights and reproductive freedom. I can't believe she's down with this alliance with the Patriots of Liberty."

"You really think she'd give up her girlfriend, though?" Rodeo looked doubtful. "Over a difference in politics?"

"At one time, I would've said no. But outside of the trans issue, the Patriots of Liberty are the antithesis of feminism. If I can convince her that her girlfriend has sold out women and the queer community for her anti-trans agenda, maybe she'll budge."

Rodeo shrugged. "I guess we'll find out."

I led us across the street and into the DekaHedron building. The same young woman with the mold-green hair sat behind the glass reception desk. She gave us one look and rolled her eyes. "Can I help you?"

"We're here to speak with Naomi Hoffman."

"About?"

"A criminal matter." I figured what the hell. No need to be completely discreet.

"Of course."

I shot her a smile she didn't bother returning. I didn't expect her to.

Mold Hair Girl made a call. "Hey, there're some cops here to see you." She hung up and glanced at me. "She'll be right up."

A few minutes later, an electronic lock buzzed, and Naomi Hoffman stepped through a frosted glass door into the reception area. The instant she saw me, anger flared on her face.

"What the hell do you want? You gonna tear this place up too?"

I held up a hand. "We're only here to talk."

"I got nothing to say to you people."

"You may change your mind after what we have to show you."

She actually laughed. "I doubt that."

"You care about women, right?"

"You know I do. *Real* women."

"Of course." I resisted the urge to emphasize that trans women were real women. "Reproductive rights, equal pay, representation, holding rapists accountable, all of that."

"Yes."

"Also care about gay rights, too, I imagine," Zahara added. "The right to adopt children. Right to have same-sex marriages recognized. The right not to be discriminated against in employment, housing, and medical care."

She crossed her arms. "What's your point?"

"I gather you're not a big fan of the Patriots of Liberty Caucus," I replied.

Her face turned to stone, but I could see the wheels turning. "What's this about?"

"Perhaps you would prefer to discuss this in private?"

Hoffman glanced at Mold Hair Girl. "Fine. Follow me."

She swiped a key card on the reader by the frosted glass door. It buzzed, and she led us through. We passed by a large room of workstations, each with multiple screens. We continued on past doors marked as studios one through eight. Finally, we reached a door marked Meeting Room One. A green sign beside it showed it was available. Hoffman slid it to reveal a red In Use sign.

Inside was a glass table and six chairs. Two flat screens were mounted onto one wall, with a ten-foot-long white-board on the adjacent one. No one sat.

Hoffman slammed the door shut. "I don't know where Blair is, and even if I did, I wouldn't tell you. What the hell is this thing you have to show me?"

"Blair's teamed up with the Patriots of Liberty," I replied.

"Bullshit."

"It's true." Zahara shook her head with disdain. "You people claim to be feminists, but you throw women under the bus to hurt trans people. You ask me, Womyn Born Womyn ain't nothing but a bunch of bigoted sellouts."

"What are you talking about?" She didn't appear to be bluffing. She genuinely didn't know.

On my phone, I pulled up a copy of the bank statement listing the check to the PLC and showed it to Hoffman. "Your pseudo-feminist buddies are giving money to the enemy."

She examined it then handed it back to me. "Proves nothing."

"Nothing?" Rodeo said with a chuckle. "Forty grand says a lot."

"So does this." Zahara played a video on her phone of Elise Holbrook and Mandy Hudson walking out of the Patriots of Liberty office, followed by our confrontation with them and members of PLC.

"And the text conversations between WBW leaders and the PLC say a lot more," I added, pulling them up on my phone.

I noticed a chai pendant hanging from a gold chain around Hoffman's neck. "Did you know Josiah Faulkner is also an anti-Semite? Tends to blather a lot about wealthy Jews controlling Hollywood and the mainstream media. And yet he's buddy-buddy with your girlfriend and her little band of TERFs."

Hoffman's expression didn't change, but her cheeks colored. "I'm not as active in Womyn Born Womyn as I once was. Too busy with work. It's more Blair's thing."

"Ah yes," I said. "Dear old Blair, who it turns out was hiding out in your trailer up near Camp Verde. I found a recent prescription bottle with her name on it, so I know she was there. Until she and Elise fucking shot Tanisha Nolan. After Elise nearly murdered my father. Considering it was your trailer, the cops may charge you as an accessory after the fact."

The righteous indignation on Hoffman's face was rapidly fading. "I wasn't at the trailer. I don't know what happened there. But I'm sorry about your father."

"Yeah, you seem real broken up about it," Zahara said with uncharacteristic venom. She put an arm around me. "Your girlfriend and her cousin murdered one person and nearly killed two others. Now they're hanging out with neo-Nazi lobbyists. Must make you so proud."

"Not to mention you creating that deepfake video of me appearing to seduce a young girl." Anger rose in my gut. "I'm going to sue the hell out of you. Life as you know it is about to come crashing down around you."

She tried to look unfazed, but I could see her flinch.

"Unless..." I added.

"Unless what?"

"Unless you help us bring in your girlfriend."

She stared at the far wall.

I added nothing else, letting her squirm under the legal implications. Zahara and Rodeo took my cue and remained silent as well. The awkward silence crackled in the room like an approaching thunderstorm.

"You all are full of shit. You got nothing but lies. That video of Mandy and Elise at the PLC is probably a deepfake." Hoffman's tone lacked the confidence of her words. "I will not betray Blair. Not for a delusional man who thinks he's a woman. You need serious therapy."

I had to admit, her misgendering me stung more than I expected. And her dedication to her sellout girlfriend was sadly impressive.

I poked her in the chest. "You had your chance. I don't envy what lies ahead for you. But trust me, you will have earned every miserable moment. Remember that." I turned to my crew. "Let's blow this joint."

When we got out on the street again, Rodeo started to speak, but I cut him off. "If you say you told me so, I will strangle you to death with a Pride flag."

Rodeo raised his hands in appeasement. "I wasn't. Just wish it had gone better is all."

"Sorry she misgendered you like that." Zahara punched the button to stop traffic for the crosswalk. "Now what?"

"I got no fucking idea. But I'm still not giving up on catching Blair."

The lighted pedestrian sign switched to WALK, and we crossed.

"You could make another video," Zahara suggested.

"Of what?"

"All the stuff you mentioned to Hoffman. Tanisha being found dead. The prescription bottle. The money from PLC. All of it. Then post it to social media and tag DekaHedron. How soon you think they'd fire her after finding out she's involved in a murder conspiracy and using their facilities to make deepfake videos? Not the kind of publicity they want, I'm sure."

I considered it. This whole video and social media war wasn't really my wheelhouse. And publicly admitting to poking around the crime scene where Tanisha was shot could get me in trouble. But it was worth considering.

"I'll think about it."

My phone rang as we climbed the stairs of the parking garage. It was Picardo the document forger.

40

"Tell me you got something for me," I told Picardo.

"A woman contacted me asking for a UK passport and related documents. The photos I took of her matched a face recognition of the woman you identified as Blair Marshall, though her hairstyle's different."

"Thank God."

"As always, you don't grab Marshall until after I've made the exchange and left. No jumping the gun. Otherwise, word gets out that I'm selling out my clients, and I'm out of business. Or worse, previous clients decide to take care of loose ends, namely me, so that I don't snitch on them."

"Yeah, whatever. When's the exchange?"

"Tomorrow afternoon in Old Town Scottsdale. At the benches on the north side of Fifth Avenue at Marshall Way."

"You're meeting Blair Marshall at Marshall Way?" I couldn't help laughing. "A little ironic."

"A mere coincidence."

"Kind of out in the open like that. Aren't you afraid all the tourists will notice you?"

"No. They'll all be staring at the horse sculptures in the middle of the roundabout. They'll pay no attention to a couple of people sitting on the benches. It's very discreet. As should you be. If this comes back and bites me in the ass, I can make your life miserable too."

"Geez, Picardo. No need to go all agro on me. You know I'm discreet."

"Last time I did this for you, I got a furious phone call from Florence State Prison. Took me an hour to convince the guy I did not know you would be there. If that happens again, our working relationship is over. And if you turn me in—"

"Relax, dude. Everything will be fine. Send me the exact time once you got it nailed down. All right?"

"Fine."

"Who was that?" Zahara asked when I hung up.

"Picardo."

She shook her head. "I don't like him. He gives me the creeps, and he helps criminals escape justice."

"He also helps us catch fugitives. I'm not saying I'm happy about the people he's helping escape, but for now, better some than none."

"You think this will work?" Rodeo asked.

"I hope so, although I'm hoping that Hoffman will come around. If I can nab Marshall before she meets with Picardo, I won't have to pay him."

My phone pinged shortly before we reached the vehicles. "Looks like Maurice at Pima Bail Bonds has one for us. DUI and vehicular assault. No priors. You two think you can handle it? I'm going to keep after Marshall."

Rodeo glanced at Zahara and nodded. "Yeah, we got it. If we need help, we'll call you."

"I'll be in touch."

I climbed into the Gray Ghost. Right when I turned the

ignition, my phone rang again. I figured it might be Picardo calling back with the details of the meet. "Ballou here."

"Ms. Ballou? It's Detective Wong."

"Yeah, detective, what's up?"

"I wanted to give you a heads-up. We had to cut Elise Holbrook loose."

"She's out on bail? She shot my father. Who knows who she'll go after next?"

"We had to release her without charges. She had an alibi. There were witnesses."

"What? That she was at a meeting in Tucson all day? She could have slipped out."

"We checked out the alibi. There was enough collaboration from other people at the meeting, and we simply couldn't prove otherwise."

"It's on the video. She was there."

"I understand. The image from the video was a little jumpy and blurry. Could have been someone who looks a little like her."

"I was there. It was her."

"Unfortunately, eyewitness testimony isn't very reliable. We have a tendency to fill in gaps. Our best guess is it could have been someone who bore a strong resemblance to Holbrook. I'm sorry, Ms. Ballou. I wish I had better news for you."

"What about Tanisha Nolan? Has the Yavapai County Sheriff's Office reached out to you?"

"They have. The good news is that Ms. Nolan is stable and expected to recover. But right now, Yavapai Sheriff's Office hasn't narrowed down a suspect."

"What about ballistics?"

"Ms. Ballou, with all due respect, I've shared with you as much as I'm able. These are ongoing investigations. I ask you not to interfere, especially with your father being a victim. We will do everything in our power to bring those responsible to justice."

I felt like throwing my phone out the window and pounding my steering wheel into junk. But it wouldn't change the situation. I took a deep breath and let it out along with all of my frustration. "Thank you for getting in touch with me, detective. Let me know if you get any new leads."

"We'll be in touch as soon as we have a suspect in custody. And if you learn of anything that can assist our investigation into your father's shooting, please get in touch."

"Yeah." I hung up, drove out of the garage, hopped on the freeway, and headed back to the Hub.

By the time I walked into the coworking space, an idea had sparked in my brain. It was a long shot. I called Picardo and asked him to forward to me the photos that Blair Marshall had sent him to use for creating her fake documents.

"What do you want those for? I told you the facial recognition matched up."

"Humor me."

"Fine."

Ten minutes later, an email with the photo attachments arrived. I opened the images. They looked like standard passport photos. Bland background, the image a little over-exposed. And if I were a betting person, I would have sworn at first glance that I was looking at Elise Holbrook, not Blair Marshall. The long blond hair had been cut into a teal-blue side shave identical to Holbrook's. Their faces were remark-ably similar. And the minimalistic makeup Marshall had previously worn was replaced with an edgier look. More eyeliner, darker lips. They could pass for twins. Or the same person.

I pulled up the photos I had previously located and compared them with what Picardo had sent.

"Fuck me."

"What's up?" Becca asked, poking her head around her wall of monitors.

"Blair Marshall cut her hair."

"And that's significant why?"

"She's the spitting image of Elise Holbrook, who happens to be her cousin."

Becca slid around to my side of the table, the casters of her executive chair clanking and grinding as she did. "Wow. That's Blair Marshall? She looks exactly like Holbrook. Maybe the nose is a little different. But the same eyes, same cheekbones, same hair. The resemblance is uncanny. What does this mean?"

"It means Blair Marshall may be the one who shot my dad. And may have also shot Tanisha Nolan."

"You're going to let that detective know, right?"

I continued to stare at the photos, comparing and contrasting Marshall's new look with her cousin, searching for ways to tell the two apart. I wasn't coming up with much. It was like distinguishing Tegan from Sara. Easy when they were side by side but trickier when only one was in a photo or video shot.

"Jinx," Becca pressed. "Call Detective Wong. Let her handle it."

"I will. Eventually."

"Jinxie, you found the smoking gun. They can arrest her."

"So can I."

"Chica, don't. I'm begging you. Let the cops handle it."

"I'm the one who uncovered this lead. I want to follow it up."

"For the bounty?"

"No. Because it's something I gotta do."

I waited the rest of the afternoon for Picardo to send me the time of his meetup with Marshall. While I waited, I started assembling a new video from photos and bits of video I had acquired, as well as some voice-over I recorded at the Hub. I hadn't decided yet whether I would release it or, if I did, when.

I felt guilty for neglecting both my father and my husband. Shit, that word sounded weird. Husband. Not boyfriend. Not fiancé. Conor was my husband.

Shortly before two o'clock, Rodeo texted they had found the fugitive for Pima Bail Bonds. Apparently, the guy had been at home sleeping off a bender. Completely forgot about his court date.

Around four, my mother called. "Jenna, are you coming to the hospital? Your father's been asking about you."

I stared at the video production app on my screen. "Be there soon, I promise. Had some work to catch up on."

"I heard the police released the woman who shot him." The anger in her voice was palpable. "How could they do that?"

"Elise Holbrook didn't shoot Dad."

"What? But you said…"

"I know. But it wasn't her. It was her cousin, Blair Marshall."

"The woman you've been chasing?"

"Yes."

"Are the police going to arrest her then?"

I wasn't sure how to respond. I wanted to be the one to slap the cuffs on that transphobic bitch. "I'm sure they will."

"How do you know it was her cousin?"

"They look a lot alike. And Holbrook had an alibi. She was down in Tucson. Lots of witnesses."

"But you were so sure before."

"Marshall cut her hair to look like Holbrook. I didn't realize it until a little while ago. I think she was trying to throw me off the trail. It worked. Until now."

"You are going to let the police handle this, right?"

Wow, there must be an echo. "I'm going to let the police handle their investigation." I opted to leave it at that. But I knew my mother was smart enough to read between the lines.

"Please come here soon. Your father misses you."

"How's he doing?"

"Better. They're talking about sending him home in the next few days."

"Good. I'll be there soon."

I called Conor and let him know I wanted to go see my father. He thought it was a good idea and promised to join me once they were done with their whirlwind tour of the valley.

"How's your mom?" I asked.

"Tired, but she's had a blast seeing Phoenix. Took her to the botanical gardens, shopping in Old Town Scottsdale.

Even drove up to see the red rocks in Sedona. She thought it was brilliant. Keeps saying how different it is from Ireland."

"That's a helluva lot to pack into a single day. No wonder she's tired."

"Aye. I'm taking her back to her motel room now. Once I get her settled, I'll join ya at hospital."

"Sounds good. I'll see you there."

I posted the video I'd created to my social media accounts, tagging DekaHedron and Hoffman, and packed away my laptop. I had little hope it would accomplish anything. But I got a certain satisfaction out of putting the truth out there for the world to see.

"Heading out?" Becca asked when I packed up my laptop.

I told her I was heading to the hospital. She offered to join me for moral support, but I told her I was good.

"See you tomorrow, then."

I hugged her and walked out to the parking lot.

The drive to the hospital sucked. The highways were clogged, and the surface streets were worse. I remembered to stop by Maisie's and picked up a to-go order for my father, as promised.

Once I got on Tatum Boulevard, the traffic thinned a bit, though there were a lot of cars puttering along at the speed limit or below, even with no one in front of them. I preferred to go about ten above. Cops tended to leave me alone, even at that speed. Maybe it was the soccer-mom vibe of the Gray Ghost. I might attract more attention driving Conor's vintage Charger.

When I finally walked into my father's room with the food from Maisie's, a burden slid off my back. Seeing him joking around with Jake, my mother, and Grand-Mère Marie helped everything feel a little more normal.

"There's the blushing bride," he said, a wide smile lighting up his face. "Mmm, something sure smells good."

I hugged him in the bed. "How're you feeling?"

He took a deep sniff of the air. "Better now that you're here."

I set the bag on the bedside table and pulled out a carton of fried green tomatoes with the pimento cheese on the side. "Bon appétit, Dad."

"Merci beaucoup, cher." His eyes blazed with joy.

My grandmother eyed it. "Not bad, I suppose. Better than the tripe they been serving my boy. You know they had the nerve to pour some leftover chicken noodle soup onto a hamburger bun and call it chicken and dumplings?" She shook her head in disdain. "Absolutely disgraceful. Bun still had sesame seeds on it and ever'thing."

I shrugged. "Yeah. Hospital food. What can you do?"

"An incentive to get better sooner." My father bit into a fried green tomato slice and moaned with pleasure. "Mmm-mmm. That's some good home cooking. Not as good as yours, Ma, but good nevertheless."

"I was afraid it'd be cold by the time I got here. You want me to have the nurse nuke it?"

"It's fine, cher, just as it is."

"I also got you their crawfish gumbo." Now my stomach was rumbling as I took the lid off the plastic container. The aromas were reminiscent of my dad's cooking. I resisted the urge to help myself to a taste. Just to make sure it was still warm, of course.

"Oh, my dear girl, you know how to treat your old dad. I am a lucky man to be surrounded by such a loving family."

"Sorry I wasn't here earlier." Not even the best Southern cooking could staunch my guilt.

"No harm done. You have your work. I had plenty of company. And the best care in the world. And now the best cooking. I am blessed." He beamed. "How goes your hunt for the fugitives of the world?"

I shrugged. "It goes. I've got some new leads. We'll see what happens."

"That's my girl. Where's that handsome husband of yours?"

"He'll be along. He's been giving his mother a tour of Phoenix and Sedona."

"Ah, of course. Delightful woman."

"Yeah, she is."

Conor and Siobhan showed up before long. We spent the next few hours talking with them. All the while, I wondered why Picardo hadn't called back with the time for his handoff of the fake papers. I understood his need to not besmirch his reputation as a primo forger, but waiting to slap the cuffs on Marshall was leaving me frustrated.

At the end of visiting hours, a nurse informed us that only my mother was allowed to stay. My brother and I both made a stink.

"You should all go home and get some rest," my father assured us. "I'm in good hands. I'll probably drift off to dreamland soon enough. No need for you to stay here and watch me snore."

I didn't want to go, though. I felt guilty for spending so little time with him. What if something bad happened? Another stroke or he caught C. diff or another disease. But my father insisted.

"You need to be at your best to catch your fugitive."

42

———

On the drive home, my phone rang. I was hoping it was Picardo, but the caller ID was an unfamiliar number. I hesitated to answer it. I was no longer sending calls outside my contacts list to voicemail. Most of the reward seekers and harassing calls had stopped.

"Fugitive Recovery. How may I help you?" I left off my name, hoping it would discourage harassers.

"Is this Jinx Ballou?" The female voice was familiar, but I was too tired to recognize it right away.

"Who's asking?"

"Naomi Hoffman."

"Well, well, well. Did you like my latest video? Probably not up to your professional standards, but I thought it made some intriguing points, don't you?"

"Is Womyn Born Womyn really working with those neo-Nazis at the Patriots of Liberty?"

"Unlike you, I don't make fake videos. I don't have the skills or technology to do it, even if I wanted to. Google it if you don't believe me."

She cursed under her breath but loud enough that I heard it.

"More importantly, your girlfriend murdered LaTonya Garrett, shot my father, and was involved in shooting Tanisha Nolan. And you continuing to protect her makes you equally guilty in the eyes of the law. You could go to jail for a very long time." I paused for effect. "Unless you help me return her to custody."

"I don't know where she is."

"You expect me to believe that? More importantly, do you expect a jury to believe that?"

"It's true. All I know is she's staying in a motel."

"What motel?"

"I don't know. She didn't tell me. She sent an encrypted message to an old email address I used to use."

"How is she paying for the room?"

"A member of the group, I imagine."

"What's her email address?"

She gave it to me. "For what it's worth, I'm sorry she's hurt all these people. The purpose of the group was to protect women. I don't know how things got so out of control."

"Your being sorry doesn't change things. Womyn Born Womyn has been hurting innocent people since it started going after trans people. Transgender women are not the threat you've made us out to be. We're women, same as you. We just want to live our lives."

"I don't know what to believe anymore."

"Believe this: unless you help me put your girlfriend behind bars, you will suffer the consequences of her and your actions. I guarantee it."

"I gave you the email address. That's all I have. I haven't seen her..." Her voice broke, and she began sobbing. "I haven't seen her in over a week. I didn't want to believe the things everyone was saying about her. She's really a good person."

"Murderers are not good people, Naomi."

"I know. I know."

"If you hear from her again, you contact me immediately and give me her location."

"I will."

I hung up and continued to drive home.

When Conor and I arrived at the Bunker, I forwarded the email address to Becca, asking her to see if she could get a location. It was a long shot, but unless Picardo came through, it was the only lead I had left.

That night, Conor and I made passionate love for hours. It almost felt like we really were on a honeymoon. I pushed all the shit in my life into the furthest reaches of my mind —a little trick my father had taught me. I knew not to permanently suppress feelings that needed to be worked through. But for one night, it was what I needed.

More than anything, I needed to feel safe enough to open myself up and be completely vulnerable with this beautiful, kind man. This man who made me laugh every day, who could melt me with a kiss. The one whose very scent I ached for when I thought he was dead. Whose voice was like a choir of heavenly angels singing into my soul.

That night I came several times. By the time we collapsed into unconsciousness, I felt the joy I had been missing since before the wedding. A joy without worries of wedding plans or dealing with cops or fugitives or bigots. A feeling of being one with my wonderful husband and, at the same time, a complete person in my own right. I couldn't make sense of it logically, but I didn't need to. My father had taught me that some things simply needed to be experienced.

Becca called the next morning while I was sitting at the

kitchen table drinking coffee with Conor and laughing at something his mother had said the day before.

"Sorry, bestie. I tried to get a geolocation on the email address. The most recent location was somewhere in Scottsdale. No more specific than that. The encryption service Marshall used is a freaking fortress. I tried to hack into it but no luck."

"Well, thanks anyway."

"You hanging in there? You two should be in the Keys."

"I'm doing okay. Better actually than I have been. And we'll get to the Keys eventually. If you get any more hits on Marshall, let me know."

I hung up and went to my computer, running the more prominent members of WBW again through SkipTrakkr, looking for recent charges to a motel on their bank statements. There was a charge a week earlier for a hotel in Lake Havasu City from one of the chapter's officers. Another one in Cabo for someone else. But nothing local. Blair Marshall was somewhere in the valley.

At nine, Picardo called me. "The meet is at noon. I already gave you the location."

"Yeah, the fountain at Fifth Ave and Marshall Way."

"I want to be gone before you move in."

"Yeah, yeah, you said so before. Trust me on this." I wasn't happy about it. It could give Marshall too much of a head start. I considered calling Detective Wong and letting her coordinate the takedown with Scottsdale PD. But I wanted this.

"If she gets away, though," I added, "I don't pay you squat."

"Wait a minute, that wasn't part of the deal."

"It is now. You want me to wait, your fee is dependent on me taking down Marshall. I get the girl, you get paid."

"Fine."

"What name is she putting on her passport?"

"Janice Kimberly Rowland."

"Good to know. Let's make this happen."

43

I called Rodeo and Zahara and caught them up on everything. We agreed to meet at eleven o'clock at the Sun West Cafe, a block away from the fountain, to go over the plan. "We want to do this low-key. Tasers as primary weapons. Firearms as backup only. Too many civilians around to turn this into a shoot-out," I told each of them on the phone. "Last thing we need is someone else getting killed over this shit."

I also called Becca back to see if she could find a Janice Rowland registered at any of the valley's motels or hotels. She checked but came up with goose eggs.

I geared up and hugged Conor. "Thanks for last night," I said. "I really needed it."

"Trust me, it was my pleasure." He smiled, and I nearly tossed off my gear to jump his bones right there. "Good hunting, love. Watch your six."

"Always. You wanna come with, or are you giving your mother another tour of the city?"

"She's flying back home today. I'm giving her a ride to the airport."

"I'm sorry I couldn't spend more time with her. She seems really nice."

"Aye, it would've been lovely if you could've spent more time together. Perhaps we can visit her in Dublin this summer."

"Wow, I'd love that. I've always wanted to travel to Ireland. Are the men all like you?" I asked with a grin.

"Oh no. Most are much better looking than me."

"No doubt."

"Cheeky girl."

"Smart-ass." I kissed him hard, and my insides turned to liquid. It took all my strength to pull myself away, even after several minutes. "I gotta go."

"Aye. Go take that dodgy TERF woman off the street."

"I intend to stop her one way or another."

"Don't kill her."

"She shot my father. I'll do what I have to."

"She may not deserve to live. But do you deserve the burden of being responsible for her death? This is a job. No room in it for vendettas."

I kissed him once more. "Duly noted."

At eleven, the three of us were sitting at a table at the café.

"So, it's a gunfight at high noon," Rodeo joked. "Sounds very Wild West."

"Let's hope it's not a gunfight," Zahara replied. "Too many people been hurt already."

"Agreed," I replied. "I want this to be quick and surgical. And if Marshall shows before Picardo, we grab her. Save me having to pay him his fee."

"He won't be happy about that," Rodeo replied.

"I don't really care. I want her off the street."

I pulled out a map of the area I'd picked up at one of the shops selling tourist tchotchkes.

"Rodeo, I want you in your vehicle east of the intersection. If there's a space there, grab it. If not, park where you can and hang out at Krueger Antiques. Should have a good view of the bench."

"Roger that," Rodeo said.

"Zahara, you'll be west of the roundabout. If you can't grab a space there, try to get a table at the Cotton Cafe. Kelly Cotton, the manager, is a friend of mine."

"Will do," Zahara replied. "Where will you be?"

"On Marshall Way, south of the intersection in front of the Boisjoli Gallery. If Marshall runs, we should be able to box her in. I am also planting an electronic bug in the planter immediately behind the bench. A little something Becca bought me a while back. It transmits to an app on my phone so I can listen in live."

Zahara gave me a sly smile. "I really hope we get her this time."

"Me too. Any other questions?"

When there was no response, I said, "Let's get in position and take down this bitch once and for all."

After planting the bug by the bench, I sat in the Gray Ghost facing south by the Boisjoli Gallery, watching the bench through my binoculars. If Marshall got past us, I could chase after her.

"Pack Leader here, check in and confirm position," I called over the radio.

"Coyote Two, check," Zahara said. "Sitting at a table by the door of the Cotton Cafe."

"Copy that, Coyote Two. Coyote One, you there?"

"Roger, Pack Leader. Parked outside the antiques shop."

"Copy, Coyote One. And now we wait."

I opened the app for the bug. Most of what I could hear was the rustling of the plants in the breeze with occasional bits of conversation from passersby.

At fifteen minutes before noon, a woman with two kids sat down on the bench, all three eating ice cream cones from the Prickly Pear Creamery a few doors down.

"Coyote Two here. What do we do now? Did Picardo have a backup plan?"

"Not sure. Hang tight. Let's see what happens. Keep your eyes peeled for either Picardo or Marshall."

"Copy, Pack Leader," came Zahara's reply.

"Pack Leader, Coyote One. I got Picardo approaching from the west on the south side of Fifth Avenue. Beige shirt, shades, and a Diamondbacks cap."

From my vantage point, I couldn't see him, but I scanned the area for Marshall. I spotted a Volvo that looked familiar, but couldn't read the license plate.

"Pack Leader, Coyote Two here. I confirm Picardo's approaching. No sign of target."

"Coyote One, Pack Leader. There's a Volvo that looks a lot like the one Marshall used to escape from me last week. Check to see if there is anyone inside."

"Copy, Pack Leader. Will approach with caution."

Picardo came into view with a small computer bag under his arm. He crossed the street near the roundabout that encircled the fountain and stopped in front of the bench.

"Excuse me, ma'am," came Picardo's muffled voice over the bug's app on my phone. "I'm supposed to meet a friend here in a few minutes. Would you mind moving on?"

"We're sitting here," the woman replied indignantly. "Go find your own bench."

He pulled out some bills from his pocket and offered them to the woman. "I really need this bench."

"I don't need your money. We're not moving."

He leaned over and whispered something in her ear. The bug didn't pick up what he was saying. However, the woman glared at him, gathered her kids, and hurried away.

"Coyote Two here. Wonder what he told that lady?"

"Don't know, Coyote Two," I replied. "Keep your eyes peeled for the target."

"Copy that, Pack Leader."

"Pack Leader, Coyote One. Volvo is empty."

"Can you check the license plate?"

"Wilco."

A moment later, Rodeo called back in with the license plate.

"Copy, Coyote One. The Volvo license plate is not a match to the one Marshall used before."

I ran a check of the plate on the mobile SkipTrakkr app. It came up as belonging to a Toyota Camry owned by a man in Avondale. "Heads up, Pack. The license plate isn't a match for that car. Someone put on a different plate. It could belong to the target."

"Any sign of Marshall?"

"Negative."

I spotted Mandy Hudson on the other side of Marshall Way, running north along the shops. She nearly got clipped by a BMW while crossing the street.

"This is Pack Leader. Mandy Hudson is in play. No sign of target. Hudson may make the exchange."

"Who the hell are you?" Picardo said, his voice now clearer.

"A friend," Hudson replied. She pulled out a thick envelope and set it between them on the bench.

"This wasn't the plan." Picardo made no move to pick up the envelope. "Where's my client?"

"What do you care? You're still getting paid. Where's the new IDs?"

Picardo picked up the envelope, gave the contents a

quick glance, and slipped it into his inside jacket pocket. "Under your seat. Take it after I leave."

I'd been so busy looking for Blair Marshall that I hadn't seen Picardo place anything under the bench. The dude was slick.

"Why should I wait?" Hudson asked defiantly.

"Cause if you don't, I have a sniper ready to take your head off. Comprendes?"

"A sniper? What the heck?" Zahara exclaimed over the radio.

"It's probably a bluff. Everyone hold their position."

My phone rang, causing me to nearly jump out of my skin. I had meant to silence it. I sent the call to voicemail without pulling it out of my pocket. My focus had to be on the exchange.

Picardo stood. "I find out you don't get that to my client, I will find you and make you regret ever meeting me."

"Relax, dude. I'm with her."

Picardo disappeared down Fifth Avenue. Hudson pulled the computer bag out from under the bench and opened it. She then made a phone call.

"Hey, sweetie," Hudson said over the receiver. "I got the goods."

She pulled out some papers and a small black something, probably a passport.

"Yeah, it's all here," she said. "Passport, birth certificate, the works. Looks good. Okay, I'll meet you in the room. I can't believe we're doing this. I feel sorry for Naomi and Elise, but I love you."

"Holy shit," I said to myself. "Marshall is having an affair with Hudson."

"Pack Leader, this is Coyote One. Should we move in?"

"No, she'll lead us to Marshall. Coyote Two, get to your vehicle and prepare to pursue."

"Copy that, Pack Leader," Zahara replied.

Hudson strolled to the Volvo, occasionally looking around to see if anyone was watching or following her. She didn't indicate she noticed any of us. A good sign, at least.

I started the Gray Ghost while monitoring the Volvo. It circled the fountain and turned south toward me. As she passed, I noticed someone in the passenger seat. Ashley Carroll, one of the WBW members who had protected Marshall at the accountant's office. She flipped me off with a grin on her face.

I started to pull out of my space, but another car was right behind her. And another after that one. Lunchtime traffic. When, at last, I could pull out of my angled parking space, the Gray Ghost felt sluggish. Something wasn't right.

"Coyote Pack, Coyote One here. Someone slashed two of my tires."

"This is Coyote Two. Same here."

"Fuck!" I put the Gray Ghost in drive and immediately realized someone had done the same to mine. Fortunately, I had installed run-flat tires on the Ghost a year earlier after a similar incident. It wouldn't be good for a high-speed chase, but I could still follow for a distance, so long as I limited my speed.

"I'm still in pursuit. I'll keep you apprised of my location."

Hudson turned right onto Indian School Road. I attempted to follow but got caught at a red light. I considered trying to squeeze through, but the westbound traffic on Indian School was heavy. My phone pinged to let me know someone had left me a voicemail message.

I pulled it out for a second and played the message on speaker, keeping an eye out for an opening to turn.

"Ms. Ballou, it's Naomi Hoffman. Blair's staying at Scottsdale Dreamcatcher Resort, room 354. Thought you should know."

"Gotcha!" I said aloud.

The traffic cleared, and I turned onto Indian School Road. I didn't have to catch up to Hudson, but I had to hurry. Clearly, Hudson and Marshall were all ready to skip the country together. Apparently, Marshall's disloyalty extended beyond the cause of feminism. She'd betrayed Hoffman as well. Too bad. So sad. I was going to make her sorry.

I called Rodeo. "Marshall's at the Scottsdale Dreamcatcher on Indian School, room 354. Let Zahara know and meet me there when you can."

"Copy that, Jinx. Got one tire changed. Another in progress. See you soon. Watch your six."

I pushed my way through the sluggish traffic. For reasons I never understood, drivers in Scottsdale were never in a hurry. Maybe it was the snowbirds unsure of where they were going or tourists fascinated by the sculptures along the canal that the road paralleled. Or maybe they simply didn't have to worry about being anywhere on time. I, on the other hand, was in a hurry. These slowpokes were sending my blood pressure skyrocketing.

When at last I could push the pedal to the metal, the car began shimmying from the deflated tire. I hoped my haste wouldn't trigger a catastrophic tire failure and leave me stranded before I reached my destination.

I caught a green left-turn arrow onto Sixty-Eighth Avenue and pulled into the Scottsdale Dreamcatcher resort. A twenty-foot-tall sculpture in the shape of a Native American dreamcatcher stood next to the parking lot entrance.

When it opened years earlier, many local Native Americans and their supporters complained about the white-owned resort misappropriating indigenous culture. Sadly, I doubted the developers or their investors lost any sleep over their misdeeds so long as they were making bank, which they were.

I cruised through the aisles and spotted the Volvo but no sign of Hudson or Marshall.

I parked behind the Volvo, blocking it in. They'd have to do better than slash my tires if they were going to escape now. I rushed out of the truck and toward the hotel lobby with my Taser in hand. I was not letting Marshall escape again. Not while I drew breath.

It took a second for my eyes to adjust from the bright daylight to the subdued lighting of the lobby. Familiar voices caught my attention.

"How the fuck did she follow us here?" Hudson said. "I thought you cut her tires."

"Go, Mandy! Just go. I'll hold her off."

I rushed toward the voices, my eyes soon focusing in on Ashley Carroll. She held an impressive-looking knife with the posture of someone who knew how to use it. Hudson ran across the lobby and disappeared into what looked like a stairwell. I heard the clomping of steps until the fire door slammed shut again.

"Put the knife down!" I shouted to Carroll in my commanding voice. "Put it down and get on the ground! Do it now! Do it now!"

"Leave her alone!" Carroll said, standing her ground. "Women gotta be protected from predators like you."

I aimed for center mass. "Last warning. Drop the knife and get on the ground."

Carroll charged me. I pulled the trigger. Her face twisted in pain, and she dropped to the floor. I kicked the knife out of her hand and cuffed her then ran down the hallway after my actual target. No time for witty banter.

The hallway brought me to an elevator lobby. Too long of a wait. Hudson had a lead on me. And I knew where she was headed. I popped in a fresh Taser cartridge and rushed into the stairwell.

A shot rang out like thunder, echoing on the concrete walls. Another ricocheted off the metal railing. Hudson's face peeked out from above, and I aimed the Taser in her direction, but she was too far away.

The clap-clap-clap of rubber-soled shoes on concrete told me Hudson was once again on the move. I sprinted up the stairs two at a time. My heart thundered in my chest so

hard I feared breaking a rib. And yet the need to bring
Marshall down, combined with a major dump of adrenaline, drove me upward.

When I hit the landing between the second and third
floors, my chest and my left arm exploded in pain while
gunshots thundered all around me. I fell, screaming in
agony.

45

I felt detached from my body as I tumbled backward. The world transformed into a carnival ride of pain. Spinning, banging, tumbling, collapsing. I struggled to make sense of what was going on.

I eventually found myself staring up at the underside of the stairs above me. The railing was shiny with fresh blood. My blood. My left arm was on fire. My head throbbed in agony. I had to force myself to breathe because each inhalation brought a new experience of pain.

At any second, Mandy Hudson would appear and finish me off. My body thrummed and tingled but didn't respond. Even my right arm felt oddly no longer a part of me.

Somewhere in the distance, light years away, I could hear a familiar ringing. Eventually, I realized it was my phone. But remembering where it was felt like trying to do advanced calculus in my head.

Blair Marshall was going to get away, along with Mandy Hudson, her new girlfriend. And I was going to die here alone. I should have spent my time at my father's bedside instead of going after that stupid bitch. Maybe then it would be Leroy Drake lying here in a pool of blood instead of me.

Not that I really had anything against Drake. Sure, he was a smart-ass who talked a big game and delivered less than half the time, but he never misgendered me, even when he was talking smack. More than I could say about the fucking TERFs I'd been chasing.

I took in another breath, wincing and whimpering as I did so, and let it go.

"Trust the process." My dad's voice reverberated in my mind. *"Trust the process."*

"What process?" I had asked countless times.

"You'll figure it out, cher. Don't give up."

"Yeah. Figure it out."

"I am not going to fucking die in this stairwell." The fog in my brain began lifting. I rolled onto my side. My mind went into sitrep mode.

Blood ran down my left arm from a wound just above the elbow. Didn't appear to have hit a major blood vessel, or I'd probably already be dead. But the torn flesh was ugly and hurt like fuck. The side of my head wasn't feeling much better. I must have smacked it on the steps when I fell. The dizziness suggested a possible concussion. Two holes in my shirt, center mass. I lifted it to find a couple of slugs embedded in my Kevlar vest. Ribs hurt, possible fracture or bruising.

With my good arm on the railing, I pulled myself to my feet, roaring like a lioness as I did so. Far below, I spotted my bright-yellow Taser down on the ground-floor landing. Even if I managed to get down the stairs to retrieve it, I doubted I could make it up to the third floor in time to stop Marshall and Hudson. The fall probably damaged it, anyway.

I retrieved a bandana from a pocket, and with a combination of my good hand and my teeth, I tightened it enough to slow the bleeding, growling through the pain.

I took a deep breath to clear the cobwebs from my mind.

"Okay, girl. You are not giving up. You are taking down these bitches, if it's the last thing you do." I drew my revolver from the ankle holster, unsnapped the retention strap, and forced myself up the stairs, one labored step at a time.

I was almost to the third-floor landing when a door below me opened.

"Jinx? You up there?" It was Rodeo.

"Ro…" My heart was hammering in my chest so fast I could barely catch my breath. "Up. Here."

Rodeo and Zahara soon appeared beside me.

"Oh goodness, Jinx, you're hit," Zahara said. "We'll call for an ambulance."

"No. Not yet. Gotta get. Marshall."

Rodeo put a hand on my back. "Boss, this looks bad. Best you sit down and conserve your strength. Zahara will call 911. I'll get Marshall."

I shook my head. The vertigo increased tenfold, nearly knocking me off my feet. "Gotta. Finish. This."

I caught the two of them exchange a glance.

"You're the boss." Rodeo opened the fire door to the third floor. I pushed my body through.

The hallway was empty. Signs on the wall indicated where rooms were located. Room 354 was to our left. I leaned on Zahara as we trudged on, even as vertigo kept pulling me to my left. A woman in a white visor and a tennis outfit stepped out of a room, saw me, and gasped.

"Get back in your room," I growled.

She squeaked like a frightened rodent and vanished

back into her room. I heard Zahara chuckle. "Easy, girl. Don't frighten the tourists."

The bleached wooden door at room 354 looked solid, fitted with an electronic lock. In the movies, the hero would either kick it in or shoot the lock. But neither method would work on a door like this. And I was no Hollywood hero.

Angry voices shouted within, but the door was too thick to make out who was saying what.

"I'll go downstairs and get the manager to let us in," Rodeo said.

"I got a better idea." Zahara pounded on the door. "Hotel management. We've received a complaint. Please open the door." She knocked some more for good measure.

The instant the doorknob turned, I threw my full weight against it, ignoring the lightning bolts of pain radiating through my body.

Mandy Hudson tumbled to the floor, her pistol sliding across the stone tiles. Rodeo took her down.

Drawing on a surge of rage and adrenaline, I stormed across the room toward where Blair Marshall, looking so much like her cousin, stood wide-eyed in horror. I raised my revolver, ready to put two in her chest. I didn't care if she was unarmed. "Fucking bitch."

Terror blazed in her eyes. "Please don't shoot me."

"You shot my dad. Ruined my wedding. Murdered LaTonya. Probably shot Tanisha too." My voice sounded like gravel in a garbage disposal. "You want mercy?"

"I'm sorry."

"Bullshit. You're only sorry you didn't finish the job."

"Shoot her." Naomi Hoffman stood nearby, a few feet from where Hudson's pistol lay. "Fakakta bitch was schtupping my girlfriend."

"Please, don't kill me." Blair Marshall cowered on her

knees. "I'm sorry I cheated on you, babe."

Hoffman railed at her. "I loved you and believed your spiel about that tranny groping you in the bathroom, that you acted in self-defense. I kept your whereabouts secret after that judge revoked your bail. I supported you when you crashed this woman's... this man's... this thing's wedding."

The use of slurs and misgendering had me seriously considering shooting Naomi too. But I held my fire. I wanted to see where this was going.

Somewhere faraway, Zahara was calling my name. I ignored it.

"I was trying to protect women and children from the trans rights activists and their dangerous agenda."

"You sold us out to those Christo-fascists. How is that protecting women?"

"You're the threat," I growled at Marshall. "Hurting innocent people who did nothing to you." My finger slipped onto the trigger.

"Jinx, don't," Zahara called from somewhere. "She's not worth it."

My mind swirled with memories. Crime scene photos of LaTonya Garrett, her face unrecognizable from the wounds and her blood spattered across the restroom tiles like a Jackson Pollock painting. Tanisha Nolan, who now clung to life in a hospital. My wedding dress soaked in my father's blood, him looking so pale that first night in the ICU. I remembered every trans teen I read about who had committed suicide. The murdered trans people memorialized each November on the Trans Day of Remembrance.

My finger squeezed the trigger then stopped.

More memories bubbled into my consciousness. My father talking about mercy. Zahara treating captured fugitives with compassion while we drove them to jail. Conor reminding me of the burden of taking a life. Even if it was deserved.

I didn't want to be the violent monster that Marshall and her hateful TERFs tried to make us out to be. I wasn't a cold-blooded killer. I didn't want to be, despite all the harm that Marshall, Hudson, and others like them had done.

"Jinx." Zahara's voice was a whisper in my ear. Her firm hand wrapped around the top of the revolver, preventing the hammer from striking the firing pin. "You're bleeding bad. You need to sit down."

"Turn around, bitch, and face the wall," I growled at Marshall, releasing the revolver into Zahara's hand.

"You're gonna shoot me in the back? You fucking cowards."

"We're going to arrest you," Zahara replied in a commanding voice. "Turn around, hands behind your head. Do it now!"

Marshall gave her ex-girlfriend a rueful glance and turned toward the wall. As Zahara cuffed one hand, Hoffman reached down and picked something off the floor. By the time I realized it was Hudson's gun, it was too late.

The muzzle flash blinded me. I body-slammed Hoffman, sending us both to the floor. I snatched the smoking gun from her hands. My ears thrummed.

"Blair!" Hudson's scream echoed weirdly from across the room.

The air felt so chilly, and I wondered if someone had cranked up the AC.

Zahara's face appeared in my field of vision. "Hold on, girl. Help's on the way."

I saw Marshall's body a few yards away, blood pouring from a wound in her back.

"Tables turned now, huh?" I wasn't sure she could hear me, or even if I said the words aloud. "Game over, bitch."

46

The room door flew open, and two uniformed Scottsdale police officers raced into the room with weapons drawn. "Police! Everyone down on the floor now! Get on the floor, hands behind your heads."

"Need an ambulance," I mumbled. "Been shot..."

Someone forced me onto my belly. My arms were pulled behind my back while cuffs bit into my wrists.

I screamed in agony. "I'm shot. I'm shot."

I caught Rodeo's and Zahara's voices shouting above the cacophony of commands from the officers. Or maybe I imagined it.

What felt like days later, the cuffs were removed. I was lifted onto a gurney and was rushed out of the room. Overhead lights blazed past. The vertigo intensified, and for a moment, I felt like I was on a Tilt-A-Whirl, spinning, spinning, round and round.

"You're gonna be all right." A fresh-faced EMT who looked about twelve years old stared down at me. The theme song from the show *Doogie Howser* started playing in my head.

"All right, Doogie," I replied.

Every time the gurney went over a bump, I ground my teeth in pain. "Can't you give me something?" I begged after they lifted me into the ambulance.

"Soon." Doogie shot me a sympathetic smile.

The rest was a blur of pain, vertigo, medical personal sticking me with IVs, then me drifting off to sleep.

When I woke, I was in a hospital bed trying to remember how I got there. I pressed the nurse call button. A woman in slate-blue scrubs appeared. "You're awake."

"Where..." My throat felt like someone had taken a belt sander to it. "Where am..."

"Scottsdale Osborn Medical Center. Do you know why you're here?"

My mind was full of cotton, probably from whatever painkillers they'd given me. My left arm was in a sling and wrapped in a thick layer of gauze. I had a bandage on my temple as well. "Shot."

"Can you tell me what day it is?"

"Tues—no, Wednesday. Is it still Wednesday?" The confrontation at the Dreamcatcher Resort felt like it was decades ago.

"It is. On a scale of one to ten, how's your pain level?"

It took me a moment to figure out how I felt. "Three. Arm hurts. Head and ribs sore."

"Let me know if you need anything for the pain."

"How bad am I?" I had vague memories of events in the Scottsdale hotel.

"The doctor will be in shortly to fill you in."

I sat back, listening to the beeping of vitals monitors in other rooms and drifted off again.

"Ms. Ballou?"

I woke up to see a man in green scrubs and a stethoscope around his neck.

"I am Dr. Carpenter."

He asked to verify my name and date of birth then explained that while there was some soft tissue damage from the gunshot wound, the bullet missed the humerus and all major blood vessels. I had a slight concussion and bruised ribs from where my vest saved me from the gunshots to my chest.

"You should be good as new in about four to six weeks. I want to hold you overnight to make sure there aren't any complications. But you should be able to return home tomorrow."

"Thanks."

He disappeared. A few minutes later, a nurse returned and put a syringe of morphine into my IV line. Kirsten walked in soon after.

"Oh my goodness, Jinx! How are you feeling?"

"Sore. Sleepy. Had better days."

"No doubt. Do you remember what happened?"

I searched my memory, but it was like reassembling the details of a dream.

"Followed Blair Marshall to hotel. Her friends tried to stop me. One with a knife. Tased her. Another shot me in the stairwell. Hudson. In the arm in the stairwell." I was having trouble getting the words to make sense. I raised my arm and winced at the sting of pain. *Don't do that,* I told myself. "Lost my Taser."

"Mandy Hudson shot you?"

"Yeah."

"Conor, Zahara, and Rodeo are all in the waiting room desperate to see you. Becca, Easton, and Jake are on their way."

"Send them in." The more friendly faces, the better. I needed my peeps.

"I will. But first, Detective Wong from Phoenix PD and a

Detective Yazzie from Scottdale have some questions."

"What questions?"

"For starters, who shot Blair Marshall?"

"She alive?"

"Last I heard. Possibly paralyzed from the waist down, I'm told. A bullet's lodged in her spine."

I tried to remember. "Hoffman. Naomi. She shot her."

"A revolver registered in your name was found at the scene. Did you shoot anyone?"

"Um... no. Didn't fire revolver." I vaguely recalled Zahara taking it from me.

"Do you feel up to speaking with the detectives, or are you too doped up?"

"For a bit. Not too long. Tired." My mind was now floating on a cloud of pain meds. *Ohhh yeahhh...*

Detective Wong walked in along with and a man dressed in a black suit. His high cheekbones and no-nonsense expression gave him an air of authority. Serious downer harshing my mellow. Couldn't we all just get along?

"How are you feeling, Ms. Ballou?" Wong asked.

"Was feeling like shit. Feeling pretty good now."

"Ms. Ballou, this is Detective Yazzie with Scottsdale PD. He has some questions about the incident at the Scottsdale Dreamcatcher Resort."

"Hey," I said with zero enthusiasm.

"Sorry to bother you while you're recovering," Yazzie said, "but I need to get your account of what occurred earlier today."

I gave them a brief description of the events, from getting the voicemail from Naomi Hoffman to confronting the women in the hotel room. The memories were like pieces of a jigsaw puzzle that kept shifting around. Wasn't sure if my answers were in any way coherent but wasn't all that concerned either way.

"Did you return fire when Hudson shot at you in the stairwell?" Yazzie asked.

"No. Dropped my Taser."

"Did you tase the woman found handcuffed in the lobby?"

"Yeah. Came at me with a knife. Big one. Like Crocodile Dundee."

Yazzie showed a photo of a knife next to an evidence marker and a ruler used to show scale. "This knife?"

"Uh-huh. Now that's a knife," I said in a goofy Australian accent. I cracked myself up. None of the detectives laughed.

"You say that Naomi Hoffmann shot Ms. Marshall. Why would she do that?"

"Marshall cheating on her with Hudson. Running away to England. Fake papers." I wondered if Hudson or Marshall would roll over on Picardo.

"So it was a lover's quarrel?"

"Sorta." I wanted to explain how Marshall's pseudo-feminist hate group had partnered with a right-wing fascist lobbying organization, and that Hoffman took issue with that. But I didn't have the brainpower to explain it.

"Where did Hoffman get the gun?" Although I'd already told them, Yazzie was circling back, checking for inconsistencies. A classic interview technique. Ask the witness for the sequence of events, then ask them again out of order, look for what changes.

"Hudson dropped."

"Was this the gun Hudson shot you with?"

My eyelids were growing heavy. The morphine was kicking in big time. "Tired."

"That's enough, detectives," Kirsten said from a hundred miles away. "You already have statements from Zahara Washington and Nathanial Kwan."

When I woke a while later, Conor, Jake, and Becca were seated around my bed.

"Oi! Jinxie! Ya gave us quite a scare, love."

"Yeah, me too. I'll live." The fog was slowly burning off from my mind. And everything hurt like a fucker.

"Glad to hear it," Jake said. "After nearly losing Dad and then this." His voice broke with emotion.

"How'd you know I was here?"

"Rodeo called," Conor replied.

Conor set a fruit basket on the bedside table and pulled out a banana with a mischievous gleam in his eye. "Hungry, love? Ya look like you could use some potassium."

"Funny. I may be doped up on painkillers, buddy, but I'm not falling for that gag again. I know you already opened it from the back and ate it."

"Suit yourself." He split the back open and pulled out the fruit. "Really good, though," he added with a mouthful of banana.

"You got me again." I couldn't help but laugh at the practical joke. "Where's Rodeo and Zahara?"

"In the waiting room," Jake answered. "I'll go get them."

He reappeared moments later, holding Rodeo's hand with Zahara next to them.

Zahara squeezed my hand, her fingers sending strength into me. Or so it felt. "I'm so sorry this happened to you. How you feeling, girl?"

Looking into her eyes, a surge of gratitude welled up inside me. "You saved me, Z."

"I think those pain meds are messing with your memory, girl. You were the one who saved me by jumping on Naomi Hoffman and taking that gun away from her."

Had I done that? It was all so fuzzy. "You saved me from killing Marshall."

She smiled. The warmth in her face nearly melted me.

"After the knee injury ended my MMA career, I was so bitter and angry. At the woman who tore my ACL. At the ref. At my doctors. At God. At my girlfriend. I started drinking and using, but my real addiction was to the anger. It was eating up my soul.

"When I finally got clean, my sponsor told me I had a choice. I could stay angry, or I could stay clean. I couldn't do both. So I let go of all that bitterness. Wasn't easy either. Took me a long time to work through it all. I had layer upon layer of resentments. But when I finally was free of it, I knew I could never go back."

"Yeah," was all I could say. My father had been trying to teach me the same lesson, only I hadn't been listening.

"While I will do everything I can to apprehend the fugitives we're assigned to go after, I will not hate them. I will not let anger or bitterness poison my attitude, no matter what these people are accused of. I can't afford to. My addict is just waiting for any excuse to get me to use again. It's out to kill me, as sure as even the most violent killer on the street."

She half sat on the edge of my bed. "In that hotel room, I recognized that fire in your eyes. That furious fire of hate. So familiar. I'd seen it in myself for the longest time. Right or wrong, I knew it didn't lead to nowhere good. I didn't want you to suffer the way I suffered. Didn't want you to risk going to jail either. So I did what I did."

"I'm glad you did. Glad you're on the team."

47

A few months later, I was sitting in a meeting room at the Las Vegas law firm of Brady, Bennett, and Shaw. Kirsten and Priya Choudhry, the senior civil litigator from her firm, sat on either side of me. A pile of papers stood stacked before them.

My arm was no longer in a sling from the gunshot wound, but the muscles and tendons were still healing. I was limited to light duty for another few weeks. Fortunately, Rodeo and Zahara grabbed the fugitives we were assigned with little trouble.

My father had also been released from the hospital and was undergoing physical and occupational therapy to get him back to his normal self.

The gunshot Blair Marshall sustained now confined her to a wheelchair. That didn't stop the Maricopa County Attorney's Office from bringing additional charges against her for shooting my father and Tanisha Nolan. Naomi Hoffman and Mandy Hudson faced charges of attempted murder.

Several other members of Womyn Born Womyn, the

Patriots of Liberty Caucus, and White Nation had also been arrested for violently crashing my wedding.

Justice has been served, I thought as I stared across the conference table at Gerard Boyce. His arm was still in a sling, though I had the feeling his was more for show. Next to him sat his attorney, Peter Shaw, a guy with a wan, reptilian face.

"We are willing to settle for ten million dollars," Shaw said, "as compensation for my client's pain and suffering, as well as his loss of income from being unable to perform in the next season of *Into the Black*."

I tried not to show the flash of fear that ran through my body. Ten million fucking dollars? I'd never make that in my entire life. And I shouldn't have to pay. The fucker had tried to rape me. Not my fault he picked the wrong woman to target.

"You're fucking delusional," I replied, resisting the urge to spit in his face. "Even if his wrist wasn't broken, he wouldn't be on the show. The producers fired his ass for trying to date-rape me. It was in all the papers."

Kirsten put a calming hand on my good arm. "Jinx…"

"I think ten million sounds fair," Choudhry replied.

I looked at Choudhry like she'd lost her damn mind. *She* was the senior civil litigator at their firm? Selling me out at first blush?

A crocodile smile crept across Shaw's face. "Glad we agree."

"But to clarify," Choudhry continued, "we agree that Mr. Boyce should pay Ms. Ballou the ten million dollars for emotional pain and suffering for drugging her and attempting to rape her." She tilted her head while turning her attention to Boyce. "Because we all know that the only reason your wrist was broken was because you assaulted my client first, thinking she was easy prey. Not Ms. Ballou's fault you targeted a woman who knew how to defend herself."

"He said, she said," Boyce replied with a smug look on his face. "I'd like to see you prove it."

Kirsten pushed a stack of papers toward the center of the table. "The police tox screen showing levels of ketamine and Valium in my client's system shortly after the incident."

"She could have taken them herself. Not my client's fault she has a drug problem," Shaw retorted.

"Fucking liar!" I shouted, but Kirsten hushed me.

"We also have testimony from other women." Choudhry put several paperclipped stacks of paper on the previous one. "Two dozen women, in fact, stating that Mr. Boyce drugged and sexually assaulted them. These are the transcripts of the depositions, but we can provide the video files of the interviews as well."

"Hearsay."

"We also have another thirty women who have come forward but whom we haven't had time to interview. But the initial details reflect a common pattern. Meeting a female fan at a convention. Inviting her to his room for a cast party. No one else but him in the room when she arrives. She wakes up later with no memory but discovering she has been sexually assaulted. It's enough for a class action suit."

Shaw and Boyce whispered back and forth. Boyce's face turned red. He was clearly pissed, which made me smile.

"Two million and your client signs a nondisclosure agreement."

I scoffed. "Like hell I will."

"Ten," Choudhry insisted. "And your client records a public statement admitting what he did to my client and apologizes for it. But we can keep the amount of the settlement confidential if you like."

"You're asking my client to throw away his career over a misunderstanding."

"A misunderstanding?" Kirsten replied. "Is that what you call attempted rape? The settlement amount is now twelve."

"Hey!" Boyce protested. "That's not how negotiations work."

"You want to go for fifteen?" asked Choudhry.

"Fucking bitches!" Boyce exclaimed.

Shaw whispered terse words to him. "Fine. Twelve mill."

I couldn't believe it. Was he really going to pay me twelve million dollars? Holy fuck!

"And a public statement." Kirsten pulled out her phone. "Shall we record it now?"

An hour later, I walked out with a cashier's check for two million dollars. It didn't seem real. The rest would be paid in installments. Of course, a portion of the settlement would go to Kirsten and Choudhry, but I wasn't complaining. And Boyce was still at risk for criminal charges from his assault on me and several other women he'd recently raped. His career was over.

I was sad in a way. I had liked his character. And his appearances in media interviews had left me thinking he was a great guy who respected woman. Oh well, I could dry my tears on all these fat checks.

Conor was waiting for us in the lobby. "How bad is it?" he asked.

"I've had worse days." I smiled and showed him the check.

Two weeks after making sure the check cleared, Conor and I were sipping mojitos and eating conch fritters on the outdoor deck of a restaurant in Key West. A Cuban jazz band played as we watched the sunset over the Gulf of Mexico.

Conor's eyes glittered as golden sunlight bathed his sunburned face. His hand gripped mine, creating a bond unlike anything I'd experienced. This was paradise.

Not because of the amazing fresh seafood or the rum or the smell of the sea or the wonderful Cuban music that always invigorated me. Not because I was now a multimillionaire or that Gerard Boyce had been arrested on multiple accounts of sexual assault.

No, this was paradise because I was with this amazing man. My husband. The word still seemed so odd. Husband. Almost laughably absurd. But every time I looked at him, endorphins flooded my brain like a summer monsoon storm.

This. This was paradise.

AUTHOR'S NOTE

This is a work of fiction, but the violence, vitriol and legislation harming transgender people is all too real. In the past year, dozens of anti-transgender bills have been introduced all across the United States alone.

Many of these bills are trying to prevent trans youth from having access to life-affirming treatment (e.g. puberty blockers) and preventing them from competing in sports. The ultimate goal is to increase trans teen suicides and increase public animosity and violence against trans people in general.

It should be noted that transgender women of color are the most common targets of anti-trans violence.

But the United States is not unique in the rise in transphobia. The United Kingdom has a small, but very vocal anti-transgender movement (often calling themselves gender critical rather than transphobic or TERFs).

Among them is author J. K. Rowling, who has repeatedly shared anti-trans content on social media. Her latest novel, *Troubled Blood*, features a male serial killer who dresses as a woman to get close to his victims.

The trope of trans women as men who cross-dress to prey on cis women is blatantly false. But it has long been used as justification for anti-trans legislation and violence.

As a transgender woman who has endured decades of violence and discrimination, I ask you to give this book an honest review and to speak out against transphobia whenever you see it. You will be saving lives. Thank you.

Dharma Kelleher

ABOUT THE AUTHOR

Dharma Kelleher writes gritty crime thrillers including the Jinx Ballou Bounty Hunter series and the Shea Stevens Outlaw Biker series.

She is one of the only openly transgender authors in the crime fiction genre. Her action-driven thrillers explore the complexities of social and criminal justice in a world where the legal system favors the privileged.

Dharma is a member of Sisters in Crime, the International Thriller Writers, and the Alliance of Independent Authors.

She lives in Arizona with her wife and a black cat named Mouse. Learn more about Dharma and her work at https://dharmakelleher.com.

ACKNOWLEDGMENTS

Even in the world of self-publishing, bringing forth a new book into the world is always a team effort.

Let me start by thanking every member of the transgender community. It is not easy for us to live as our true selves. It takes courage, persistence, and deep level of self-trust. But it also takes the generosity of community to reach out and lift each other up. We are stronger together.

For their brilliant editing skills, I want to thank my editors at Red Adept Editing.

For their assistance with research, I want to thank Adam Richardson and Patrick O'Donnell, as well as all of the helpful people in the Writer's Detective Bureau and the Cops & Writers Facebook groups.

For their wisdom and guidance with growing my author brand, I thank Joanna Penn, Orna Ross, Michael La Ronn, and Sasha Black from the Alliance of Independent Authors; Tammi Labrecque and the Newsletter Ninja Facebook group; David Gaughran; Mark Dawson and James Blatch of the Self-Publishing Formula; Lindsay Buroker,

Andrea Pearson, and Jo Lallo of the Six Figure Authors podcast; and Erin Wright, Suzie O'Connell and the people in the Wide for the Win Facebook group.

Last, but certainly not least, I want to thank all of my loyal fans, especially my newsletter subscribers. Enjoy!